BOTH SIDES OF THE COIN

BOTH SIDES OF THE COIN

By Honey Seltzer

ISBN 978-0-557-13575-2

For my children and grandchildren
Always follow your heart

Special thanks to those of you who encouraged me
to keep trying
And to Lori for her time, her infinite patience and her love

"Only the invented part of our Life –
The unreal Part – Has any scheme, any Beauty."

--Gerald Murphy

"Being deeply loved by someone gives you
Strength; loving someone deeply gives you
Courage."

--Lao Tzu

❧ 1 ❧

It was the middle of the night in Los Angeles, when the shrill sound of the ringing phone brought Matt McKenzie out of a deep sleep. He fumbled for the phone, barely able to mumble hello to whoever had dared intrude on his much-needed sleep. He had just fallen asleep after a long day on the set of the latest movie he was directing. It had been a miserable day with the spoiled star of the film, and he had come home exhausted and cranky.

"Matt? is this Matt?" a female voice asked.

There was something in her voice that woke him at once. He felt his heart begin to pound. Somehow he instinctively knew what this might be about, and he felt a rush of fear. "Yes," he assured his caller, "it's Matt."

"It's Jennifer, Ann's daughter."

"Jennifer, oh no," he answered with a trembling voice. "Something's happened to her, hasn't it?" In his heart he knew the answer before she could respond.

She couldn't speak at first. He could hear her trying not to cry, so that she could talk to him.

"What's happened? Tell me," he said softly.

There was silence on both their parts. His eyes filled with tears. At that moment, the woman lying beside him in the darkened room sat up. She reached for the lamp on her side of the bed and turned it on. He squeezed his eyes shut.

"Shut it off," he told her.

"Who is it?" she asked in an annoyed voice, totally ignoring his request. When he didn't answer, she grabbed the phone from his hand. "Who is this!" she snapped.

"Don't!" he threatened as he pulled the phone away from her.

"I'm so sorry, Jennifer. Please tell me what's happened."

"Please forgive me, I didn't mean to create any problems."

"No, no, it's fine," he told her, almost shouting. He was furious at Jeramie for grabbing the phone and upsetting her. "You can call me anytime. Please, what's happened? Tell me."

Jennifer began to cry. She had tried so hard not to fall apart, but she couldn't help it.

"Honey, please don't cry. Just try and tell me what's happened to your mom."

"Oh Matt," she sobbed, "she's gone. It just happened a little while ago. I didn't want to wake you. I know it's the middle of the night for you, but I knew you'd want to know, and I knew she would have wanted me to tell you." She started crying again, and he didn't try to stop her, as his own tears flowed from his eyes. "I wanted to be the one to tell you. I couldn't let you hear it on the news," she said, when she could finally talk again.

The woman in the bed looked at him with fury, and stormed out of the bed and out of the room. He shook his head sadly. He'd deal with her later. Right now he had to focus on what Jennifer had just told him. "Tell me what happened."

"She didn't feel well; hadn't felt well in some time and never said a word to any of us. She just ignored the pain until she couldn't stand it any longer, and then went to the doctor. But by that time it was too late to do anything for her except keep her as comfortable as possible. I don't understand her. She wasn't stupid. It just doesn't make sense to me. How could she have been so dumb?"

He didn't have any answers. He had always believed he knew Ann better than anyone, but she had fooled him as well.

"When did she find out?"

"About three months ago."

"What! No, that's impossible." He couldn't believe what he was hearing. He needed to get off the phone as fast as he could, before he really broke down.

Somehow he got through the rest of the conversation, but not before promising Jennifer he'd fly to New York as soon as he could get a flight.

He felt totally bewildered. Closing his eyes, he lay back on his pillow and let the tears come. It's just not possible he told himself. He had spoken to Ann two days ago and she'd never said a word to him. They had talked for about a half-hour and he'd never sensed that anything was wrong. They had had a wonderful time on the phone. She had been so funny and so sweet and, he now recalled, very much in the mood to reminisce. Why hadn't she told him? Damn her. There were so many things he would have said to her, and now they would never be spoken. It wasn't fair. How could she have left him so incomplete? Did he tell her how much he loved her, had always loved her? Did he tell her how much his existence depended on her very being? He couldn't remember. What if he hadn't? Now he'd never be able to.

He hadn't heard Jeramie return to the room. She sat in the chair across from the bed, staring at her husband. She realized he didn't even know she was sitting there, and it hurt. It hurt deeply. How could she, Jeramie King, one of the top agents in Hollywood, stay married to a man who, after twenty-five years, still loved another woman? Most of the time, she had convinced herself that he loved her. Their life was good, if not perfect, but she knew, as she watched him, that it wasn't true and probably had never been.

He looked up at her and started to tell her what had happened, but she got up and once again left the room.

He couldn't deal with her feelings right now. All he could think about was Ann.

Reaching for his phone, he pushed a button that linked him to his assistant, Alexis, who lived in the guest cottage on the grounds of his estate.

"Alexis, it's me. So sorry to wake you but I need a plane to New York as soon as possible."

"What's wrong?"

"It's personal. I just got word a dear friend has passed away, and I've got to get there. Please get on it right away. It's really urgent."

He hung up before she could answer him.

He rushed into the bathroom and turned on the shower. He needed to get himself under control. All he felt was a terrible sadness and the need to cry, but he fought to control himself. Within ten minutes he was dressed. The phone rang as he was packing his briefcase and computer.

"It's me," Alexis said. "I was so lucky. The studio had a plane all ready to leave for New York to pick up some big shots and they are holding it for you. I'll pick you up in five minutes. Is that okay?"

"You're fabulous. I can't thank you enough. Can you bring me whatever mail I haven't looked at? I can do some work on the plane. I'm not going to sleep, that's for sure."

"I'll bring you everything I have. See you in five."

True to her word, he heard the car honking its horn in five minutes. He turned to say goodbye to Jeramie, but she wasn't anywhere in the room, and as he ran through the house he didn't see any sign of her.

"Damn her," he thought. "Why doesn't she understand I have to go?"

He raced out of the door and into the waiting car.

When he got to the terminal where the private plane was waiting, he took the papers from Alexis, thanked her again, and raced to the Plane.

Jeramie had seen his face, and listened to his voice on the phone and felt disgust, more for herself for staying with him for so long, than for him. She was his wife because she had fulfilled a need in him that most women would never have accepted; she had always recognized that. From the beginning, she had been the breadwinner and leader of their lives. He had happily accepted all her demands and allowed her to make the rules --except for one. He had never fully given up Ann, as he had promised. He couldn't, and she knew it.

☜ 2 ☞

Matt sat back in his seat and closed his eyes. He had told the stewardess not to wake him for any meals. He just wanted to have this time to think of Ann, without feeling the piercing eyes of Jeramie. He had never been able to explain his feelings for Ann to her. He had tried at the beginning of their relationship, he really had, but when he realized she couldn't understand, he stopped explaining himself. Why would she, or any woman for that matter, understand? It was so complex. He really loved Jeramie in many ways, and he was forever indebted to her for the things she had done for him in the early days of their life together, but he also loved another woman in ways he could never describe. Ann was imbedded in his soul, always to be there.

Why was it Ann had always understood, or at least tried to understand? he wondered. He couldn't stop thinking of her, his lovely Ann. It was absolutely impossible to believe that she was gone. He couldn't accept it. He didn't think he could go on, knowing he would never see or speak to her again. They hadn't seen each other in months, but time had always stood still for them.

Somehow, he fell asleep, and awaking only to the announcement that they would soon be landing in New York. For the moment, he couldn't remember why he was on the plane. Then the realization of what he had to face in the next days came crashing down on him.

He left the plane. At the gate, he saw the familiar face of Marco, the driver who always met him when he flew in to New York. He was so grateful to see someone he knew. They greeted each other warmly. He had his carry-on with him and Marco quickly led the way to the waiting car. As soon as he got settled in the car, he called Jeramie. The machine answered. He felt so helpless. He hadn't asked her to come with him, and she hadn't offered. She hadn't wanted to discuss Ann with him when he tried to tell her about her death. She'd just turned away from him, and he'd stopped trying. He knew she wasn't part of what he had to face, and yet it had always been a part of all of them.

Marco dropped him off at his New York apartment. He preferred having his own place when he came east on business. It gave him a sense of privacy no hotel could ever afford. When he came east with Jeramie, they stayed in a hotel.

He called Jennifer to tell her he was in New York. She gave him the address of the chapel and told him the family would be there that night from seven to ten. The funeral would be the next morning. He promised to see them that evening. When he hung up, he realized it was getting late. He took a shower and shaved, then realized he was hungry. He hadn't eaten all day. He walked into the kitchen and looked in the refrigerator. He found fresh fruit and cheese and smiled. As usual, Alexis had arranged everything. He couldn't help but think of Ann. When he'd first met her, it seemed to him she always ordered grilled cheese. She loved it. He had thought her so sweet and unsophisticated. Would he think of her for the rest of his life every time he did something or ate something they had shared, he wondered? He found himself wanting to cry and forced himself to not to. He knew if he started, he wouldn't be able to stop. He had to get dressed and leave.

ಬ 3 ಚ

When he walked into the chapel, people turned to stare at him. He normally found it laughable when he was recognized. It had ceased to bother him, but this wasn't the time to be noticed. He wanted to be here as family. He wanted it to be for Ann, and he hoped people would leave him alone.

A somber young man escorted him to the room where Ann's daughters were sitting with their families. He hadn't seen Jennifer and Liz in years. It seemed strange to see them with their own children. He had known them for such a long time.

They saw him at once. He was hard to miss. Liz had always described him as 'gorgeous.' Now, in his early fifties, he was so much more. As he approached, everyone in the room stopped talking and looked up. The girls jumped up from their seats and he gathered them in his arms and held them. When they stepped back, his eyes filled with tears. "God, Jennifer, you look more and more like your mom; and you Liz, you're an absolute knockout." As if on signal, both women began to cry. Once again he pulled them into his arms. When they finally stopped sobbing, they pulled away and looked at him, trying to smile.

"We're so glad you're here," they said, simultaneously.

"Me too," he answered.

He felt totally lost. He didn't know what to say to them. To say he was sorry was so inadequate, and to say how much he loved their mother seemed inappropriate, and yet he had to let them know how loved she had been.

"I loved her very much," he finally mumbled.

Jennifer spoke for them both, when she told him that they knew. "Mom loved you always. We've always known that, and how happy you made her."

"Are you sure? There was so much I didn't give her."

Their eyes filled again. Jennifer spoke at once. "She had your love. I think she always felt that was enough." Liz shook her head in agreement.

He stayed with them for a while, but found it impossible to fight his feelings. He had to get out of there. When he felt it wouldn't look awful he left, assuring them he'd be at the funeral in the morning.

As he started to walk back to his apartment, he stopped in the middle of the street. He couldn't go back home until he did something else. He hailed a cab. He had to see his old apartment; the first little place he had had in New York, the place where they had fallen in love.

When he reached his destination, he got out and walked up the street until he found what had once been his building. It was now rebuilt, with a modern brick façade, no longer in any way resembling the place he had lived in. The sense of loss was overwhelming. Ann was gone; this house, this place where they had first made love, all gone. He couldn't bear it. He began to run, sobbing as he ran, until he could no longer move. He hailed another cab, managed to climb in and give the driver his address. Never had he felt such anguish.

❀ 4 ❀

He hadn't slept a wink the night before. His eyes were swollen from fatigue and tears. It was only six o'clock in the morning. The funeral wasn't until ten, but he couldn't sleep. He got out of bed, went into the kitchen and put up a pot of coffee. Once he had showered and sipped the coffee, he knew what he had to do. He picked up the phone, called the funeral chapel and asked for the director. Although he would have preferred anonymity, he explained who he was; he knew his name would get him what he wanted. The director assured him his request could be honored. "Just get here at eight-thirty and no one will disturb you," he was assured.

At eight-thirty sharp, he was shown into the room that held Ann's coffin. His legs gave way as he walked towards her. Someone had placed a chair where he could sit and look at her. He found himself alone and sat down. It took him a few minutes to bring himself to look at Ann. When he finally did, he was okay. She looked like his Annie, just sleeping. Whoever had dressed her, had chosen to make her look as though she were on the way to lunch, casual and beautiful as she had always been.

He bent down and kissed her forehead and then took her hand. He sat quietly holding her hand and feeling her presence. He knew she was somewhere near him. He felt it so strongly. "Oh Annie, how could you leave without telling me," he cried. They had always had a very special way of communicating. He could be sound asleep, and in his sleep sense her calling him, needing him. He'd awaken and pick up the phone and dial her number, and she'd answer, "What took you so long?" If he had ever told anyone, they would have thought he was crazy, but he knew he could really hear her when she needed him. Why? Why hadn't she called for him while she lay so ill, knowing she was dying? How could she not? He felt so angry. As he thought these thoughts he felt a tap on his shoulder. He looked up startled and found Jennifer at his side.

"I knew I'd find you here," she said.

"Are you okay?" he asked. He didn't like the way she looked.

She tried to smile for him, and his heart broke because, at that moment, he could have sworn he was looking at Ann.

"I have something for you."

"What?"

"Mom asked me to give this to you when this day was over. She knew it would help you, and it made her feel better knowing you would have it." She handed him a package.

He looked at her puzzled.

"I only know it's a CD she made for you. I hope it helps."

He held it to his breast and looked down at Ann's sleeping body.

He then heard noises and looked up. People were beginning to arrive in the room. He got up from his chair and hugged Jennifer.

"I'm not going to the cemetery. I can't. I'll just stay for the services. I hope you and Liz understand. I'll keep in touch, and I hope you'll call me whenever you need to talk. I'll always be there for both of you".

"We'd like that. You will say goodbye to Liz. She'd feel terrible if you didn't."

"I will, I just want to say goodbye to your mom one more time."

Jennifer shook her head and walked away, allowing him his final moments with her mother.

ಬ 5 ಜ

The services had been beautiful, but heart wrenching. Matt had been so grateful he hadn't been asked to speak, because what he felt for Ann was his, and his alone. He couldn't wait to get back to his apartment so that he could look at what Ann had left for him.

It was only Noon, but he didn't care. He poured himself a shot of scotch and put the CD in the machine.

He gasped when her face appeared before him. There she was, his Ann looking into his eyes and smiling. She was sitting in her most favorite place in the world, the deck of her beach house in East Hampton. He had finally forced her into letting him buy it for her. She had only given in because she had known how much it meant for him to give her something special, and something that she had always dreamed of having. He had somehow miraculously found the house they had spent a magical weekend in many years before. It had been on the market, and he knew he had to buy it for her.

"Without your belief in me, and your loan so many years go, I never would have made it. You've got to let me give this to you." he had pleaded.

She told him over and over again that he didn't owe her anything, and never would. What ever she had done for him was because she had loved him so much, and believed in him. His success was her reward.

He finally wore her down. "It's too late, I've bought it, and it's yours. It will be just for us." He implored. "Remember the first time we spent at the beach?" he reminded her.

He won. How could she ever forget?

Once she accepted the house, her happiest moments were to sit on her deck and watch the ocean. There was tremendous peace simply watching the beauty of the ocean; the wave's sometimes so gentle, and sometimes so forceful landing at her door were breathtaking. At night, listening to them crash, as she lay in bed, were to her the most beautiful sounds in the world. The rare nights she shared her bed with Matt were the most special. Cradled in his arms, the breeze of the sea air filling the room, the sounds of the ocean pulling them deep into sleep were heavenly. Rare as they were, they were so special.

As he sat in his living room alone, in New York, looking at this beautiful woman talking to him, he could hardly hear her voice through his own cries. He stopped the machine until he could finally get the courage to turn it back on.

"Matt dearest, I know what you're feeling right now. Please don't be angry with me for not telling you. I couldn't. I couldn't stand to see your face filled with horror and fear for me. I couldn't watch you looking at me, seeing me fade. I needed to know your memories would always be of me as I was, as we were. We had something so very special, so very unique. I just couldn't bear to have anything take that away, even death.

I know you think you could have helped me through this, but no one my darling can do that. Please, please forgive me. You have given me a love I never expected to have. Before meeting you, I dreamed of what it must feel like to love passionately, and to have that person love me equally. I have been so blessed to have found you, and to have known throughout all these years that I was deeply loved.

❧ 6 ❧

On the day you walked in to my life I had been working for Peter Simmons for almost two years, and loving every moment. I couldn't believe I could be this happy.

I had spent so many years living in a marriage that had brought me constant crisis and sadness, that I was convinced my life would always be that way. I had been so wrong. I had finally found my place, and I still found it unimaginable that all the pain and misery had ended. Yet unbeknownst to me, so much more of a different kind of happiness was coming my way. The beginning of something I had longed for, but never believed possible, was about to find me.

What you saw that first day we met, in no way resembled what I had been just a few years earlier. I tried so hard not to think of the bad times, they were gone. I did not want to remember a Sunday morning years earlier, basking in the excitement of being pregnant with my second daughter, when two men appeared at my home asking for my husband Charlie. When he came to the door they simply handed him a piece of paper, and left. His face went white. When I asked him what this was about, he shoved it in to my hand. At first I didn't understand what I was looking at. The paper seemed to say that our house no longer belonged to us. I ran to the back of the house calling for him. During a lot of words that made no sense to me, he tried to explain that our family business, one that his father, brothers, and he had spent years building from very little to a big success had now been destroyed. We were all financially ruined. We had gone from riches to rags. Puff, and down we went. No one ever really explained the how or why's to me, and if they had it wouldn't have changed anything. It had happened.

I was so young, and innocent, and hopeful. I was so sure we'd be fine. I hadn't come from money, and hadn't had it long enough to become spoiled. I, in my innocence, believed that we could build a life with our children that could be meaningful. We didn't need a lot of money to be happy, I thought. I was sure he would find a job, and we'd survive and be fine. It wasn't that simple. He had been the spoiled, youngest son of a rich man. He had never really been given a great deal of responsibility. By the time he joined the family business it was a proven success, and he just did whatever his father or older brothers asked him to do. He was happy go-lucky, and kind, and generous. He was always the first to put his hand in his pocket and pay for a dinner with his friends, never expecting anyone to pay him back. He was a sweet man and gentle man until his world came tumbling down, and he didn't know how to handle it. Everything he had believed in had been taken away from him. The friends he once showered with affection and money, turned away from him. It not only broke his heart, it broke his spirit, and we, my children and I, for the next twenty years paid the price. Nothing I could say, or do helped. He spent every waking hour for the next twenty years thinking of ways to become rich again. He borrowed from anyone who would lend him money, and tried time and time again to start new ventures that failed. I begged him to let me get a job, but the thought of his wife working was humiliating to him. He thought if I worked, it would only prove to everyone that he was a loser. I felt so sorry for him, and so I would keep quiet, until the next rent came due. During most of those bad years, I rarely knew if we could pay the monthly rent on our small apartment we now lived in. I would get very frightened, and I would once again try again to persuade him to let me find a job. It was always the same. If I tried to take a stand, he would get very upset, and I would feel so bad that I would give in to him.

A few years after the loss he developed a variety of illnesses, including a bad heart. He had become so bitter and angry, that most people preferred staying away from us.

One of his brothers managed to rebuild his life and out of sympathy for the children and myself, finally gave him a demeaning job in his company, that consisted of a paltry salary and the payment of our rent. I was so grateful not to worry anymore about being dispossessed from our apartment.

I tried to take a stand and look for a job, but I was so beaten down by then, that I just couldn't get the guts to fight. I was petrified that I would be the cause of his death, and so I stayed quiet, and struggled, fearing every phone call would be from another creditor.

One day I opened an envelope that arrived in the mail. When I realized that it was a cancellation notice of his small, but necessary life insurance policy, I could scarcely breathe. I barely recall the scene that followed, but I remember screaming at him for the first time in my married life. I raced out of the house shaking. I had to get away from him. I hated him. I hated him, not just for this, but for all of the past twenty years. This was the first time I had allowed myself to be honest with myself. My entire twenties, thirties, and now forties had been taken away from me. I had pretended all these years not to care, to be supportive and nurturing. I never allowed myself to feel sorry for myself. I couldn't pretend any longer.

I had no family left by then, and I desperately needed someone to talk to. I was too ashamed to tell my friends. I had covered for him for so long, and I couldn't break the faith. I found myself at our family doctor's office, in hysterics. My hands were shaking so badly, and my heart palpitating so rapidly, that he became frightened for my life.

He had known our family for years. My husband was his patient, as well as my children and I. He knew how bad it was in our home. He now looked at me, and I could see that I was scaring him.

He sat me down, and waited for me to calm myself. When I finally stopped trembling, he asked me to tell him what had happened that could have upset me this badly. My eyes filled with tears, as I told him about opening the letter from the insurance company. "He never told me he hadn't paid the bill. He had hidden the bill from me," I cried. "If I hadn't gone to the mailbox first, I would never have seen the cancellation letter. And it was for such a small amount of money. What kind of man is he?"

"What did you do when you read the letter?" he asked me.

"I went ballistic. I ran into the bedroom where he was resting, and I threw it at him. I screamed at him, as I have never screamed at anyone before in my life. 'How could you?' I cried, over and over again; 'how could you do this to us? You know how sick you are, and you didn't care enough about me and your children to tell me about this?'"

"He just looked at me as if I were insane, and then he picked up the letter and looked at it. He couldn't answer at first, and then just shrugged. I totally lost it. I became hysterical. 'This was for your children, you bastard.' I cried, and then he slapped me across the face in a rage. I held my cheek, which still burned with pain, and do you know what he said? 'My wife doesn't curse.'"

"Oh my God, he hit you"?

I shook my head yes. I could tell he was shocked, and I was totally drained from just talking about everything. He got up, and brought me a cup of water and a pill, and urged me to take it. All the while he talked to me very quietly, but firmly. His main intention was to convince me to finally take control of my life, not just for myself, but for my children as well.

"I'm so sorry. He's a very sick man, in every way. You must know, he's not going to be here much longer. You can't do anything more for him. You have been a great wife. Now you've got to get on with your life. Go out in to the world, and look for work. You're bright, you're attractive, and you're lovely. I'm sure there is something out there that can bring you a decent living, and peace of mind. Do not, please don't, listen to him anymore. You simply cannot. He'll destroy you, and your children need you."

The tears ran down my face, as I listened to him talking. My greatest wish was to obey him. "How can I do that? He'll die." I cried.

He raised his voice at me, "Ann, listen to me. You are not the one who'll determine when he dies. He will die, within the next few years; that I know, but it won't be because of anything you do. He's just a very sick man, with a very bad heart. I can't save him, so how can you? Please listen to me, my dear. I don't want to bury you first." I burst into tears, and cried until there was none left to shed.

When I finally left his office, I knew he was right. I walked the streets of my neighborhood for hours, just thinking about what he had said to me. By the time I reached home, I knew what I had to do, but I wasn't about to discuss it with Charlie. I knew I had to move fast, before I lost my resolve. It took so little to scare me. I knew how easily he could manipulate me, and I couldn't let that happen this time. He tried to apologize for hitting me, and I pretended to accept his pathetic words. All I wanted at that moment was peace, and a new life. I had to find something that would bring me a future.

The next day I bought the *New York Times* and, while Charlie napped, I circled secretarial jobs. I'd been a very good secretary before we got married, and I knew my typing skills were still good.

I made some calls while he was still sleeping, and set up interviews for the next day. I quickly wrote a resume. I knew it looked pretty pathetic, but what could I do? I had done volunteer work in community affairs, so I added that to the resume, hoping that being President of the grade school Parents Association might impress someone enough to give me a chance.

In the morning I lied to Charlie, and told him I was going to the high school to do volunteer work. He never objected to anything I did, as long as it didn't bring in money.

I spent the day going from one employment agency to another, and was totally discouraged by the end of the day. It seemed that more than my lack of current experience, my age seemed to be the bigger problem in finding a job. I was competing against young women in their twenties. I saw them in every agency I went to. It wasn't hard to notice the difference between how they were treated, and how I was. I wasn't asked to go on one interview, but watched as the young ones sailed out of the agencies, with slips of papers in their hands and smiles on their faces. By the time I got home, I felt totally defeated. I was only a little past forty, and I was being treated like an old woman. When I looked at myself in the mirror I tried to be objective. It wasn't a great image, I had to admit. The smiling blonde girl I had once been no longer existed. What I now saw was a tired woman with dark circles under her eyes. My once-shiny hair looked drab, and almost colorless. It hadn't been cut properly in years, and it had no style at all. I had become so thin I looked emaciated. "Oh God!" I thought. "No wonder no one wants to hire me. I'm a mess!"

I wanted to crawl into bed and cover my head with a blanket, and stay there forever, but I also knew that's what I had been doing for the past twenty years. "No more," I cried to myself.

I marched into the bathroom again, and looked at myself carefully. I couldn't do much but I would try. I left the house and went to the local drugstore, and bought a hair color kit and some fresh makeup. That night, when the girls and Charlie were asleep, I cut my own hair, colored it, and soaked in a bubble bath for an hour.

Both Sides of the Coin

In the morning, I took tremendous pains with my makeup, blew my hair carefully, and got dressed. When I once again said I was going to the school Charlie got angry. "I promised," I lied. He looked at me suspiciously, but never commented on my hair or makeup.

At the end of another fruitless day, I fell into a deep depression. Somehow, I forced myself to try one more time, and pulled myself together the next morning. Once again, I lied to my husband and went back into the city. After hours of getting nowhere, prepared to go home, I tried one last agency. The two women who owned it were actually friendly. They greeted me cheerfully, and I felt the sadness begin to leave my body as I responded to their kindness. I sat quietly, while they looked at my pathetic resume and at me. By this time, most of my makeup had disappeared, and I'm sure my hair was a mess. My lack of nice clothing hadn't helped my image either, but there wasn't anything I could do about that. When they asked me to take a typing test, I became hopeful. This was the first time anyone had shown an interest in my skills. They set a clock for three minutes, and asked me to type the prepared test they placed in front of me. My hands were shaking, but somehow they did not fail me, and my fingers began to fly across the keyboard. When the bell rang announcing that my time was up they checked my paper, and were really astonished at how quickly and accurately I had typed. I hadn't made any errors. Even I was amazed.

They left me sitting in a reception area, as they went into their office to consult. They had a job that had been impossible to fill. Maybe I was the right fit?

ೞ 9 ೞ

The next day, I walked into the offices of Peter Simmons Films, scared out of my wits. I had no idea how much my life would change starting that day. I knew nothing about film making, and had absolutely no experience in the world of motion pictures, other than my total love of movies. As with millions of other people, going to the movies had always been my place to escape to from real life.

The women in the agency had taken a chance on me, because the job in question was working for a woman who was known to be a pain in the ass. Pat Owens, the right hand to Peter Simmons, a famous movie producer, was, as it turned out, a real pain. However, if one got to know her long enough, a kind and decent woman lived beneath her tough exterior. Then there was Peter himself, a man who was generally impossible to please, and who preferred to have beautiful woman surround him. Of course I knew none of this that day, or I would have run for the door at once. I'm forever grateful I didn't run.

None of the beauties that had been seen so far had been hired, and the women at the agency had a feeling that Pat would prefer someone that appeared to be gentle and complacent. God knows there was nothing threatening about me, and I would do anything she asked of me, as long as I had a job.

I sat in the reception area, literally trembling. When Pat came out to greet me, I looked at her, and felt totally overwhelmed and shabby. She was one of the most beautiful women I'd every met. She stood about five feet eight inches tall, and had a body that seemed meant for men to fantasize over. She had a perfectly shaped oval face with high cheekbones, grey, almond-shaped eyes, and long shiny auburn hair that looked as if it just fell in swirls without any effort. She was dressed in a stunning gray suit that matched her eyes, and she smiled. All I could think was, "what am I doing here? I'm such a mess."

Pat, no fool, seemed to recognize my fear and tried to put me at ease before I bolted. She desperately needed an assistant and was getting tired of interviewing people. At first glance, she wasn't sure that I would work out. I looked, as she told me months later, pretty pathetic. Yet, after we spoke for a few minutes, she made a hasty decision. She asked me to wait, and she walked to Peter's office.

"I want you to meet a woman I'd like to hire as my assistant."

"Why do I have to meet her?" he snapped. "I don't care who you hire as your assistant. This is the tenth one that's been in. Just hire someone and get it over with."

"You have to see her, too."

"You keep telling me this, why?"

"Well, because she'll also be working for you, once I get her comfortable."

He looked at her and grinned. "You mean you don't want to do the typing and steno anymore?"

"I think I'm above that, don't you?"

"Okay, okay. Bring her in."

"She's shy, so can you please take it easy."

He glared at her and shook his head okay.

Pat went back to her office and got me.

"I want you to meet Peter now. He can be a real ass sometimes, really impossible. Please, Ann, and this is important, please try not to let him ever think you're afraid of him. He'll eat you up if he thinks you're scared."

She saw the fear in my eyes. "Oh shit, I didn't mean to scare you. I can understand you're nervous, just try not to show it. I just wanted to tell you the bad things. Honestly, there are times, and most times when Peter is one of the kindest men. He's like the proverbial little girl with the curl -- when he's good he's very, very good, and when he's bad he's dreadful."

I listened to her, but my heart turned over wondering how I would hide my fears. I so desperately wanted and needed this job. I had to try to get it. I forced myself to calm down.

Before I could think any further about what was happening, I was following her down a long corridor filled with enlarged photographs of movie stars, as well as posters of successful motion pictures. In spite of my fears, I felt tremendous excitement, an emotion I had thought was gone forever in my life. For a moment, life seemed livable, and the possibility of a small amount of happiness seemed possible. At the end of the corridor, we came upon a closed double door made of thick, dark gleaming mahogany. Pat threw open the door and sauntered in. I timidly followed her, a stance I would take for quite a while.

20

Seated behind a massive eighteenth-century desk, was a man in his early forties. His thin frame was clad in a dark navy, double-breasted, pinstriped suit. His tie, a subtle blend of light blue silk with thick vertical stripes of darker blue, rested on a perfect white shirt. His black curly hair framed a finely chiseled face. When he looked up, his piercing blue eyes apprised the two of us. In a second, they seemed to take in everything. He didn't smile. I sensed disinterest on his part, and it hurt me. In one second I had, once again, been made to feel totally insignificant.

He beckoned us in with one hand, as the other grabbed a ringing phone.

We walked to the deep thick cream-colored chairs facing his desk, and when Pat sat down into one of them, I did the same. I felt so awkward, and simply folded my hands in my lap. In an effort to calm myself, I looked around and studied the imposing office. His deep, resonant voice, speaking on the phone, intruded on my efforts, so I tried concentrating on his conversation. When I realized he was talking about people I had seen in the movies or had read about, I couldn't help but become excited. To him it seemed so every day, but to me it was the beginning of a life of fantasy.

When he was finished speaking on the phone, he turned to us, and Pat introduced me.

He leaned across the desk and shook my hand, and then turned to Pat and said, "Let's clear my desk."

For the next half hour, I sat mesmerized as Peter went through almost every paper on his desk, handing each one to Pat with different instructions. At times, he'd dictate a letter regarding a particular document, and Pat would quickly take down whatever he said. She appeared to do everything effortlessly, and I watched in total awe, wondering how in the world she did it.

At last they were finished. Everything that had been on his desk was now in piles on the floor next to Pat's chair.

Peter then turned to me. Until that moment, he hadn't said a word to me since shaking my hand. "Do you think you could do all this?" he asked.

I was totally startled by his question, thinking he must be crazy. I could never do what I had just seen her do, but I couldn't tell him that. I looked him straight in the eyes, and from a part of me hidden so deeply I didn't know it existed, I found the courage to say "yes". I wanted this job so badly; I'd do anything to get it, even lie. "Please God," I said to myself, "please let them give it to me."

A mere week ago I had gone from place to place, finding only rejection. I can still remember walking down the streets of New York, feeling as though there was nothing left for me in this life, yet knowing I had two beautiful children to take care of. I had looked up into the sky, and thought "somewhere in this big city, there has to be something for me." I had been right. My gut told me this was the job I was meant to have. Even if I wasn't skilled enough, I knew I'd figure it out. I had to have it.

Peter turned to Pat and said, "Fine, let's see how it works out."

And that was that. The job was mine. All I had to do was tell my husband.

He went ballistic. "You're making a loser out of me," he shouted. "You lied to me," he screamed. With my new found strength and determination, I wanted to scream back, "but you are a loser." I couldn't. I couldn't be that hurtful. I simply looked him in the eyes, and very quietly told him it wasn't open to debate. With that I walked away from him, and into the kitchen to prepare our dinner.

ઇ 10 ઙ

It hadn't been easy at the beginning. Peter hadn't particular taken to me, and I once overheard him telling Pat he found me mousy. Although probably true at the time, it hurt me terribly. I was earning very little money, and the last thing I could afford to spend money on was my appearance. I did the best I could.

Sometimes he'd call me in to his office, and begin dictating, at lightening fast speed, lengthy letters and documents, using motion picture jargon that made no sense to me. I hadn't taken steno since I was seventeen years old, and fresh out of high school. I'd run out of his office as soon as he finished dictating, and quickly try to scribble down the words I could vaguely remember hearing him say, praying I'd get it right. At night I'd sit glued to the television set with a large legal pad in my lap, and as the newscasters spoke I'd try to get down their words in shorthand as fast as I could, so that my hand would get used to their speed, and it did.

Slowly, things at work became easier. I no longer trembled while taking shorthand, and Peter hadn't complained in months. I was also learning about making movies, which was fascinating. Best of all I had made some new and wonderful friends. I felt the first sense of happiness in such a very long time, and it felt so good.

On the home front, the torture continued. A few days after I was offered the job, Charlie proceeded to have what appeared to be a heart attack. The lack of my usual hysteria soon stopped the attack. Not to say he didn't have a serious heart condition but, so many times in the past, he had faked it in order to get a reaction from me. This time he was taking revenge on me. I had lied to him. I had gone behind his back, and found a job. He couldn't forgive me this sin. In the past, I had always given him the benefit of the doubt, and had been solicitous and caring. I just couldn't keep it up any longer. I had reached my breaking point the day he hit me. I could no longer put his life ahead of mine and my children's. I could no longer give him my life. I had two daughters who needed at least one parent. My actions towards him were so against everything I had ever been. It was just as hard for me to understand that I was capable of selfishness, as it was for him. But he wasn't going to win this time. I had taken a stand for the first time in twenty years, and nothing could possibly change my mind, because I knew it was a matter of life and death for my girls and me.

During the first year I worked, he tried making my life miserable, every chance he got. He could tell I was happy away from him, and he resented it terribly. Every night when I'd get home, he'd make some snide remark about how tired I looked, how neglected the house was, how insolent the kids were, and on and on. I stood my ground with him, and refused to give in to him and quit the job. "I'd sooner die than give it up," I told him.

He tried everything to elicit sympathy from me. One night I came home to find him in bed under the blankets.

"Are you in pain?" I asked him.

"I'm just resting," he said, in a way that meant it was more than resting that had put him in the bed.

I never knew if he was play-acting to make me feel guilty because I was working, or if he really felt lousy. I looked at him, and wanted to scream with anger, "just be honest."

"You're late," he snapped.

I wasn't going to fight with him, so I just turned to leave the room to go to the kitchen and start dinner.

He wouldn't stop ranting. "I'm surprised the big shot let you come home at all," he said, sarcastically.

"Typical," I thought. Every night it was something else. I kept my face hidden from him because I knew I couldn't hide my fury.

At that moment I heard my daughters call from the other part of the apartment. They had just come in.

Liz, the younger of my two daughters, turned to her father upon entering the bedroom, and said something he didn't like. She had met a neighbor on the way in, who had told her he had helped Charlie into the house that afternoon.

Charlie immediately snapped at her, and told her to shut up. He could be so horrible to both of them, but mostly to Liz.

I tried to stop them before it became too heated. They had never gotten along, because she spoke up to him. Jennifer, on the other hand always placated him, and tried not to argue. I asked him what he had been doing outside, since the weather had been cold and windy.

"What do you think I'm going to do, stay in this house all day, while you're out there being Miss Bread Winner?" he shouted.

"That's not fair," I started to say, as I felt the tears well in my eyes. He could be so cruel.

He began gasping for breath, and the three of us stopped and watched him, realizing this might be an actual attack. I quickly ran to the night table for his pills, and handed him one to put under his tongue. As the pill began to work, the heavy breathing eased off.

"What are you all hysterical about, it's nothing," he said smugly. Once again, mission accomplished. He had gotten our attention.

I could feel my own heart racing. This only happened to me at home, never at work, I realized.

I had to get out of the room. I could barely breathe. Every day with him became even worse than the last. I went into the kitchen to begin dinner, my hands still shaking, and my heart still racing. The girls followed me.

"How do you stand it?" Liz asked. "He loves getting you all worked up. He's glad he finally has something to ride you about."

"Liz, please. You know how sick he is."

"Yeah, so what's his excuse for the rest of his life? All of my life he's been sick, even when he really wasn't. All of my life I've had to watch what I said to him, because I might make him sick. And you, Mom, what's he ever done for you, but drive you crazy every day?"

"He wasn't always like this, sweetie."

"How would I know? It must have been before I was born, that's for sure."

I didn't know what to say. I felt so terrible, and guilty for my daughters, particularly Liz who always got the brunt of his nastiness.

One night, when the girls were out of the house, and Charlie and I were having dinner alone, the phone rang. It was Pat. She called to ask me to please take care of an important contract the first thing next morning, since she would be late and it had to be done by nine. I was thrilled to be given the responsibility, and assured her I'd take care of it. I was beginning to feel more and more like part of an accepted team, and I loved it. We kept talking about little things and I, without realizing it, was ignoring Charlie. When I finally hung up, I was smiling.

As I began to pick on my unfinished dinner, he lashed out at me. "You can't even stand to have a quiet meal with me," he shouted. "All you care about is your God damn job."

Before I could begin to defend myself, he began gasping for breath. I was so used to his behavior, I didn't really believe it was anything other than another way of getting my attention. I calmly reached for his pills, and handed one to him. As I had lost my appetite, I turned away and began clearing the table, when I heard a crash. I quickly turned back to find him on the floor, gasping for breath.

I knew at once this was very serious, and quickly grabbed the phone and dialed 9-1-1. I explained as best I could, without sounding hysterical, where I was and what was happening. I bent down to the floor and cursed myself for never learning CPR.

I spoke very softly, and he made it clear that he heard me and was conscious, but I knew in my heart of hearts that this was very bad. The ambulance arrived in minutes, and I rode with him as we raced through the streets, holding his hand, and trying to reassure him that everything would be okay. He looked so small and childlike, and I felt so sorry for him, and for the life he had so cheated himself of, and for the life I knew he would never have.

He had been a kind, generous, and decent man when I first met him. He'd had loads of friends who'd constantly raided my refrigerator, sprawled all over my brand new sofas, and enjoyed our home as much as we had. If anyone had needed a helping hand, he'd been the first to offer it. He had never loaned people money, he'd given it to them; no strings attached. He hadn't deserved the treatment he'd received from these so-called friends, when they'd realized he was no longer rich. They had all turned their backs on him. No one had offered him a helping hand. There was one friend that had meant the most to him; the one he had actually given money to so that he might start a business. This friend had become a multi-millionaire thanks to Charlie, and when Charlie had gone to him for help in paying our rent, he'd thrown a check at him and told him never to come back for more.

I think that was the day I lost the man I married. That was the beginning of twenty years of living with a destroyed man, both physically and psychologically. For the rest of his life, his only aim was to become rich again, and that never happened. As I held his hand in the ambulance, he looked at me and whispered "thank you" and was gone.

In the wake of his death, I felt so sorry for him. Yet, in a way, part of me felt tremendous relief that an end had finally come to a very long road of unhappiness for him, as well as for me and my children. The old me would have felt tremendous guilt at his passing. After all I had defied him by getting a job, knowing how miserable it would make him. In my heart I recognized that no one person had been responsible for his death. He was a very sick man, who had hopefully found some peace and, hopefully, so would we.

❧ 11 ☙

Two years after I had entered the world of The Peter Simmons Film Company, you, Matt McKenzie, were working at odd jobs in the movie business. You were a graduate of NYU Film School, and were an aspiring writer. You had met Louise Simmons, Peter's daughter, at a party. She was very attractive and lots of fun, as well as being totally uninhibited. You were a perfect companion for her. There you were, an extremely rugged, good-looking, tall, dark haired, dark eyed guy, with as much charm and intelligence as her father. Until the next guy came along, for her you were it.

You were having a ball with her, and since you were in no position, nor did you desire to settle down with one girl, she was heaven sent. Not only was Louise attractive, she provided fun, plus great sex, and expected no emotional or permanent commitment. She promised she'd introduce you to the right people, and she kept her word. She took you to all the fun parties, the after-hours clubs, and off Broadway shows. You both went to screenings in private screening rooms, and you walked down the red carpet with her at premieres of new films. Slowly, you made friends with guys and girls who were all on the verge of success in the business you loved so much, and were meeting people who had already achieved the kind of success you coveted.

Louise had read your latest script, which you had written on speculation, and she had really liked it. Until this time she hadn't introduced you to her father. She preferred keeping her boyfriends away from Peter. However, she had a feeling he might like this script. Without telling you, she brought it to our office, and gave it to me instead of Pat. She knew Pat wouldn't take the time to read the script. Pat wasn't very fond of Louise, and had never hidden her feelings, whereas, Louise figured that, since I was fairly new to the job, I would probably want to ingratiate myself with the boss's daughter.

When she gave me the script, she asked that, if I liked it, would I give it to Peter. I was thrilled. I was still so naïve I took it as a compliment. I really liked Louise, in spite of Pat's constant criticism of her. She was so 'out there', so unafraid of life, and always so sure of herself. She had all the attributes that I had never had. I envied her lack of self-consciousness. It never seemed to occur to Louise that anyone would ever say no to her.

"Is the writer someone special?" I asked, smiling at her.

"For now," she laughed. "Easy come easy go. You'll give it to dad if you like it?"

I assured her I would, after I read it.

That night I took home the script. I didn't get a chance to pick it up for two days, but when I did I was entranced. It needed work, but there was something special about it.

Peter had started to give me scripts to read, and he had liked what I had to say. It was very exciting for me to have his approval on something that I considered really important. I was starting to feel more confident, and I was getting so much more positive feedback, not just from Peter, but from clients I now spoke to on the phone, and from everyone I worked with. I was happier than I had been in years. I just loved the movie business, and I loved the people I worked with. I was in absolute awe of Peter, who after finally deciding I wasn't too bad, had even given me a substantial raise after my first year. I was so excited when he called me in to his office, and told me that I had exceeded his expectations and deserved a better salary. He had done this without me asking for a raise, and I loved him for it. Left to my own devices, I don't know if I ever would have had the nerve to ask. Thanks to the raise, I had started paying off all the bills that had accumulated during the past years, and I was actually beginning to see the light of day.

My girls were growing up. Jennifer was now at Vassar, on a full scholarship, and Liz was in her last year of high school, soon to follow Jennifer. I was so proud of them both. My heart was light and freer than I could remember. Everything, little or big made me smile. I couldn't believe that I could feel such joy. I had conditioned myself to believe that life had very little to offer me, and I now realized I had been wrong.

After reading your script, I gave it to Peter with my notes. He read it, and liked it too, and told me to call you in for a meeting.

ಬ 12 ೞ

My life seemed to undergo new changes every day, and I welcomed each and every one of them. I had awakened from a very bad dream, and whoever that woman had been during the years of the nightmare was slowly disappearing. I didn't know what was still to come, but I sensed that my newfound courage was going to take me places I had never dreamed possible.

I remember the night I went to dinner with my childhood friends Roz and Fran, and their husbands. I know you remember them, Matt, especially Fran. When you finally met her, you hated her on first sight.

I couldn't help but smile as I listened to Ann giggling as she said this.

"They took me to a very "in" restaurant—their words. Fran, as usual, was dressed to the nine's, and her arms were weighted down with all her diamonds. Poor thing, she only felt secure if her ring had the biggest stone of anyone she knew. I'd known her since we were kids growing up in the Bronx, when her father drove a cab and her family could barely make ends meet. Everything at this stage in her life was about her lifestyle and the desperate need to eliminate any memories of her earlier poor days. Even in my worst days I had actually always felt sorry for her. She probably thought I was jealous of her, but what she didn't understand was she had nothing I ever wanted. It was exhausting being Fran. Keeping up with the Joneses is not an easy feat. Milton, her pathetic husband, had made it big in the garment industry. They were always arguing, yet they had somehow stayed together, at least until then. On the other hand, Roz and Stan were totally different. She was, and still is, one of the sweetest people I know, and her husband Stan is also just a really good guy.

That night as we sat around the table eating, Fran, as usual, was telling me how to live my life. I think she recognized before I did that something was happening to our friendship. She was working very hard to keep control of me, something I hadn't realized or thought about until that moment. She wasn't happy with the new me. During all the years of my marriage, I was the underdog as far as she was concerned. I was "poor Ann," and she was successful Fran, even if only through her marriage, and she liked it that way. She loved to give me advice, offer me money, and offer me clothing. She was always trying to do things for me that would make me feel beholden to her consciously or unconsciously. I can't say for sure, but in hindsight I believe it nourished her need for importance. Most of the time my pride would say no, but it was a very hard fight on my part because Charlie was always ready to accept anything and everything, and there were times when I had to accept her offer of money or I couldn't have fed my kids.

Now things had changed. I was working for a movie producer. Just the words "movie producer" were enough to upset her. It was something she wasn't a part of and it sounded so glamorous. She didn't see me when I spent five hours standing on my feet feeding legal documents into the copy machine. She didn't see me going on personal errands for Pat or Peter. That part wasn't glamorous, but I loved every moment.

"Little plain Ann, how can she be part of a fairytale life?" she must have wondered. It certainly wasn't intentional on my part, but I think I was beginning to drive her crazy. I was now able to support myself, and I looked better and felt better. My whole attitude about myself had improved. I felt proud of what I was accomplishing. I was just so happy to finally be at a point in my life where I didn't owe anyone any money. It was the most wonderful feeling in the world, and it really bothered Fran. She liked me better when I was suffering. I understood what she was feeling, but she didn't and there wasn't anything I could do about it. I wasn't going backwards to make her or anybody else happy.

That night, as we sat in the restaurant, she lectured me on working too hard. I can still hear her saying with a lot of attitude and her ever sparkling diamonds, "You need to find a rich husband. Wouldn't you love to have a maid and a decent lifestyle? Why should you have to drag yourself to work every day on those damn subways with all those degenerates?"

Before I could answer, she continued ranting. "For God's sake, you lived with the creep for over twenty years, and what did you end up with but a bunch of bills?"

I finally couldn't keep quiet. "Fran, stop it. He's dead now, and I did get two beautiful daughters. Please. I'm happy working. I love what I do. I don't care about the things you care about."

"Well, you should! Look at you," she snapped. "You're as thin as a rail."

At that point poor Roz, who had been quiet all this time, finally spoke up. "Fran, you're wrong, she looks beautiful. She looks like a model." She protested.

That was something Fran did not want to hear, especially since she'd always had a weight problem.

I interrupted them. "Please, stop it. You all don't understand. I don't want a husband, at least not now. I love my life. I'm using my brain, and I'm getting paid well and people respect me. Don't you understand? I feel like a person, *me* Ann, not poor little Ann."

Fran was all set to interrupt me again, but I wouldn't let her. It was important to me that she understood how I felt. "I'm not afraid anymore. I'm not a little mouse anymore. I can take care of myself and my kids better than anyone else has ever done. Do you know how wonderful it is for the first time in over twenty years not to have to worry about how I'm going to pay the rent, not to owe you any money, not to live with a man who is either putting a pill under his tongue, gasping for breath, or listening to his breathing night after night, never knowing when I'm going to have to rush him to the hospital?" I stopped. I couldn't go on anymore.

Dear Stan tried to come to my rescue by assuring me they were only worried about me. They wanted to be sure that there was someone to take care of me if I couldn't work any longer. I thought to myself, "I'm only forty-four years old; are they crazy? What are they worrying about now?" It was later that I found out that he had given some man, some rich man that he vaguely knew, my phone number. I guess all this was to prepare me for a call from a stranger. I was just about to get really angry when a large group of people entered the restaurant. It became totally silent and everyone turned to stare. Two of the men in the group were prominent movie stars. One of them saw me as he passed our table and stopped. He smiled at me as if I was really someone important, and then bent down and hugged me. It was Richard Stewart, who at that time was very famous. "Ann," he said and took my hand, "How are you, dear? You look beautiful. Give my best to Peter." He kissed me on both cheeks, smiled at my friends, and walked away to join his group. For the first time in Fran's life she was speechless.

✿ 13 ✿

The very next day after this delightful dinner, Sally, our receptionist, called me in my office to say that Matt McKenzie had arrived for his appointment with Peter. I walked outside to get you, and you stood up, all six foot two inches of beauty. I can see you cringing, but you were beautiful. You still are.

I introduced myself to you. When you looked at me, your face lit up with a grin, and you took my hand to shake. For the briefest moment I felt a sense of recognition. Something passed between us that neither one of us recognized, but which I now know was the moment when we had become reunited in this lifetime. The moment passed as quickly as it had arrived. We didn't realize it then, but a new lifetime was beginning for us. Oh I know the skeptics would laugh at us, but we believed and that's all that really matters. Your dark brown eyes seemed to twinkle as you smiled. They still do, my darling.

I know I brought you in to meet Peter, and then I went down to Pat's office. Beautiful, exotic Pat, sat behind her massive marble desk, her feet up on the desk and the phone tucked behind her ear. She smiled when I came in.

As soon as she got off the phone, I told her what I had felt when I met you. "It was so weird. When he took my hand, I'd swear I'd held it before. Something about him is so familiar. Crazy I guess?"

"Maybe from a past life." she jokingly said. I laughed with her.

By the time I got back to my desk, my buzzer was going wild. It was Peter, summoning me in to his office. You were standing up holding a folder with pages inside.

"Thank Ann," Peter said to you. "She's the one who loved your script."

You looked at me with those wonderful eyes.

"Find him an office," Peter said, 'he's coming to work with us."

You looked so happy.

Peter had offered you a job working for the company, as part of the writing team that he employed. Although he said he would option your screenplay for a nominal amount of money, he also wanted you to work on other projects the firm was developing.

You were so excited that you probably would have said yes to anything he said, and who could blame you. Peter was considered one of the most respected movie producers, and any young writer would have been thrilled to have any kind of agreement with him.

He told me to call our attorney, Jim Fink, and have him draw up a contract for a year's employment, with an option to renew, as well as an option on your screenplay for twenty thousand dollars up front. I doubt if you really heard a word he said, but Peter made it clear to you that, other than the twenty thousand dollars, you would be working exclusively on salary for the first year. He also said that if one of the in house projects you worked on went into production and was ultimately released you'd get a bonus plus points. I remember that he did keep asking you if you understood what points were, and you kept saying you did. This was a new language you were yet to really understand.

ఙ 14 �

That was our beginning. You had this tiny little office, in the back next to the copy room. As I recall, it had a desk, a lamp, a file cabinet, and a chair. I don't think it had anything else, and I know it didn't have a window. It didn't matter to you. You were in seventh heaven. You were working, making new friends, and charming everyone, including me. You had taken the twenty thousand dollars that Peter had given you and rented an apartment downtown. It was your first apartment with no roommates, and you were thrilled. Until then, you had always managed to fall into the apartment of some friend or another and stay until you felt you were overstaying your welcome. Sometimes it was with a girl who thought your stay was a commitment, but you hadn't thought about it the same way. Once you realized what was happening, you would leave. You were young and free, and that's what you wanted and needed. One of your friends was a decorator. Oh God, you had so many "friends" in those days, mostly female. She did a wonderful job of making your tiny apartment really lovely. I didn't know that until much later, when I finally got to visit. But that's another story, isn't it, probably my favorite of all our stories. Not yet, dear Matt, let me do this my way.

I don't know how it began, but you had asked me if I had a little free time to type some of the pages of a script you were writing. You preferred writing on a yellow legal pad, and you couldn't type very well. Ah yes, the days before computers. I wasn't that busy that day, and said "sure". From that day on, your pages landed on my desk, and I would type them, even when I was busy, never letting Peter see what I was doing. I enjoyed doing it, because I felt like I was helping you become successful. I believed in you from day one. You'd hand me new pages, and I'd type them and bring them back to your little office in the back. Sometimes, if I weren't in a rush to get back to my desk, I'd sit across from you and we'd talk about the story. It was fun, and exhilarating for me. For you too, I realized much later on.

Everything between us was harmless. We were just very comfortable with one another. Never did I envision you as my potential lover, husband, or date. I had never been good at flirting, even when I was really young. I certainly wasn't flirting with you. I had never seen myself as the kind of woman men fell madly in love with. I couldn't imagine some guy looking at me and thinking "isn't she hot, isn't she beautiful, I've got to have her." I was the good girl. The girl you brought home to Mama, the girl you married, the virgin. When I was young and single, if I met a certain kind of man that aroused a sense of sexual excitement in me and made me long for something I'd never had, I'd become painfully shy and he would quickly lose interest. I was so afraid to show my sexuality, because I thought men would think less of me as a person. I was so pathetically a product of my generation. I just drowned in my self-consciousness, and so I had accepted what had been offered to me, my husband. That was an easy choice, because I didn't care enough, hence it was attainable. I had stopped looking at the untouchable. In retrospect, one of the saddest things that happen to any of us as human beings is that we can't blame anyone but ourselves for most of the choices we make in life. We are all capable of doing horrible things to ourselves, albeit often unwillingly. I married because it was the thing to do. My friends were getting married, my parents wanted to make a wedding and I wanted to have children. That was the path I chose. I didn't have had the courage to fight the society I was part of. I met a man who pursued me relentlessly, and I in the end was responsible for my lack of courage.

With you it was so easy, so comfortable. I could talk to you, admire your beauty, and look into your eyes when you spoke to me, because you were so much younger than I. You were safe. Although you were everything I had dreamed of when I was a young girl, I was no longer that young girl. It never crossed my mind to think of you as anything but the young writer who I loved working with. I was always myself with you. I was never self-conscious with you, because I never for a moment thought you'd think of me as anything but a friend.

❧ 15 ☙

On a Saturday morning in May, my phone rang at home. It was Sally, our receptionist. Sally was young, full of fun, and always loved to try new things. She was currently house-sitting a friend's houseboat, in the marina on the West Side in Manhattan, and she felt like having a party. She was calling everyone in the office to join her the next morning for brunch on the boat.

So far, five people had said yes: Pat; you; Miguel, our comptroller; Tony, Peter's associate; and Drue, Tony's assistant. Sally wanted me to join them as well.

It sounded like fun, and I asked her if I could also bring Jennifer, who was home from school that weekend. Liz was away at a friend's house on the Island, and I didn't want to leave Jennifer alone.

"Of course bring her. You can also bring the bagels. I've given everyone else their assignments."

I laughed and told her we'd be there. When I hung up I told Jennifer, who also thought it would be fun. She was a little surprised that I was willing to go on a boat since I'd always been leery of boats, really afraid. I laughed, and said something to the effect that I was on a new campaign to get rid of a fear a week. I also reminded her that the boat wasn't moving from the marina.

The next morning was a perfect day. Jennifer and I arrived at the 79th Street basin, and found the houseboat anchored amongst many other boats. We walked down the plank with our arms filled with groceries, since we had decided that bagels weren't enough to bring to a party. We were both dressed in jeans, tee shirts and sneakers, and we were laughing and excited. When we reached the boat, we saw Sally waving from the deck. We heard loud voices behind us, and turned to see Pat, Miguel, Drue, Tony and you, arriving together. We waited. Everyone was in a festive mood, as we all greeted each other. I introduced Jennifer to the group, or rather the ones she hadn't met before. Sally heard us, and called to us to come on board as she was starving. We all started climbing up the ramp. When we got to the top of the ramp, you were suddenly in front of me, and gave me your hand so I could jump on board. It was the first time since the day we met that our hands had really touched. I felt something I didn't understand. I tried to ignore it, and joined the gang. We followed Sally to the galley, where she immediately started putting all the food on plates. We found seats, and there you were seated next to me. I didn't think too much about it, until I noticed Drue looking at me in a strange way. Drue a very pretty, golden girl from a rich Connecticut family, had met Tony at a gallery opening a year earlier. She had ended up, not only sleeping with him, but soon becoming his assistant. Everyone knew she was very ambitious, and she was aggressive enough and pretty enough to make it big time, if she played her cards right. What I didn't know was that she had tired of Tony as a lover and you, my love, were on her list of things to do. Several times during the past year, she had come into your office while I was there and glared at me until I felt so uncomfortable I'd leave. I couldn't understand what was bothering her about me. You never seemed to notice. Sometimes I'd see you both leave the office together at night. She'd always make sure that I noticed. She'd have her arms around you, and my understanding of her body language was that you might be sleeping together. It wasn't any of my business. I knew you saw a lot of girls, because many times I'd hear you on the phone when I was in your office. You and Louise still got together, but your relationship definitely wasn't exclusive. You were young and attractive, so why not? In retrospect, I think Drue sensed, way before either of us, that something was going to happen between us and she was working very hard to prevent it.

I did once ask you if you were seeing her, and you vehemently denied it. I didn't believe you, but it wasn't my business, not then.

I turned away from Drue's glare and joined in with the fun everyone at the table seemed to be having. I looked at Jennifer sitting across from me, and she seemed happy and comfortable with everyone. It meant a lot to me to see my daughter happy. She had lived through so many sad moments in her life, and had always handled it with such grace. I was so proud of her. She was beautiful, brilliant, and most of all lovely. I felt very lucky as I looked at her smiling face.

Drue began asking you questions about your work, and of course everyone at the table had to make some comments about Peter. We all had such mixed feelings about him. You were in the midst of working on a new script, and he was being very difficult. It was the beginning of your discontent.

Drue tried to impress everyone by implying she'd had conversations with Peter about your work, and that he just "loved everything you did."

Pat, who was never one to sit quietly and disliked Drue intensely, immediately jumped on her. I can still hear her, as she said in her deep theatrical voice, accompanied with daggers in her eyes, "and my dear when did you and Peter have all these insightful conversations?"

Tony immediately came to Drue's defense. It was suddenly becoming really awful. Miguel, dear man, tried to stop them from having a real catfight, and changed the subject. Of all things, he asked me about a date I had had the week before, courtesy of Stan. I had finally run out of excuses, and had agreed to go out with his friend. The night had been a total disaster. Never again would I let anyone talk me into something I didn't want to do.

Miguel, who had become a dear friend to me and my family, and a confidant as well, meant no harm in asking. However, at that moment I could have killed him for asking. I had just realized that you had your arm around my chair, and the last thing I wanted to do was talk about the awful date that Stan had set up for me.

Before I could attempt to answer him, Drue loving the opportunity to be hurtful to me cut to the jugular. "You had a date?" she said in a voice filled with utter shock, making it sound as though it were an impossibility. I really got angry but wouldn't give her the pleasure of showing it.

Pat got furious at her. "Don't you ever give up?"

"It's nothing Pat," I said smiling. "He was very nice. There's really nothing special to tell you all about."

Drue wouldn't stop. She went on and on. "Did he make a pass? How old was he? I always wondered about people your age. I mean do you still do it?" She was simply horrible. She wasn't going to quit.

Oh Matt, I thought you would kill her. I felt your arm squeeze my shoulder, and I looked up and saw your blazing eyes. I don't remember ever feeling so protected in my life. I put my hand on your thigh without thinking, just to keep you seated. You looked at me, and covered my hand with yours. I don't remember another word that was said at the table, until Miguel finally suggested we all go up on to the deck.

Everyone seemed relieved to finally leave the galley. Sally opened a closet stacked with mats and handed them out to all of us.

Jennifer whispered as we climbed the stairs, "Mom, are you alright? What a bitch. How do you work with her? What's her problem?"

What could I say to my daughter? Could I tell her that this young, very beautiful girl, for some reason found me a threat? I didn't understand it, so all I could do was calm Jennifer down. I told her not to worry, and that I was fine.

A few minutes later, I had almost forgotten all about Drue and her nastiness. We had placed mats out on deck, and someone had turned on music. I was lying on a mat, looking at what was to me absolutely beautiful. The harbor filled with boats, gentle waves falling against the softly rocking boat, all made for a sense of peace and tranquility. I felt such contentment at that moment. I turned to Jennifer and said, "Isn't this nice? Before she could begin to answer, I followed with "What do you think of Matt?"

She smiled at me. "Mom, he likes you."

I looked at her in amazement. I didn't know what to reply. I knew what I had felt down in the galley, but I didn't think it meant more than a friend protecting another friend. I actually felt myself blushing. It just seemed so impossible.

"Jennifer, do you know how old he is?"

"Mom, you're blind. He really likes you. It's okay. He's not a kid Mom." she tried to assure me. My own child was encouraging me to look at the world a little differently than I had ever done before.

I didn't know what to say. I turned away from her, and watched as Drue got up and walked to you. You had been sitting on a mat, staring into space. She pulled you by your arm and said, "let's dance."

I heard you answer, "there's no room for dancing," but she wouldn't take no for an answer, and you let her pull you up.

The music was soft, and slow, and she moved her body as close as possible into yours. I couldn't help but watch. We all did.

You looked so uncomfortable dancing with her, but she didn't seem to notice or care. When the music stopped, Tony came to claim her for the next dance. She looked annoyed as you made a hasty retreat back to your cushion. They began dancing, and we could all see how familiar their bodies were with each other. It was obvious they'd been together many times.

I looked over at you. You were once again sitting on your mat, quietly thinking. Jennifer had gone over to Pat, and joined her and Miguel and Sally to play cards.

I closed my eyes and allowed the sun to rest on my face. It felt so wonderful. I sensed a presence, and opened my eyes and you were standing over me. You extended your hand, and mumbled, "let's dance."

Before I could answer, you had pulled me to my feet. I could feel my face burning, and yet I was filled with a sense of excitement I couldn't explain. You took me in your arms and I, who was five foot six inches tall, had never felt so tiny. At first we were a little stiff, but within moments our bodies relaxed and moved comfortably together. The movement of the boat seemed to push us even closer. I looked up and met your eyes, which seemed to be studying me. I smiled nervously before looking down as we continued to dance.

We were so engrossed in a beginning, a start of a meshing of bodies that seemed to know each other so easily. Our movements were all about feelings. "Who are we, what's going on?" We weren't very good dancers, and then again we knew it wasn't about dancing. I could sense Drue staring at us. I didn't want to look at her, or at anyone. I didn't want to see the fury in her eyes. I didn't want to know if anyone else was paying attention to us. I just wanted to stay lost in this moment. I didn't want anyone to ruin it.

The music ended, and as I stood breathless and still in your arms, you abruptly told me you had to leave.

I felt myself go limp. I was confused and disappointed, and I tried not to show it.

"I have a lot of work to do," you said aloud. Then you lowered your voice, so no one else would hear you, and told me that the only reason you had come in the first place was because you knew I'd be here.

I didn't know what to say. My face burned. This was all so unexpected. We'd known each other for over a year, and this was the first time you'd said anything so personal to me.

You didn't wait for any answer, you just bent down and kissed the top of my head, and walked away to say goodbye to everyone else.

When Drue heard you telling people you were leaving, she jumped up and ran after you. "Wait! I'll go with you. I have to get home and do my laundry."

We all looked at her in amazement. Laundry! We felt sorry for Tony. He immediately jumped up as well. "I'll take you home." he said.

Oh no, this wasn't what she had in mind. She wouldn't hear of it. She made him stay. "Why should your day be spoiled?" she insisted. He felt like a fool in front of everyone, and stopped arguing with her. You hadn't waited for her, and had already left the boat. She just ran after you. We could all hear her calling your name, as she raced down the pier. Obviously, she couldn't care less what anyone thought of her.

I wondered for years what happened that day between the two of you. Whenever I asked, you swore to me that you did not sleep with her. I had wanted to believe you, because I knew her reason for pursuing you was to hurt me. I wanted to believe you knew that and would not let her win. I have to tell you now, dear, that I never believed you. You were young and needy, and at that time we were just a dream. No matter what happened that day she didn't win at all. And, when you finally told me it was a relief.

I wanted to shout into the screen," I'm so sorry Ann. I'm so sorry." I had tried so hard to get rid of Drue that afternoon, but she had caught up to me. I'd wanted to get home, and think about the feelings that had erupted in me when I'd held Ann in my arms. I had never wanted to take someone to bed as badly as I had on that dance floor. She had looked so tiny, so innocent, and so sweet. She had felt so right in my arms. I'd had to get away fast. Then I'd had this bitch running after me.

"Do you have to walk so fast?" she'd yelled from behind. Just then I'd seen an empty cab and hailed it. As I'd opened the door she had reached my side and slid in. There had been no choice but to follow her.

"Where can I drop you?" I'd asked.

"You're joking?" she'd responded

I had looked at her and thought, "Oh, what the hell. I'm so horny anyone will do." Yes, dear Ann, I tell you this now when you can't hear me, but I was sorry that day and forever after. I hope you knew it meant absolutely nothing to me.

❧ 16 ☙

I didn't realize it then, but I fell in love with you that day Matt. It had never occurred to me that you, of all people, would see me as anything other than the woman who worked for Peter, who you enjoyed talking to, and who also helped type your scripts. Of all the women you encountered, what could you possibly see in me I kept asking myself? I was just me, a fairly average looking, halfway intelligent, but not brilliant woman, who had just started to learn to smile and was building a new life. Most importantly, I was sixteen years older than you. It was absurd. Much as I told myself it was senseless, impossible and could never be, it didn't stop me from having feelings that I had never believed I was capable of feeling. After that day on the houseboat, I looked for signs in everything you did, in every word you uttered to me. I waited, wanting to believe that your words were the beginning of something more. I didn't begin to visualize what that "more" could be, but a yearning had been created. I waited, but nothing happened. Instead, at the end of many days, I watched you meet different young women and go off with your arm around whoever she might be. The parade was endless. I felt so stupid.

You have always been a very touchy person, and many of the times when we were together in your office you instinctively touched my shoulder, touched my hair, or kissed me on top of my head. I would take these moments very seriously, and I'd look at you, too embarrassed to say anything, simply waiting for you to say something. It wasn't happening.

As I walked down the street at the end of a day, I'd find myself admonishing myself, questioning how I, who had lived such a strait laced sexual and personal life, could have such overwhelming feelings for someone so many years younger than myself. I was behaving like a kid in the first heat of their life. Miss Perfect was how I had been viewed. I had spent my life wearing the white gloves of my perceived perfection. I had done nothing to change that image, until the day I had taken control of my life, and had defied Charlie and found my job with Peter.

Until that moment in time I had only slept with one man in my entire life, my husband. I had been a virgin when I got married. It had been expected of me, and I always did what was expected of me.

One night during my engagement to Charlie as we "necked," *can you believe that's what was you did back then?* He asked me if I were still a virgin. I was outraged to think he could even question such a thing. I began crying, and he felt terrible for having asked. That was the woman I had once been.

I had never known or felt a love that was exciting and unbelievably sexual. I never believed that I would ever be madly in love with someone who would love me back as passionately. That was the one dream I had always secretly coveted. I was a hopeless romantic. If I saw a couple walking down the street, holding hands and looking into each other's eyes in that special way that lovers do, I felt pure envy. I would have given anything to feel as that woman did. Ha! Even now, some twenty years later, I still am that hopeless romantic. But thanks to you, my darling, I've been the woman I so envied.

One evening, as I was getting ready to leave the office, Pat waylaid me. "What are you doing tonight?" she asked.

I laughed. "The same thing I do every night. I'm going home."

"No you're not. You're coming with Miguel and me. We're going out for drinks and dinner."

I hesitated for a second, but then I said yes. I wanted to have some fun. I was so tired of just going home every night. Jennifer was back at school, and Liz was going to a friend's house for the night to do a project, and sleep over. I had no good reason to say no, and Miguel and Pat were fun people.

Pat was thrilled that I had finally said yes to something social. We picked up Miguel, and the three of us first went to the bar at the Regency Hotel. It was the first time I had been there, and I felt very sophisticated. We found a table, and I let them order the drinks and fried zucchini. This was all so new to me. I rarely drank, and had never eaten zucchini, no less fried. As I say all this now, I realize how naïve and unsophisticated I was. You would have thought we were ordering caviar and champagne. I got excited those days over the most mundane thing. Everything seemed fabulous, and exciting to me. It's no wonder a twenty-six year old man, who had traveled all over the world, didn't think I was too old for him. I was a juvenile in a grown up life.

I looked around at all the other people in the room, and imagined they were all rich and famous, which I now realize was silly. But it was fun thinking that way. As we were ordering, I looked up, and there you were standing over me. I could feel my heart begin racing, and my face burn as I smiled and tried to say "hi."

Pat asked you what you were doing there, and you told us you were waiting for Louise, who was late. Pat immediately told you to sit with us

44

until you had to leave. You smiled, and we made room for you. Once again, as you had on the houseboat, you managed to sit next to me, with your arm around my chair. Every so often I could feel your hand touch my shoulder, making it impossible for me to concentrate on everyone's conversation. My blissful state was soon shattered when Louise appeared. She was decidedly annoyed with you, and wasn't ashamed to show it. It seems you were supposed to meet her outside. She had been cooling her heels in the lobby for some time and there you were with us, apparently having a good time.

You gave her your best smile as you jumped up, and your arm was now around her shoulder as you calmed her down and said a quick goodbye to all of us. With my first stirrings of jealousy, I watched you go.

Pat picked up my feelings almost at once. "You like him, don't you?"

I tried to act shocked at her question. I wasn't a very good actress.

She totally ignored my reaction, and got right into it. "You know what you need?" Before I could answer she just went right on. "You need to get laid."

I laughed and blushed at the same time. "That's your answer to everything. Anyway, I don't think I remember how."

"Believe me," she laughed. "You never forget. I think that young man that just ran out of here is the perfect person for you."

"Are you crazy? Do you know how old he is?"

"So he's younger than you. Big deal! Admit it Ann, you want him. I've watched you. You're hungry, and you protest too much my dear."

"That sounds so awful."

"What's awful about desire? You're such a fool. My God, you're the only woman I know who's only slept with one man in her entire life. For Pete's sake go out there and have an affair. Damn it, it won't kill you honestly."

"I can't," I moaned. "What will people think?"

"You're hopeless. You are so Victorian, I'm nauseous."

Miguel agreed with her.

"No one's asking anyway," I replied, like a child.

"Ah ha," Pat screeched. "You do want to sleep with him! I was right. What do you need, a gold engraved invitation?"

I looked at her, and knew she was right. What was I supposed to do, just go up to you, and tell you what I felt? I couldn't. It had to come from you. That's the way I was. During all the years of my marriage if I wanted sex I could never bring myself to ask Charlie. He made it clear from the beginning that it had to come from him. He thought it unbecoming for a woman to be the aggressor. Ladies didn't do that he told me, and I believed him. How could I possibly know if he was wrong? I didn't know any better, because he was the only man I had ever slept with. He had set the rules, and I'd followed them. He had so many rules. His wife must never curse, never wear sexy clothing, and never initiate sex.

I was ready to break all of those rules if I could get the nerve.

ങ 17 ങ

Weeks went by. I tried to stop thinking about you other than as a lovely young man who I worked with. I convinced myself I had imagined your interest and that I was just a silly woman. I pretended not to pay any attention to the young girls I saw you with, particularly Drue, who never stopped throwing herself at you, especially if she thought I would notice. If you found her interesting, it was none of my business.

Working for Peter was great. He had become so much nicer to me, and in my own way I worshipped him. To me he had become my knight in shining armor. He had allowed me to become a part of a company that was exciting, challenging and part fantasy. He had given me a new life and I was eternally grateful. Almost everyone in the firm had become my extended family. We all shared each other lives, and other than Drue and Tony, we were all really fond of each other. I loved the industry, and to spend my days working with people all over the world who made movies was beyond my wildest dreams. I worked really long hours, sometimes even on the weekend. It didn't matter. I loved the job so much, that time just flew by. Each day was more interesting, and exciting than the last one had been. I felt so lucky, so blessed.

One particular night Peter asked me to stay very late. He needed the contracts I had been working on for a meeting the next morning. He had to finalize them, but he had a date picking him up shortly, and he didn't want to cancel her.

"Do you mind staying late? I shouldn't be gone more than a couple of hours," he told me with a grin on his face. The implication being, it was not dinner he was looking forward to.

I was getting used to watching the people I worked with live lives I personally never could have entertained. I got a big kick out of them. It was as though I was part of a soap opera, but I was the audience. I couldn't really participate, but I lived vicariously through their adventures.

I assured him I could stay.

"I want you to look her over when she gets here," he said. "Let me know what you think."

I laughed. A few minutes later, a very pretty, voluptuous blonde woman walked through my office, in a black dress that appeared to have been sewn on to her body, and asked for Peter.

Peter heard her, and came out of his office to greet her. He took her back into his office to show her around, and before too long they came out again. He introduced her to me as Joy. Her name seemed so appropriate to his reaction. She was actually very sweet, and seemed concerned about my working so late. I had seen some of his other dates, and although they all physically seemed to be the same type, she seemed to be a little less self-centered. Sexy, as they all were, she was nicer.

They were leaving, but he'd be back later. "Why don't you go out and grab a bite of food, and then come back and wait for me," he told me.

I said I would in a little while. He gave me that great smile that made it all worth doing. He had that way with people that made them give him their best.

As they turned to leave, you walked into my office. You were working late and had heard voices.

Peter seemed as surprised to see you as I did, and asked you why you were still in the office.

When you answered, "I do my best work at night," Joy's eyes devoured you. That was your magic. Woman just couldn't get enough of you. She mumbled, but I heard her say, "I bet you do." I suddenly disliked her. She was no longer sweet, as far as I was concerned. This new aspect of my personality was beginning to spring up too frequently. That green-eyed monster, jealousy, had edged its way into my psyche and I wasn't able to shove it away. I had never been a jealous person, but that was the old Ann.

Peter just ignored the exchange and took her by the arm and ushered her out of the office.

The moment they left, you turned to me. "Working late again?"

I just nodded.

"You look tired. Do you want to go out and grab something to eat?"

I couldn't believe I had heard right. I stared at you and then looked down at my desk. I had to hear you ask again.

"I have all these contracts to finish." I finally mumbled, as I felt the jealousy leave my body and a great deal of relief arrive to replace it.

"You have to eat some time. Come on."

I looked up at your face and wanted nothing more than to go out with you. All my vows and words to myself these past months simply vanished. I pushed the papers back, and took off my glasses. You were standing at my desk and I smiled.

You put your hands behind my neck and started to massage it. I couldn't breathe, no less talk. I sat quietly, trying so hard not to show what I was feeling. When you finally stopped, you ruffled my hair and said, "Come on, let's go."

I looked up at you and somehow managed to get up from the chair.

We walked to a cute little restaurant a couple of blocks away from the office. You put your arm around my shoulder as we made our way. There was something about that gesture that felt so right. I didn't want the walk to end. I kept telling myself not to read anything into this sudden invitation, and even though I'd seen you walking this way many a night as you left the office with some girl, to me it seemed special.

A few minutes later, we were sitting at a table waiting for our food. At first we simply sat staring at one another, and then you broke the silence and told me once again that I looked tired and that you thought I worked too hard.

My first thought was "oh my, I must look awful." I pushed my hair away, and tried not to focus on what I looked like.

"It's just been a long day."

You must have read my mind, so you quickly made sure to tell me that you weren't saying I looked awful, but that you were concerned for my health.

I had to smile at your attempt at chivalry. It was sweet, and you weren't really the sweet type.

"All this work doesn't leave you much time for other things."

"Like what?" I asked. "I don't have that much else to do anymore. My kids are growing up and they have their own lives. Liz is going off to college in September, and the house will be empty then. At least work occupies my mind." As I was saying all this to you, I realized that I was really screwing up any relationship between us. By referring to my children, I had just made myself seriously older than you, and probably bored you with my honesty.

You didn't react, but kept right on asking me questions. And suddenly I stopped trying to undo anything I had said. "This is who I am." I thought, 'and he's really interested."

When you next asked me if I ever missed not having fun, I tried to explain that I was having my own kind of fun.

"Just coming to work every day is fun for me. I get to meet people most people only read about." I looked at you, feeling a sense of urgency. Even though we had talked so many times in your office after I'd typed your pages, the talks were usually about you. This time I wanted you to understand something more about me. "You see it, don't you, the excitement? It's fantasyland."

You tried to interrupt me, but I couldn't stop talking.

"You don't understand. You're so young, and everything is in front of you. When I went out there looking for a job, after years of just being a wife, and mom, most of the doors were closed. They looked at me as if, oh, as if I had one foot in the grave. I was only just forty and I was considered old. It was awful."

You looked at me in amazement, and told me you couldn't understand, since you didn't think I was old and you thought I was beautiful.

I couldn't believe you had called me beautiful. I don't think anyone had ever called me beautiful before. I felt the heat rush to my face as you said this.

I had to keep talking. I don't remember anything I said, but you seemed to listen to every word as though I were totally fascinating.

I finally ran dry and stopped talking; or almost.

I'm sorry, I'm ranting. I must sound like an idiot to you".

You were so sweet. "No you don't. I think you're terrific." you assured me.

"Don't you have anyone; a guy?" you then asked me.

I shook my head no. I wanted to say I'd had enough togetherness to last a lifetime, but I didn't.

"What about sex?" you persisted.

"I just don't think about it," I answered quickly. What a liar I was. I was sitting next to you, and all I could think of was what it would be like to have you make love to me. I couldn't believe I was thinking all this, but I was. Instead I said something really stupid to the effect that I didn't see anyone falling all over me, so I didn't have to think about sex.

"Maybe you don't give anyone any encouragement."

"Did you mean yourself?" I wondered, but I was too afraid to find out.

"Promise you won't laugh," I answered. Your eyes told me you wouldn't. "I just don't know how to encourage a man. I feel like such a jerk. I'm always afraid I'll make a fool of myself. I mean, what if I thought they were interested and I encouraged them, and then I was wrong? I'd feel so dumb. I'm not good at talking to most men. I get so tongue tied."

"But you're talking to me."

"But that's different."

"Why, because I'm younger than you are? So you think I'm not looking at you in a sexual way?"

I didn't know how to answer you. I wanted to say, "Are you looking at me in a sexual way?" But I couldn't do that. I couldn't take the chance you'd laugh at me. I said nothing.

You looked at me as though I were pathetic. "Don't you ever look in the mirror? You're very beautiful, you have a great body and you're very desirable."

I could feel myself beaming at you and blushing like a fool.

"I'm embarrassing you. Don't be. I love talking to you, and looking at you. "

You then covered my hand with yours.

I felt myself grinning at you. I think I knew at that moment that I could say almost anything to you, and you'd understand. We had talked many times before, but this night was different. We had found a sense of belonging that, despite the bumps of life that would come to us in the years that followed, would never take away what we had discovered. For me, it was a sense of finding someone I had always known, but couldn't find. When people talk about soul mates I understand it completely. You were mine, and I yours, and we had recognized each other the first day you walked into Peter's office, and tonight in one moment we had come home. From that day forward we were always able to find each other despite two lives that were often worlds apart. You also became my best friend that night, and I, yours.

Once again I had to stop the machine. I'd been sitting and watching, and listening to Ann relive all those precious moments of the beginning of us. I closed my eyes, and saw us there as clearly as if it all happened a day ago, and I cried. I had loved her from the moment I saw her, as she approached me in Peter's waiting room. I probably appeared to her as a brazen, nervy kid. She had no idea how frightened I was at the prospect of meeting the great Peter Simmons. Yet, something about her, that was impossible to define, calmed me down and gave me the guts to go in to his office and sell myself as a future writer. That took a lot of nerve. Always, from that day on, I sensed I had this wonderful woman in my corner, cheering me on. Now she was gone, and I felt lost. I needed to talk to someone, but there was no one I could call. I'd kept so much of our relationship just between us. I know women talk to their friends more easily than men do. I hope that when I hurt her, as I did so many times during all the years, she had someone she could go to. I had to turn the machine back on.

I had totally forgotten about eating, until the waiter arrived with our food. As we ate, you began telling me stories about growing up in a tiny town. You told me about your family, and they sounded so nice and loving. You, to hear you tell it, were a horror and made your parents crazy with fear. I laughed at your stories about your disastrous experiences with girls.

"I'm sure you're not that way anymore. I see you with Louise and Drue," I managed to say. I was asking to get hurt by bringing them up, but I couldn't help it.

You rolled your eyes. "Drue? No way. I can't stand her. As for Louise, she's fun most of the time, and the great thing about her is that she doesn't confuse sex with love."

I was going to say something, but you wanted to keep talking, and I wanted to hear what you had to say.

"Look, I guess I use Louise, but she uses me too. I know that sounds awful, but it works for us. It's that simple. We each get what we want, and for me probably it's better that way. I'm not good in relationships. I always seem to hurt people. I don't mean to. It's just that I can't seem to give as much as people want, or need. Louise needs a guy on her arm, so it's been easy, but I'm trying not to do that anymore." You looked at me with those dark twinkling eyes, and reached across and squeezed my hand. "It's hard to change."

When you said that, I wondered if you were trying to warn me, to tell me something, but I didn't know how to ask you.

"You're not cruel."

You smiled at me as if I were a child.

"Do you want to do something some night?"

"Just us?" I asked like a fool.

You broke out laughing. "Yes, you idiot, just us."

I searched your face and, to me, I saw life. I think I knew then, that picture of you would be the one I would pull up for the rest of my life. Your face looking at me with something no one had ever given me before. I had never felt so unbelievably loved and happy.

"Okay" was all I could answer.

That settled, we began talking about your work. I told you how much I loved your latest script, and that Peter liked it too.

"He does? He hasn't said anything. All he does is grunt. Can I tell you something I couldn't tell anyone else?"

I shook my head yes.

"I get so scared. I mean how do I know I have any talent? What makes me think I'm so special I'll ever write a great script? Maybe I really stink."

I couldn't believe you felt so insecure.

"No, no. You are good. Everyone gets scared. You asked me why I work so hard. Part of it is I'm scared too. Scared I won't be as good as someone else, and they'll replace me. I think most people who are halfway intelligent need to prove themselves more than most. Don't ask me why I know it, but I know you're good. You'll be fabulously successful someday. So please remember I'm the one who said it." I laughed. "Remember when you win an Academy Award think of me."

You laughed. "I'll tweak my ear and you'll know it's for you." You took my hand in yours, and told me you could talk to me forever. I remember thinking how nice it was to be with someone who listened, really listened. And then I could feel tears welling in my eyes, because I was remembering my marriage, my husband who never heard a word I said, and I felt so sad. You saw the change in me at once, and tried to get me to tell you what I was thinking about.

"It's nothing," I said.

"I hate people, especially women who say 'it's nothing' when you know damn well it's something."

I wanted so much to tell you everything about me, everything that ever happened to me, but I couldn't. I took your hand, and told you that the one subject I couldn't talk about was my marriage.

You squeezed my hand and again nodded.

"If you ever want to talk about it let me know."

I shook my head yes.

❧ 19 ☙

It was the night of the firm's annual Christmas party. A large hotel suite had been converted into a nightclub atmosphere. We had arranged for a buffet dinner as well as a DJ, and everything looked beautiful. The rooms were filled mostly with Peter's friends and clients, as well as the entire office staff.

I was talking to Pat and Miguel, when you came over to us. Weeks and weeks had passed since that night in the restaurant. You'd never said another word about getting together. Yet every time I turned around, you'd seem to be there. I was like a teenager with a terrible crush. I couldn't get you out of my mind. Part of me was ashamed of myself, and the other part refused to think about the age difference. I had feelings for you I had never before had, and I didn't care about anything else. I had never known it was possible to feel this way about someone. I simply had to look at you and I could have devoured you. I was on a crash course to love.

We were laughing and enjoying the party, when I felt your arm go around my shoulder. Just feeling your arm on my shoulder was enough to make me happy. I looked across the room and saw Drue and Tony. As usual she was glaring at me. I turned my face away. I just wasn't in the mood to let her spoil my evening. She was constantly trying to hurt my feelings, "but not tonight," I vowed to myself.

It didn't take long before she came over to us with Tony at her side.

He immediately started complaining about the party. He thought we should have had it at the Four Seasons restaurant, as we had the year before.

Pat couldn't keep quiet, and reminded him that he was the one who had said the restaurant had been too expensive.

That shut him up. He only said what he had said because Drue knew I had helped plan this party, and she wanted me to look stupid.

You, bless you, in order to protect me, dropped your arm so that it fell around my waist and you pulled me closer to you as you told them what a great time you were having.

Drue's eyes narrowed, her face filled with venom. "Well Peter obviously didn't share your enthusiasm, he just left."

"He thought the party was great. Don't you ever have anything nice to say? It happens he has to make an early plane," Pat quickly answered.

She ignored Pat and turned back to me. "I hear you may be joining him in LA, is that true?" she asked with a look that was filled with scorn.

"Maybe," I replied. I was, but it was none of her business. This was going to be my first business trip and I was very excited. I had never been to Los Angeles and I couldn't believe this was happening to me.

"Won't it be hard to leave your kids?" she asked, sarcastically. Before I could answer she put her hand to her mouth as if she had committed a terrible faux par and looked at you with a knowing grin. Then she turned back to me. "Oh, I keep forgetting they're all grown up, and you're old enough to be our mothers."

I wanted to punch her in the mouth. She was so unbelievably cruel. Before I could do or say anything, you pulled me aside, and took me on to the dance floor.

"Are you all right?"

I could feel tears welling in my eyes.

"What did I ever do to her that makes her so hateful?"

"You are too nice and that's something she can't deal with. Do you want to get out of here?"

"Oh yes," I said. I felt such a sense of excitement and happiness. The hell with Drue, I thought.

"Let me tell Pat and Miguel I'm leaving."

We agreed to meet in the lobby, and you walked away, as I ran to Pat.

"I'm leaving now." I told her.

She grinned at me. "With him, I assume."

I just grinned back at her.

She walked with me to the coatroom. I was getting very frightened.

"Pat, is it okay? He's so young. What am I doing? Oh God, I'm a wreck."

She just laughed. "Why does everything have to be a big deal with you? Just go for it. It doesn't have to be the love affair of the century, to sleep with someone."

"It does for me," I told her. "You don't understand, all of my life I've been wrapped up in white gloves. It's so hard to take them off. What will people think of me?"

Pat got really furious with me. "Listen to me you idiot. You don't owe anyone an explanation but yourself. Look at you. You've spent your whole life doing what people expected of you. What did it get you, Miss Perfect? Ann, if you can live with it, damn the world. Go for it sweetie. You know you want this."

I wanted so badly to listen to her.

I hugged her and thanked her. She was such a great friend.

You were waiting for me in the lobby. All I can remember is that it was snowing outside as we began walking aimlessly through the city streets. I hardly noticed it once you put your arm around my shoulder.

Once again I had to stop the machine. I knew what was coming and I needed a few minutes before I could turn the tape back on. I wondered if Ann had known that that night of all nights was imbedded in my mind as clearly as if it happened yesterday. Had I ever told her how much it had meant to me, I wondered?

I knew I had to go on. Watching Ann's face as she talked about their beginning was amazing in itself. She lost years and became a young woman again as she relived those precious days.

I hit the button and began watching and listening to her again.

We must have walked silently through the snow-filled streets for about five blocks, when you stopped. I held my breath, waiting.

"You never saw my apartment. Want to come up?"

"Oh my God," I thought. "It's going to happen." I shook my head yes, and the next thing I knew you were hailing a cab.

ಬ 20 ಛ

We rode the elevator to your apartment without saying a word to one another. Whatever we were thinking was another matter. You fumbled with the key, but finally opened the door. I couldn't stop staring at the back of your head. So silly. Every part of me was wired with senses that were beyond description. We walked into the dark apartment. You ran ahead to turn on the lights. I was really surprised at how nice it all looked. Your "friend" the decorator had furnished the living room almost entirely in white and black, except for a beautiful oak table that was set up as a desk. The room, although small, looked much larger because of its furnishings. I didn't expect you to have such a neat home. To me there was a sense of adventure in you. I saw you as a bohemian, a guy with torn jeans and leather patches on your jacket. You had lived so much for your years. You had been all over the world and had relationships that were somewhat exotic. You were young, but definitely not a kid. What did I know about a life like yours? I'd spent the last twenty odd years being a mother and wife. No travel, no adventures, and only one man.

I complimented you on the room, peaked into the tiny kitchen, and then smiled to myself as I looked at the sink filled with unwashed dishes. This was more of what I had expected from you. This sloppiness lived up to the image I'd conjured up. I followed you into the bedroom that was the size of a large closet. All that fit into the room was a bed and a tiny table next to the bed that held your phone. On the wall in front of the bed were shelves that housed your television set and some books. Your clothes were thrown all over the bed, and when we walked in you quickly shoved them on to the floor. We threw our coats on top of the rumpled clothing.

You walked to the TV set and turned it on as Johnny Carson began his show. You sat down on the bed and flicked on your answering machine. I stood awkwardly, watching you. I didn't know what I was supposed to do. A girl's voice came on the machine. The moment she said "Hi Matt," you turned it off. I could tell you were embarrassed. I decided to take my chances and sat down on the bed next to you. You propped up a couple of pillows and leaned back, I sat next to you pretending I, too, was looking at the television, but I wasn't. I didn't know what came next. I was so uncomfortable. I'd never gone to a guy's apartment before. I had no idea who did what. "Why am I here?" I asked myself. I knew I had to find out.

I finally whispered, "Could you move over?" I was totally out of my league. I just didn't know what to do or how to act. I was so afraid that I was making a fool of myself, but you quickly moved over and made room for me.

"Can I have one of the pillows?"

You gave me one and I put it under my head and stared ahead, again pretending I was watching Johnny Carson.

We just lay there. I just wanted my heart to stop beating so loudly. I was sure you could hear every beat. And then I felt your arm reach around my neck and I instinctively rested my head in your arm. Your hand began to gently stroke my shoulder and I could barely breathe. I was having trouble swallowing, and my heart kept beating so fast I was sure you could see it through my blouse. I finally dared to look up and found your eyes searching mine. We didn't have to say a word. Your face came towards me and our lips finally touched. Everything I had imagined happened. When we finally broke away I looked into your face and you were smiling. You ran your fingers through my hair and looked at me with a look that made me shudder. You pulled me fiercely into your arms where we found one another in a rush of passion that carried us to a special place, our place then and always.

Hours later I looked up at you and you took my chin in your hand and studied my face.

"What are you looking at?"

You smiled so tenderly. "You're wonderful," you told me. "I've been dreaming of this since the first time I saw you."

I couldn't believe you had felt this way about me and for so long. I couldn't understand what it was you had seen in me that had opened your heart to me. You were young and beautiful, talented and smart. You could have had almost any young girl you set your mind to. What was it you saw?

Oh Ann" I cried in to the screen. "I saw you. "

"Thank you," was all I could think to say to you.

You looked at me with surprise. You couldn't understand why I was thanking you.

I tried to explain my feelings, but it wasn't easy. I wanted you to know how much these past hours had meant to me, and also for you to understand how frightened I was that you would be disappointed in me. It had been so long since I'd been with anyone, and I was afraid I wouldn't be very good.

You looked at me with bewilderment. And then you lifted my face and looked at me lovingly. You pulled me toward you and held me all the while caressing my hair and kissing my neck, and then my lips.

"Oh God," you mumbled. "Did he do a number on you. Don't you know you're a beautiful, desirable woman? "

I felt tears building, and you kissed my eyes as they fell on my face and gently wiped away the remains. You held me in your arms and once again we made love.

Hours later, we were still lying in bed when we both realized we were hungry. You threw me one of your shirts that lay on the floor, and I put it on and followed you into the kitchen. I never told you this darling, but I still have that shirt. I never laundered it, because whenever I needed you and missed you, I'd hold it in my hands and bury my nose into it and breathe in the aroma of you. All these years later, I swear I can still smell you.

We were eating sandwiches, when I heard the noise of the TV from the other room and realized how late it was.

"Oh my God, I never called the girls. They'll think something awful has happened to me. I forgot all about them."

You tried to convince me that I was worrying for nothing, and you begged me to spend the night, but I couldn't. This was all so new to me, and I didn't want them to know I had spent the night with a man, especially you.

I called home, and when a very frightened voice answered, I felt terrible. The joy of this special evening almost evaporated. I lied and said that my watch had stopped; that I had gone to Pat's house after the party and didn't realize how late it was. I told Jennifer I'd get a cab and would be home soon. "Go to bed sweetie and please forgive me." I could hear Liz in the background complaining about my behavior and I thought, "Oh what would she say if she really knew?"

I pulled on my clothes and left on your shirt as well, which is how I came to keep it. You threw on jeans and a sweater so you could take me downstairs to get a cab. As we were leaving the apartment you pulled me in your arms and, in a barely audible voice, you told me you didn't want to hurt me. I didn't know what to say to you, as it was inconceivable to me at that moment that you could possibly hurt me.

"I'm not good at relationships. I screw them up."

I stood on my toes and kissed you. "Don't," I said. "No thinking tonight. Not you and not me. Don't let's spoil it. You won't screw it up. You'll see.'

"I hope not," you mumbled.

I rode home in a state of bliss. As the car drove through the darkened streets, I closed my eyes and relived the entire night. It was one of the most perfect nights I had ever had. I couldn't stop smiling as I remembered each moment.

ೞ 21 ೦೩

You did screw it up. So did I. Neither one of us meant to but this was the beginning of a relationship that would be filled with constant ups and downs. We had something so rare and special but we didn't know how to deal with it. It took us so many years and so many different ways to handle our many incarnations.

I was sixteen years older than you and I was the child. I was in love. That's all I knew. I had committed to you with my body and soul. I was the teenager expecting a 'boyfriend'. If we slept together, didn't that have to mean something? It did, but it was so much more complicated than that.

I came from a world where I had slept with one man, my husband and not until our wedding night. I knew the world had changed and I thought I could deal with the new world, but I was still that naive young woman of yesteryear. I expected that our night together would lead to other nights and when you didn't talk to me about it or ask for more I felt, not only bewildered, but cheapened and so very foolish. It never occurred to me that you might be frightened by me. My seriousness was worn for anyone who cared enough to see. But I could only see my own anguish. How could I have allowed myself to think we had a chance? I was a mother and had been a wife for twenty years. What was I doing? I tried to demean myself and it worked. I had so little esteem in my worth as a desirable female that it was very easy for me to blame myself. I couldn't believe that I had been so stupid to think that someone like you would want me.

I found myself in a constant daze, and Pat noticed how sad I looked. She came into my office one day. I looked up at her and she stared at me as though I were the most pathetic thing she had ever seen.

"You slept with him, right?"

I had never discussed that night with her and she hadn't asked.

My face turned red. No response was necessary.

"And?"

"And what? He obviously didn't enjoy the night because he hasn't said anything about it again." I started to cry and she sat there quietly until I finally was able to stop.

"Oh Ann, you're such a fool. It's my fault. I talked you into it. How was I supposed to know you'd fall in love with him?"

"I thought he cared. He said so and it was all so wonderful."

"Don't you understand that sex and love are two different things? I'm sure it was just as wonderful for him as for you."

"I don't agree with you."

She just shook her head at me. She was so much more sophisticated than I.

Just then the door to Peter's office opened and you came walking out into mine. You walked over to Pat and gave her a big hello, and even kissed her on the cheek. You gave me a faint smile. I felt frozen in my chair. I couldn't believe how coldly you were acting towards me. I was totally bewildered and hurt. No sooner had you cruelly ignored me, when the other door to my office opened and Drue stuck her head in. She saw you. "Oh good I was looking for you," she said. "Remember we have a luncheon date in fifteen minutes." The bitch gave me her superior smile and left.

To say you looked uncomfortable would be putting it mildly. You looked like you wanted to run from fire.

I could feel myself trembling and Pat quickly tried to get you out of my office. You looked at me, and saw my hurt. You almost stopped to say something but thought better of it and left.

"It's nothing," Pat said.

"Nothing, nothing! How could he? He told me he couldn't stand her and he knows how hard she's worked to hurt me. With her it's a contest. Did you see her face, the bitch? She's just gloating."

Pat tried to calm me down.

"I care for him so much. What did I do wrong?'

Pat just looked at me without answering and I asked her to please leave me alone.

I just couldn't get the scene out of my head. Watching the two of you going off to lunch had been so hurtful.

Just before this little scenario I had been typing a script for you. We had a routine where you would leave your handwritten yellow pages on my chair in my office, and I would type them up for you and return them to you. I now picked up the loose pages you had left and walked to your empty office. I took the pages and with vengeance threw them all over your floor, slammed the door and walked back to my office. I had never known I could feel such jealousy and rage. Emotions I had never ever experienced rose up with such force that I had no more control over them than an erupting volcano. Years of not feeling anything but despair and hopelessness during my marriage were now replaced with feelings of life that included love and all that goes with it. As I tell you all this, I can't help wondering how you tolerated me. I seemed to cry at the drop of a hat or scream, something I had never done before. I really was an emotional wreck and, through it all, we seemed to have survived, haven't we my dearest?

"Because I loved you!" Matt shouted at the screen.

Later that afternoon you charged into my office. "What the hell was that all about?" you shouted. You could get angry too.

I looked at you with such fury and said something to you I had never said to anyone before in my life. "Go fuck yourself." It just came rushing out of my mouth, and oh my God, it felt good.

"You don't talk like that!" you shouted back.

I looked at you incredulously. I almost thought I was back with Charlie, who made sure I never cursed, or made sure I never wore tight clothes because someone might notice I had a good figure. It was too much. I started laughing hysterically. I couldn't stop and you just looked at me, really scared, not knowing what to do. Fortunately for me, Peter had left for a trip about an hour earlier so he heard none of this.

We were on an emotional roller coaster. Always would be, my darling.

"Why are you acting this way?" you finally asked. "I thought we were friends."

That was the worst thing you could have said to me.

I was furious. I remember shouting at you, and again this was something very new to me. It had taken me twenty years to finally answer Charlie, and here I was screaming at someone who had entered my life just a short while ago. "Friends, Oh my, I am out of date. It's that age difference I guess. I didn't know you go around screwing all your friends. Would you believe I'm so stupid I thought sex was for people who cared for each other?"

You tried to touch me and I pulled away.

"Don't put a finger on me," I cried. By now I was hysterical. "Go screw your little friend down the hall."

"Ann, stop it. You don't know what you're talking about."

"Yes I do," I sobbed. "That thing, that awful bitch, how could you, and with her of all people? I feel like such a fool." I sat down at my desk and couldn't stop crying.

You looked so helpless. You walked to the door of my office, peered out, and then closed and locked it. You walked to me as I sat still sobbing in my chair, pulled me up into your arms, and held me like a child.

"Listen to me, please," you begged. "If I keep refusing her it could make her more vicious. You must know I don't care about her. I'm not trying to hurt you. I've tried to avoid hurting you but I'm not doing a good job of it, am I? I knew the minute you left that night that we were going to have problems and I was right."

I had stopped crying as you starting talking to me, and I was trying to understand what you were saying, but it wasn't making any sense. I opened my mouth to say something but you stopped me.

"No," you said. "Let me talk, please."

I kept quiet.

"I know you think I've been ignoring you. If I thought we could have a casual affair it would be different. But look at you. I was right; I'm not good at loving someone. You don't talk about it, but I know you've had enough shit in your life. I don't want to be responsible for adding any more. I just don't want to hurt you. I care too much already."

I think your last words were all I really heard. I hadn't been a failure and you really cared. That was so important to me. I already knew how much you meant to me. I would do anything to have you in my life. "Help me," I pleaded. "I want to grow up. It can be on your terms. Please be patient with me. I have so much catching up to do. I can be casual."

You laughed when I said the last part. You already knew me pretty well.

"I just don't want something that feels so wonderful to go away because I acted like a baby." I couldn't believe I was saying these things to you, but I was in love. "I want you so much and I think you want me, right?"

You shook your head yes and all was right with the world. We had a chance.

"Can't we have an affair like other people do? No promises, no commitments?"

She looked so vulnerable, and my heart burst with love for her. I'd never felt this way about any other woman. She had no idea, but I had fallen in love with her the first time I had laid eyes on her. That love would never leave me, although throughout our lives I would come to abuse it and put it on the back burner, sometimes for months and often years. Yet it always came back as strong as it had been at the beginning.

On that day, we had no idea how long our love would last. Our concern was only how to make it work for the now.

You pulled me to you and held me tight, and kissed my neck and my hair.

"Does that mean yes?" I asked you.

"Come with me," you said, and I let you pull me into Peter's empty office. I had lost all sense of sanity.

❀ 22 ❀

I realized that day that I must never make you feel responsible for me, or make you feel you had lost your freedom. Not an easy feat and one that took a long time to master. I didn't rationalize any of this, but deep down I think I knew, even then, that we were not meant to end up in a traditional relationship. I would learn to accept or try to that you had to do "your thing." I knew you had many friends, male and female, and I didn't expect to be a part of that portion of your life. I don't think I really knew what it was that I wanted from you or you from me. I know now it was moments; a lifetime of shared moments was enough for me. Not to say that I wouldn't at times cry myself to sleep because of times in your life I so desperately wished I could share and couldn't. Time and time again in the years to come, I had to watch from the sidelines. Yet I wouldn't change it for the world.

At that time, all I knew was that I was in love, something that had eluded me until that moment. It was a treasure I had dreamed of all my life. I certainly hadn't planned on meeting someone so much younger than I, and loving him as I did. But I had. The last thing I wanted was to have you ridiculed by others. I understood how the world looked at relationships between older women and younger men. It's very different when an older man flaunts his young beautiful woman. All his cronies pat him on the back and said "good job." BUT, if a younger man introduced his older woman, those same cronies would not say it aloud, but would surely think "What's wrong with him? Why is he with her?" I would have hated that for you. It didn't matter that you never looked like a kid, or that I for some genetic quirk, and despite the miserable life I had lived prior to meeting you, always looked much younger than I was; we knew. During our early days, I doubt if people seeing us walking down the street, you with your arm around my waist, me looking up at you all giddy, would have automatically thought we looked particularly mismatched. Eventually, it would have shown.

We were never going to have a relationship like the people I knew, nor did I expect my friends to understand how I felt about you. But I didn't care. All I knew was that when I was with you, or talking to you on the phone, I was happier than I had ever been. I'd take what little I got. It was so much more than I had ever had.

We had no set pattern nor did we ever establish one. That wasn't what we were about. I would wait for you to want me to share a moment with me. Sometimes weeks would go by and then, suddenly, you'd ask me to go to the movies so you could analyze the writing, the directing etc. It was fun, because you made me feel like you counted on me. We'd bounce ideas off each other and you always seemed to think my comments were important. We became a team that way. That part of our relationship has always meant so much to me.

Ah, but the green eyed monster had entered my life with a force of its own. I, who had never been a jealous person, now found myself filled with unbelievable jealousy whenever a young woman appeared on the horizon. You have always been a touchy person and it was so natural for you, when talking to a female, to put your arm on her and touch her in some way. What I didn't see didn't hurt me, but I saw enough.

In the past, although there was so much I could have envied as I watched my friends, I honestly hadn't been jealous. During all the years of my marriage when we hadn't had a dime and lived in a one-bedroom apartment with two young children, the only thing I'd dreamed of was a larger apartment so that the girls would have their own room. All I'd ever wanted was peace in my home. I so hated anger and turmoil. Most of my friends not only had the larger space, but husbands who'd taken them on vacations throughout the world and given them large allowances to spend on all the clothes they wanted. They'd all had nannies and housekeepers and had regularly gone to the beauty salon to have their facials, their manicures, their pedicures and hair done. I couldn't have cared less. I would cheer them on when they looked lovely, and at times had gone along with them to the high priced shops where I'd sit quietly as they'd bought their new season's wardrobe. I had enjoyed just being with them.

But you were my treasure. You were everything I'd ever dreamed of and fantasized about. You were the boy I never knew in high school, the boy I never expected to have in this lifetime. To find you so late was the most wonderful thing that could have happened to me, but I couldn't stand it as I watched you with those young women that always appeared out of no where. I tried so hard not to show my anger, my frustration and my needs.

I found myself reacting when I shouldn't; in ways I never believed I was capable of being. Sometimes I didn't recognize myself. There was a night when I was supposed to come to your apartment after a class I was taking at the New School. I finished with the class and called your house to tell you I was on the way. A girl answered your phone. I felt my face burn and my body tremble as I slammed down the phone. I was so hurt and so angry. "We had a date I kept tell myself. How could he?" I went to my own house.

Honey Seltzer

An hour later you phoned. You were furious.

"Where the hell are you", you shouted.

I slammed the phone down.

You called back.

I finally answered the phone, and before you could say one word I accused you of forgetting I was coming over. "How many other women come to your apartment when you're expecting me?" I cried.

You lowered your voice, because you knew one of us had to be rational. "She's my neighbor for Pete's sake. She had loaned me her vacuum cleaner and had come down to get it back. I thought you might be hungry when you go here, and I wanted to go out and get us something to eat. I asked her to stay, so that if you called or showed up before I came back, she could tell you I'd be right back." Those were the days before cell phones. I had slammed the phone down so fast she'd never had a chance to tell me anything. I felt so foolish.

I seemed to be slamming the phone down a lot. Sometimes I really didn't know who I was.

Oh Matt, I think the most important thing I learned from you during those days was that no matter what I did, how badly I acted, you didn't stop loving me and deep down I knew it. You were the first person in my life that allowed me to show anger, disappointment and love, and you always forgave me. For the first time in my life, I didn't have to hide my feelings. While it was all happening, I didn't understand how liberating this was for me. I had suppressed so many of my emotions for so long. I had always been so afraid that someone might not like me if I acted out of character. I always played the part of the good girl, the perfect young lady, the perfect woman, the perfect wife and perfect mother. Of course I wasn't any of these things. Who could be? Once I understood that, I understood that I could be the true me, or as close as anyone can be to who they really are. It was okay. You would love me as I was, even if you didn't always show it the way I expected.

During this learning process, I waited like a hopeful bridesmaid. After each moment with you, I'd wait for the next. Sometimes we'd spend an evening together at a movie or a play where I barely paid attention to what I was seeing. My only thoughts were of what might follow. If you took my hand, put your hand on my knee or smiled at me, I was filled with a longing so powerful that, as I tell you about this, I can still feel all those long ago emotions. Sometimes nothing followed and I couldn't understand why. I'd wonder if you were in a rush to leave me to meet someone else, or go to a party you hadn't told me about. It had to be more than you being tired. I was the older one and I wasn't tired. It was so hard for me. I was stupidly naïve and so totally in love, and trying so hard to give you a sense of freedom. I had this preconceived notion that because you were young you must have always been horny. I knew so little about men.

There came a night when I really lost it. We had gone to a play. When we left the theatre you hailed a cab and gave the driver your address. Then you said to him "and a second stop in Queens." You were sending me home. I froze. We had had such a good time. In the darkened theatre, I had made notes so we could talk about some of the scenes, and now we rode, I in silence filled with a terrible hurt and a terrible sense of inadequacy and rejection. You seemed totally unaware of my feelings. You kept talking and I answered in one-syllable words. I wasn't hearing a word you were saying. We were almost at your house when you noticed and said, "Are you all right?" Just then, as we stopped for a light, I noticed an empty cab alongside of us. In a flash I grabbed my bag, jumped out, and slammed the door with all the force I could muster. I ran to the empty cab and jumped in. I didn't see your face, but I heard the door of the cab behind me open as you shouted my name. I told the cabbie to ignore you and please take me to Queens. I cried all the way home. I couldn't understand why you hadn't wanted me to go home with you.

I heard my phone ringing as I was opening the door. I ignored the sound. I didn't even turn on the lights in the apartment, but made my way to my bedroom. I threw myself on the bed and cried like a baby. When I think of those moments now, I can't believe I could cry so much and so often. I had spent so many years in a terrible marriage and rarely allowed myself to cry.

Now you had opened up a wounded heart, and it needed so much attention to heal it. You did your best, but this was a lot for you to be burdened with.

You kept ringing me for hours, until I finally picked up the phone.

"What?"

"Why do you do these things?"

I couldn't answer. I started sobbing.

"Ann, please stop crying. I don't know what I did. Why did you run off like that? You scared the shit out of me."

"I was so hurt," I cried. "We had such a good time and then you were sending me home. You didn't even ask me if I wanted to go home, you just sent me on my way."

You were really surprised by my reaction. You simply didn't think the way I did. "Ann," you said, "you can't keep doing these things. You've got to trust me enough to tell me how you feel when it's happening. I had a good time tonight, a great time in fact. I was tired, it was late and I wanted to go home. It was that simple. It had nothing to do with my feelings for you or lack of feelings. But if it meant that much to you, you should have told me. I can't be a fucking mind reader."

You were right of course. It was a lesson that would take me quite a while to learn as you well know.

It's amazing how I can still remember so many of those moments, but I do. All the good and all the bad are all a part of me. I cherish each and every second I've ever spent with you, physically or on the phone or in man's latest way of communication, email. You have been the breath of my life.

We somehow got through the cab incident and went on to other days.

I think the weekend in the Hamptons was the defining moment of our relationship. That was the one that made us know we were destined to link our lives in some way, together or apart, forever.

I walked into Pat's office one morning as you were standing there. I only heard the last part of the conversation, but she was making you agree to something and you'd finally said okay.

When you both noticed me she said, "You too."

I didn't know what she was referring to. "What are you talking about?"

"We're all going to East Hampton for the weekend."

"It's winter," I stupidly said.

She shook her head at me as though I were the most pathetic person she'd every known. She was trying to set up this romantic weekend for me and I wasn't helping a bit. You didn't know that she knew about us, or whatever "us" was at that time, but she wanted to move us along.

"My brother Paul is house-sitting this fabulous house and he can invite friends whenever he wants. I've asked Miguel too," she said.

She looked at me, waiting for an answer.

"I don't know if I can." I murmured.

I thought she was going to kill me. Her eyes were blazing.

"Why?"

I couldn't come up with an answer fast enough. I wanted to go, but I had seen a reaction on your face when she asked me. I didn't know what to do.

Pat, bless her, could read my mind. "I'm not taking no for an answer," she said with her usual spunk. She looked at you, Matt, and waited for you to say something.

You were stuck. You couldn't embarrass me in front of her, and so you smiled and pretended it was a great idea.

When you left the office I stayed to talk to Pat.

"He doesn't want me to go."

"He's just being an ass. It's going to be great, I promise you."

Both Sides of the Coin

I wasn't so sure. I made her promise she wouldn't let on that she knew about us, because I knew you would be very upset if you thought anyone in the office had any idea we were at all involved. She promised, and she always kept her word.

That Saturday morning, we all met at a car rental place and piled into a station wagon. Miguel had decided not to join us, but Paul's friend Brett went along with us. Everyone seemed set to enjoy the weekend except you. You seemed very uncomfortable and sullen. I was beginning to feel I had made an awful mistake in joining this group. Pat kept the chatter going, and if she noticed that you were very quiet she ignored it.

After an hour or so we reached a charming grey-shingled house that faced the ocean. Paul came out of the house to meet us.

It was one of the loveliest houses I had ever seen. Some of the windows were open a little, and sheer white curtains billowed from the wind setting a welcoming tone. As we walked to the front door, I could see in to the living room and noticed a beautiful fieldstone fireplace. The interior of the house was everything I had ever dreamed of having. Little did I know that years later this house would be my very own. Do you remember the comfortable chintz floral sofas that flanked the fireplace? Once you sunk into them, you needed someone to pull you up. The peach colored walls were filled with built-in bookcases bursting with books on all subjects. Everything in the room was furnished in soft shades of green and yellow with splashes of peach. A fire was lit and Paul had put out sandwiches and hot drinks for us. We dropped our bags, took off our jackets and scrambled to the table. As I sat eating, I looked out the windows. At the far end of the room and beyond the windows were the dunes that appeared to have been there for centuries and, beyond them, the crashing waves of the ocean. I was mesmerized by the sight and forgot where I was, whom I was with and what I had allowed myself to worry about. I was looking at sheer heaven. I don't think until that day I had ever envisioned being at the beach in the winter. There's something so mysterious about the ocean at this time of the year. The water and the crashing waves are darker and more threatening and yet, in a perverted way, so sexual.

When we had finished our lunch and everyone seemed relaxed, Paul assigned us our rooms. We were told to put our bags away and get ready to go ice-skating; there was an outdoor rink down the road.

I found myself being led to a room on the main floor, and noticed that Paul led you to the room next to mine. He quickly scooted off with Pat and Brett. They were to stay upstairs.

Pat had a suite of her own which, I later found out, was the owner's suite. It was amazing. The bedroom was huge; the bathroom was almost as large, with an old-fashioned claw tub, and a wood-burning fireplace. The windows looked out at the ocean. It was spectacular. I would have bathed forever in such a setting, and years later it became another answered dream.

I went into my assigned room to get another sweater, to wear under my jacket. When I came out to the living room, you were the only one there. I walked over to you with a smile and you looked at me in a strange way. I waited for you to say something and you did.

"Does she know?"

"Know what?" I asked, even though I knew what you meant.

I was saved by the bell. Pat, Paul and Brett came running down the stairs.

"Let's go, kids", she cried, and we got up and joined them. Words between us still left unsaid.

We piled into the station wagon and drove to the ice skating rink where we rented skates.

The rink was really crowded with skaters. I hadn't skated in years and was looking forward to it, as I'd always been a good skater.

I was the first one with skates on, and got on the ice to warm up. I immediately felt secure and off I flew. It felt glorious. When I had gone around the rink a few times I realized none of my roommates were near me. I saw Pat holding on to the railing and skated over to her.

"Help me," she begged. "I can't skate."

I was shocked. She was the woman who was so bright and seemed to know how to do everything. She was my mentor teaching me new things every day.

"I can't believe there's something you can't do," I gleefully said to her. I was grinning like a schoolgirl.

"Bitch," she cried. "Teach me."

I laughed and took her arm and led her around the rink. She was starting to get the hang of it, when I saw you, and that was even more of a shock to me. You had grown up in the mountains. You had told me about how much you love to ski. It never crossed my mind that you couldn't skate.

I took Pat by the arm and brought her over to you and the other two guys.

"I thought all you klutz's should be together," I laughingly said.

You were smiling at me and I felt so relieved.

I took your arm and offered to take you around as I had Pat. You laughed and held my arm, and off we sailed.

You started looking as though you were finally having fun. After a while we stopped skating so we could scrape the snow off our blades.

I looked at your smiling face, and you confessed that you had been acting like a "shit head." I agreed with you.

"I know I've been miserable to you and I'm sorry. It just all seemed so contrived on Pat's part to get us here this weekend. Our relationship is none of her business."

I fibbed just a little when I said with a smile, "the only thing she knows is that you can't skate." I grabbed your arm and we started skating again. "You know," I said "sometimes for a young guy you're a real pill."

You laughed and for the rest of the time we were at the rink we all had a lot of fun.

This was the first time we'd ever been together with other people outside of the office. It felt comfortable for me. I hoped you felt the same. We couldn't hide forever.

That night Paul invited a few other friends that lived out at the beach to dinner. He was a fabulous cook and dinner was scrumptious. Afterwards we all fell into the sofas in the living room. Someone lit a fire and we drank wine and listened to music. It was a perfect evening ending with the start of falling snow. This was all so new to me. I felt such happiness and contentment. It was so hard to believe that I had fallen into this new life. Every moment seemed monumental. It was almost impossible to remember all the bad days. They were slowly vanishing from my memory. No need to hold on to misery.

Paul's friends were concerned about driving home in the snow, so they left fairly early. The five of us sat around relaxing. Pat brought out a Scrabble set and forced you to play with her. The two of you were soon arguing, each of you accusing the other of cheating. You had fun arguing, not serious stuff, and you were enjoying yourselves. Around midnight Pat began yawning and Paul and Brett followed suit. Soon they said they were tired and going to bed. Up the stairs they went, and you and I were left sitting alone in the living room.

I didn't know what I should do. Did I go first? Did you? We couldn't seem to look at one another, and finally I pulled myself up and told you I was going to take a shower and go to bed. You just said, "good night."

Ah those tears of mine. I could feel them welling up, and raced to my room before you could see me. Here I go again, I thought, never quite sure of my part in this play we seemed to be in. I got my robe, my unglamorous flannel pajamas and went to the bathroom that separated our two rooms. I took a quick shower and got into my pajamas. I remember looking at myself in the mirror and hating what I saw. Without makeup I looked so pale and so ordinary. I pinched my cheeks to make them pink and realized I was being ridiculous.

I went into my room and climbed into bed. I soon heard you go into the bathroom and I listened to the sounds of the shower. After a while you turned off the water and I heard you leave the bathroom and go into your room. When the door to your room closed and silence prevailed, I became devastated.

Until now we had never spent the night together. It was hard to tell by your charming attitude if indeed anything would change that evening. The times we had made love had always ended with me going home. I had so wanted this to be our first experience without any time restraints spoiling anything. Once again I felt the fool. I curled up in bed crying, all the while saying to myself "damn you, damn you. I hate you."

And then I heard a door opening and closing very softly, and my door opened. I could hear your breathing as you made your way to the bed and you whispered, "Move over."

I made room for you and you turned to me and took me in your arms. I remember saying "Oh Matt" as I threw my arms around you. You touched my face and felt my tears and you propped yourself up on your elbow and gently pulled my chin up. In the darkness I felt you looking into my eyes. "What's the matter?" you asked me. "Why were you crying?"

"I thought you weren't coming," I said like a child.

You pulled me into your arms and tenderly played with my hair as you waited for my tears to stop. "How could you think that? I didn't want them to hear us. I was just waiting for them to go to sleep."

"I get so confused some times. I feel so foolish."

"Didn't you know I wanted to be with you?"

You held me in your arms and assured me this was what you wanted. I wrapped myself around you and felt the peace I had forever yearned for.

Like a child, I asked you if you would stay all night. "Of course I will," you said.

"I want that so much. You make me feel safe." You were so touched by my words. What I couldn't tell you was that I had never spent an entire night in a man's arms. With Charlie, when sex was over, he went to his side of the bed and I to mine. Never in all the years of marriage did he just hold me for the night.

Being with you was everything I had never had and so desperately needed.

When I woke up the next morning, for a moment I couldn't remember where I was. Then I smiled to myself and felt so happy and so content. I had had the most extraordinary night of my life. Our lovemaking had been almost magical. All the tenderness that any woman could hope for from a man, I had been blessed with. All the crashing moments of extreme, breathless passion-creating orgasms that were never ending had visited me. I would forever hold this night in my heart and mind. It was the night that truly created our love, our eternal love.

❧ 24 ☙

After the weekend at the beach we had found our way. Our relationship became less of a game, as we each reached an understanding of what we meant to each other. We began to accept and understand how much or little we could give to one enough, trying hard not to hurt or get hurt. It was making us happy. I was feeling less insecure and it helped you to love me without fear. You were able to confide in me that I was the first person you had ever loved more than yourself. That was an amazing confession.

Then came the outside forces. I had friends and children who knew nothing much about the love I had found, "my younger man." You had friends who knew nothing about "your older woman." Slowly we tried to let them in.

I had so wanted to share my feelings with Roz and Fran. They had been my friends since high school. I could pretty much count on Roz being supportive, but Fran was another case. We hadn't seen each other in quite a while and we finally chose a date to have dinner, just the three of us. Fran loved the idea of "girls night out." She chose the restaurant, and Roz and I arrived first, which was the usual routine, as Fran was generally late for everything.

We had been shown to our table and waited patiently. Roz commented on how well she thought I looked. I grinned at her and she knew me well enough to know there was something more to my grin.

"Something I should know?" she asked.

I smiled at her and said, "I'll tell you when Fran gets here."

I no sooner said that, than Fran sauntered in. She was, as usual, dressed to the teeth. Diamonds flashed on her throat, on her ears and on her hands. One almost had to shield their eyes from their brilliance. I had to give it to Stan; he was good to her.

She paused at the table, giving the waiter a dirty look. He finally relented and pulled out the chair for her.

In a loud voice, she managed to tell us how awful she thought the service was. Roz and I just looked at each other, suppressing the urge to laugh. We'd heard this complaint before in numerous other restaurants, and she was the one who had had picked this one because they knew her. She loved going to restaurants where she got "her table."

"Are we drinking tonight girls?" she asked us.

I answered first with a "Why not?"

She stared at me as though she had never seen me before. "My, don't you sound cheerful. Are we celebrating something?"

I could feel myself blushing.

Before I could answer, the waiter came back with the wine list.

I rarely drank, so I bowed to my sophisticated friend and allowed her to do the honors, as did Roz. It made her feel so good when she thought she knew more than we did. It wasn't that she was mean. Underneath the diamond veneer was a basically decent woman who wasn't really happy. Her only fulfillment had become possessions. We had all grown up together and had had parents with little money. When Fran had met Stan, he was going to college. They had fallen madly in love and gotten married very quickly. Their early years had been financially hard, and Fran had gotten pregnant very rapidly. Within three years, she'd had two children. They'd struggled, but they had been in love. Somewhere along the way Stan became successful, and the more successful he became, the less of a husband he became. As time went, on he became a notorious cheater and a lousy liar. Fran caught him so many times that her threats of divorce had begun to sound like a broken record. Every time she caught him cheating, he produced a bigger piece of jewelry, a fancier apartment, a vacation home or a more luxurious car. Finally they reached the top of their aspirations -- membership in a prestigious country club, where he managed to screw most of the member's wives. It always amazed me that these women would want him. He wasn't very attractive and he wasn't very sophisticated. All he had was money, but so did their husbands. So what was the attraction? The only answer I ever came up with was that they were lost and lonely. How sad for them.

For her salvation Fran had assumed this faux sophistication and the need to believe she was better than most. We understood her need, and even though she could annoy the hell out of us we tried to be tolerant and allow her the self-image she so desperately needed.

Once she had ordered she looked at me with piercing eyes.

"There's something going on, I can sense it. Well spit it out. What's happening that's making you all aglow?"

I sounded like a little girl when I finally confessed that I was seeing someone. Note that I said 'seeing' someone, not 'sleeping with' someone. I just didn't have the nerve to blurt it out.

Fran didn't waste a moment to ask me who he was.

When I told her it was someone I had met at work, she immediately assumed that I meant Peter. "You're having an affair with your boss. Are you crazy? Someone like him isn't going to want you for very long, be realistic."

"I didn't say I was having an affair with anyone and certainly not with my boss," I angrily retorted. How dare she make me feel so insignificant?

Roz became furious with her.

I stopped her from defending me. I could speak for myself, something new in my life, but doable.

"His name is Matt McKenzie and he's a young writer."

As Roz began getting all excited over the prospect of me with a writer, Fran had picked up on the key word of my statement, 'young.'

"Young, how young, dare I ask?"

Before I could respond the waiter returned with our wine. We sat quietly while he allowed Madam to taste and then approve, and finally pour for Roz and myself. I was so angry with her.

As soon as the waiter walked away, I snapped, "it's none of your business how young he is. I knew you'd zero in on that. He's wonderful, he's beautiful and I'm crazy about him. I thought you'd be happy for me, but I misjudged, so let's just drop the subject."

Not Fran. She wouldn't let go. On and on she went. "It's disgusting. I'm totally nauseous. I'm absolutely sick to my stomach. It's like going to bed with my Bobbie. I knew you'd get like the rest of them once you got into show business, they're all a bunch of degenerates."

I couldn't believe the viciousness spewing from her mouth.

"You're a narrow minded, jealous hypocrite. Do you hear yourself?" I snapped. "How is it you don't call your cheating husband a degenerate? Why, because he isn't in 'show business?" I cried. I felt myself trembling with rage and hurt. I couldn't look at her. I started to get up from the table when Roz pushed me back. People were looking at us. It was awful. No one spoke. I picked up my glass and started drinking the wine, but my hands were shaking so badly that I had to put it down.

Both Sides of the Coin

It seemed like forever before Fran finally broke the silence. "I'm sorry. I didn't mean it to sound that way. It's just that I always wanted you to find someone who would give you a good life, and this is what you chose? What good is a boy in your life? What else besides sex are you going to get out of this? Is he going to take you out on Saturday nights? Are you going to join Milton and me, and are you going to go out with his friends?" she said with a sanctimonious glint in her eyes. Calling her husband a degenerate hadn't seemed to affect her at all. She was just amazing.

I should have known better than to argue, but it hurt me to listen to her. "He's not a boy. You don't even know him. He's amazing. He told me not to tell you about us, but I didn't want to listen to him. You're my best friends and I wanted you to be happy for me. How can you pass judgment when you don't even know him?"

Roz immediately assured me she thought it was great, but I didn't believe her. She was just trying to make me feel better, and she could never be as cutting as Fran. Fran, on the other hand, was determined to get her point across no matter how I glorified you Matt and how much her words hurt me.

"Call it quits now before you get hurt."

"No! I'm alive for the first time in my life. No way am I giving him up. You have no idea how wonderful he makes me feel."

She gave me a look of disgust and I felt like killing her.

"This is my life. I don't tell you how to live yours and God knows it's often tempting. I'm really tired of you always telling me how to live mine, Fran. It's just none of your business, so just drop it and stop giving me those disgusted looks. You should be so lucky as to someday have a Matthew in your life."

I think I scared her because it was probably the first time in all the years that we'd known each other that I didn't let her boss me around. She didn't know how to handle it, and I saw the fear in her face at the thought of losing our friendship. She was wise enough to finally shut her mouth.

I never told you this Matt, but a few years later when things between Fran and Milton were at a new time low she began taking classes -- one on the power to heal, another on developing one's psychic abilities. She was looking for something that was hers alone, not Milton's. She thought she had the power to heal and was a budding psychic. She would place her hand on a portion of your body that felt unwell and the heat of her hand would alleviate the pain. No one had the nerve to tell her it wasn't working. She also began predicting all kinds of sundry things that were going to happen. She was totally caught up in her newfound abilities. At class she met a 'young man" (ha!). Who other than me could she confide any of this to? His name was Brian, I think, and I met him once. He was tall, dark and had greasy hair slicked back à la Henry Winkler as "The Fonz." He had very little money and he immediately became fascinated by Fran's sparkling jewelry. Now I'm being really mean. Whatever, she fell for him like a ton of bricks. However, she didn't like the idea of paying for a hotel room and he couldn't afford one, so they used the back seat of her Mercedes to do the dirty deed; this from a woman who found the thought of you and I repulsive. Enough, I shouldn't talk like this, but she had hurt me more than I realized. Now you know I was never perfect. But then you knew that all along.

25

My children came next, or should I say Liz. I never had to tell Jennifer. She had seen us at the beginning and had known before we did that there was something special between us. Liz, on the other hand, was my youngest child, my baby; and her image of her mother did not include a young lover, or for that matter any lover. Her mom couldn't possibly be sexual. It just didn't work that way in her mind.

I rarely discussed you with her, and since she was now away at college I could see you and she wouldn't notice that I got in late on many a night. She knew you worked in my office, because I always talked about all the people I worked with. I didn't think I mentioned you any more than I did Peter, or Pat or Drue or any of the others, but she wasn't stupid, this daughter of mine, and I must have given something away.

One Sunday morning, on a weekend when Liz was home from school, the phone rang and she answered it. "It's for you," she said with a grim look on her face.

I looked at her and saw her look that told me she wasn't happy. I took the phone from her, and she walked in to another room.

It was you on the other end of the phone. It was a beautiful day and you thought I might want to go to the museum with you. I loved the idea. There was an exhibition at MOMA that we both wanted to see. I hesitated for a second when Liz walked back in to the room. She gave me a dirty look as she listened to our conversation, and I made up my mind to say yes to you. I felt she was being unfair to me and I couldn't let her dictate my life. I knew I had always been a good mother and I didn't deserve this loss of favor from her.

I told you I'd meet you in a couple of hours and hung up the phone.

When I told her I was going out, she asked me where I was going.

I told her I was meeting you and that we were going to MOMA. "Anyone want to go with us?" I asked.

"It would be nice when I'm home for a weekend if you'd hang around."

"I asked if you wanted to go."

"Sure! You know you don't want us to go with you. Who are you kidding?"

"I asked you didn't I? And you're not going back to school until Wednesday. So what's the big deal?"

"You drop everything for him."

"He's my friend and I enjoy his company."

"Bullshit."

I was now really getting upset and trying so hard to control myself. "Are you trying to imply something?"

Her answer knocked the wind out of me.

"You're either the biggest liar I know or the biggest fool."

I must have stayed motionless and silent for some time. How do I answer my own daughter? Why is she doing this to me? I haven't done anything to hurt her. I stared at her and saw the spite and anger in her face. I couldn't accommodate these actions, and finally said, in a very low voice, as it was so hard for me to speak, "Which would you prefer?"

Her faced became flushed and then she answered, "I guess I'd rather you were a liar."

"I guess I am," I mumbled.

She looked mortified as she ran from the room crying.

I called after her but she ran to her room, and I heard the door slam shut. I looked at Jennifer for help.

Bless her. She got up from the couch and hugged me. "Don't worry Mom, I'll talk to her. She shouldn't have spoken to you like that."

I was suddenly left alone in the living room and I felt terrible. I didn't think I had handled the situation well at all. But how can you handle something like this well? The truth was, I was in love with a man sixteen years younger than I. He wasn't that much older than Jennifer. Was there something wrong with me? Was I going to destroy my family because I had fallen in love?

A few minutes later I heard the front door slam and then silence in the apartment. I remember picking up the phone and calling you. I told you I couldn't meet you and as I spoke I began to cry.

You were very upset with what Liz had said and done. You talked to me until I calmed down, and you convinced me that what we felt was real and meaningful. In my heart I already knew that. I just needed to hear you say the words.

If my eyes could have followed my girls as they left the house, I would have seen them walking through the neighborhood streets until they reached the playground behind their old elementary school. There were no other people there at that time and they first sat on a bench, each with their own thoughts. Jennifer suddenly jumped up and pulled Liz with her to the swings. They each got on a swing and begin pumping until they were high off the ground. A smile slowly appeared on Liz's face. Jennifer reminded her of how I'd always brought them to the playground in the afternoons.

"How could I forget? She watched us like a hawk. Always so afraid we'd hurt ourselves," she said.

"Remember when I did hurt myself? I thought she'd die when the swing hit me in the mouth and I broke a tooth."

Liz interrupted. "I always remember when it rained and Mom was always standing outside the school with an umbrella."

Jennifer looked at her sister and wished she could make her understand that their mother has a right to some happiness. "Don't do this to her Liz. She's happier than I've every known her to be."

"How can you accept it? I'm sorry. I love her, but I think it's awful. I'm embarrassed that my mother could do something like this. I'm so ashamed of her."

"Liz you're being unfair. He's really very nice and I think she loves him. Maybe if you met him you'd change your mind."

Liz got off the swing and started walking away. She couldn't and wouldn't talk about it any more.

I heard the door open when they come back. I was in my room lying on my bed fully clothed when Jennifer walked in. "Are you okay?" she asked.

"Where is she? She hates me doesn't she?"

"She doesn't understand. Give her time."

I knew I had to talk to her and, if I had to, I'd give you up.

I knocked on the door to her room and didn't wait for her to respond. The music was blaring and when I went to turn it down, she snapped at me with such anger that I felt myself recoil.

"Isn't your boy friend waiting?"

"I want to talk to you. Please Liz, let's talk about this." I begged. "I'm not going out. You're more important to me."

"Well I don't want to talk to you. Leave me alone. I'm going back to school in the morning."

She turned her back to me and started crying. I walked to her and took her in my arms. She sobbed and I kept holding her. "Why, why couldn't you have fallen for some normal man?"

"Liz, please. I care for him very much. His age has nothing to do with it. He makes me happy. Doesn't that count for something? You don't even know him. You'd like him if you met him." I pleaded.

She just pulled herself away from me. I looked at her with such sadness. I had put my life on hold for over twenty years so that my kids could have a home with two parents. I had stood between her and her father each time they did battle, always taking her side, always stopping him from physically hurting her. I had done the best I could. I asked for nothing but understanding and that wasn't coming; at least not now. I realized that she was still so young and had so much more of life to live before she could ever begin to understand me.

"Fine," I shouted. "Do what you want. Go back to school, but I'm going to tell you something. For once I'm not going to cater to anyone else's opinion of what's right or wrong for me. I'm sick of everyone always knowing everything, because none of you know anything. I cared when Fran criticized me and looked at me with scorn, but I could take that because her own life is so questionable. But you, you've lived with me all of your life and you've seen all the things I've gone through, and for you to act like this is awful, it hurts too much." I couldn't go on. I felt the tears I had tried so hard to keep from falling fail me, and I started to leave her room.

"Mom, wait," she cried. I turned to her and she ran in to my arms crying. "I'm sorry. You know I want you happy. I didn't mean to hurt you. I'm so sorry." Then she looked up at me and with her funny little smile asked me when she could meet you.

26

Last but not least we come to your friends. I had no idea what you had told any of them about us. The first year or so of our relationship was so intense that we hadn't cared to share our lives with anyone else. We were either fighting, mainly because of my insecurities and jealousies, or we were making love with all the passion that we had used in our fights. Nothing about us was simple, and yet we devoured each moment and knew instinctively how precious they were to us.

As I say these words to you, I long for those moments, those moments that we can never have again. The moments that stay so sharply in our minds but can never be as they were. The smells, the touches the sounds can never be again, and for that I cry.

Enough of feeling sorry for myself. I'm sorry my darling. This is not what I'm trying to do.

Once again I had to shut the machine. The love I felt watching Ann and listening to her talk about us had brought back more that I could bear. I remembered my friends and the unexpected reluctance on my part to admit to our relationship when they encountered us for the first time.

We enjoyed one another so much. We liked so many of the same things. We loved going to art galleries and museums. We adored all movies, old and new, and didn't care how far back we sat in a darkened theatre. We loved it all. We would wander through Little Italy where I taught you about eating good pasta and drinking cheap wine. It all seemed delicious and exciting to you, and to me, just watching and feeling your excitement was equally thrilling. We'd walk through Greenwich Village arm in arm, me towering over you, bumping each other's hips and loving every second. I taught you how to use chopsticks in a little dive in China Town. We did have so much fun.

Yet, once again, the outside forces came into our lives. We had been walking through Central Park one Sunday morning when a group of young people called out your name. It was obvious you knew most of them. We stopped to talk to them, or rather you talked and I just stood quietly by your side. Finally it was obvious that you had to introduce me to them. You made it as quick as possible, said your "goodbyes" and marched ahead, me following behind like an idiot. They had asked us to join them for brunch but you had told them we had other plans.

Both Sides of the Coin

We left the Park and kept walking down Fifth Avenue. Neither one of us spoke a word for the next half hour. I was hurt, and you seemed angry. We kept our thoughts to ourselves. We kept on walking. We had almost reached your apartment building when I couldn't keep quiet.

"You were embarrassed to be with me, weren't you?" I finally asked.

I didn't let you answer. I could see your answer in your eyes.

"It never occurred to me that none of your friends know about us."

You looked so miserable, but I didn't care. I was too hurt to care. If you felt ashamed to admit our relationship to your friends, then what were we all about?

We reached your building and I followed you in. I had to finish the conversation. We got into the elevator and rode in silence with two elderly women. We reached your floor and got out.

You opened the door to your apartment and I stormed in ahead of you. I looked at you and waited for you to speak.

When you didn't say anything, I insisted we had to talk about what had happened.

"Why were you so upset over them seeing us? Haven't you told any of them we were seeing each other?"

"Forget it," you said. "I don't want to talk about it."

"Oh no, you are going to talk about this. It's too important," I insisted.

You looked so unhappy but I didn't care. We had to get this out in the open. I sat down on your precious white couch and waited.

"I told Todd and he thinks I'm crazy, same as your friends do."

"Why? Did he give you a good reason other than the age difference?"

"He thinks it could hurt my career if Peter ever found out, and he also thinks you're holding me back from meeting girls my own age."

I looked at you and I really wanted to smack you. At that moment you did sound like a kid, something you had never before seemed to be.

"What garbage! I could buy the part about Peter, but in all honesty he'd be more upset with me than you. He thinks I'm some sort of Doris Day. He'd be shocked to think I can't get enough of someone like you." I shouted.

I was really upset to talk like this. But I couldn't stop. "I'm stopping you from going after girls your own age? What crap? You go out with plenty of girls. I never stop you. I've never made this an exclusive relationship for you. You have all the freedom you want. You just haven't met anyone you care about, so don't blame me."

By now I was up, and marching back and forth in the room.

You were just as upset, and tried to explain to me what you were feeling. "I didn't say I don't go out with girls. I just don't know. I really don't know. I meet them, I date them and all the time I want you. Damn it, why couldn't you be twenty-five?" you cried.

"Because I'm not and there's nothing we can do about it. And you know what? When I was twenty-five you wouldn't have gone for me because I wasn't me."

You came towards me wanting to hold me, and for the moment I let you.

"Oh shit" you said. "When we're alone it's so perfect."

"I know, but it's not perfect, we can't always be alone. I try not to think about it."

"Stop it. You're so God damn accepting. I'm not your husband. It has to bother you."

That hurt me. "You're right. You know what? I'm a damned liar. I love you so much it's pathetic. I look at you, I don't even have to touch you; just being in the same room as you makes me happy. When I see you talking to some young thing, I die inside. All I can think of is 'he's going to take her to bed, he's going to fall in love with her, and I'm going to lose him and why, because I'm too old.' It hurts so much." I cried.

"I wish I didn't love you," you answered. "I wish you didn't love me. I want a wife some day, kids, a home. I want to feel normal."

I covered my eyes. I couldn't look at you. "Oh my God, you don't feel normal? How do you stand making love to me?" The tears poured from my eyes as I rushed through the apartment to the doorway. I heard you begging me not to leave. I heard you saying you didn't mean what you had said. I even heard you say you didn't want to lose me, but at that moment it was more than I could handle. I slammed the door in your face and raced down the stairs. I didn't wait for the elevator.

Sometime later I found myself sitting in Pat's kitchen, drinking tea and wiping my eyes after having told her the whole sordid mess. She had seen my face when I arrived, and led me in to her apartment and waited for me to stop crying. She had listened patiently, and to her credit didn't give me "I told you so."

I looked at her and suddenly I smiled. "You know, I'm pathetic. I just don't know who I am anymore. I've had more fights in the last couple of years of my life than I've had in all the other years before. "

"You're just a latent adolescent," she said with a grin.

"You're right, but it's time I grew up. I raised two teenagers and they never acted this way. I would have killed them if they had."

"Do I expect too much of people? God, I was so angry with him and he was just being honest. He does deserve to have a normal life, whatever that is."

She didn't have to answer me. I just needed someone to talk to and she had been there for me.

ಐ 27 ಲ

A few weeks had passed since that day in your apartment. You had called my house and left a lot of messages, but I wasn't ready to talk to you. I had avoided you at work, which hadn't been easy, but now I knew we had to talk. Peter was on a plane and I knew he wouldn't be calling me for a while so I walked down to your office, knocked on the door and walked in.

You looked up from your desk and when you saw me your face broke out in a big smile. As usual, my heart raced at the sight of you.

You tried to tell me that you had been calling me, but I stopped you. I needed to talk first. You tried to tell me you hadn't meant what you said, but I interrupted you.

"You did mean it and you were right. I've thought about this a lot. We don't belong together. We could never make it out there. The world will never let us. I've been wrong and selfish."

"Stop being the martyr."

I hate that expression and reacted with sarcasm. "It's my best role," I shot back.

"Well it doesn't suit you at all."

"Don't be silly. I was conditioned for it from birth," I countered.

You just sat back in your chair staring at me, and I realized that I was not saying what I had come in to your office to say. Once again we were fighting. I didn't want to end us with a fight. "Please let's not argue. I love you for whatever crazy reason. You came into my life and you gave me so many things I've never had, and I'll always love you for that but…"

You got up from your chair and walked to me. You put your arms around me and held me and mumbled.

"But I love you too. Do you know you're the only person I've ever cared about more than myself? Don't do this to us."

"It's no good. You'd hate me someday and I couldn't stand that. I can't give you what you need and want. I couldn't stand it if people ridiculed you for being with an older woman, and they would. Maybe not now, but in twenty years they surely would. They never ridicule men with younger women. They get pats on the back from the guys that envy them. But no one is going to envy you. I can never give you children, and you deserve to have them. It will only hurt us more if we continue, and I can't and don't want to hurt anymore."

I pulled away from you and walked to the door. I didn't want to start crying. You just stood there looking so lost. I had to get away from you before I broke down. I ran out before you could say anything.

I raced back to my office and closed the door. Why oh why couldn't I be twenty-five years old? Everything I felt for you seemed so overpowering, so urgent so passionate. Why wasn't it right for us to love each other? Why? And then I cried.

Twenty years later I still can cry when I think of all I lost because of a number. The life I so wanted and should have had was never to be, because of a number. Throughout all the years we've known each other, you've never really known what it cost me to not be able to claim you as mine. You've had both sides of the coin and were complete, but I never wanted that for myself. You were all I've ever wanted.

Ann, I begged you to come with me, to marry me. Why didn't you listen to me? I could have been with you at the end. It's where I should have been.

Weeks went by after that day, and whenever we saw each other at work we were civil and smiled, but that was all we did until, a month or so later, at about midnight, my phone rang. When I answered it I could hear a lot of background noise. I kept saying "hello" until I finally heard your voice say "Hi!"

"Hi" I managed to answer.

"I just wanted to hear your voice. You never said we couldn't talk."

I couldn't help smiling. It felt so good to hear your voice as well.

"Where are you? I hear an awful lot of noise."

"I'm with a beautiful young woman of child-bearing age and a load of young people in a restaurant downtown, and it stinks."

"Who is she?"

"A ballerina and she's a moron."

"What? I can hardly hear you," I said. I had heard the moron part loud and clear.

"I got to go. Just wanted to hear your voice," you said again, and hung up.

What I didn't know was that you were with Todd and a group of your other friends. When you hung up the phone you went back to the table. You reclaimed your seat next to the ballerina and sat quietly looking into space. Todd noticed and asked if something was wrong. You gave him a look that said, without words, that he should mind his own business. The ballerina began rubbing your arm and shoving her face in yours. The suggestion of spending the night with you was mentioned and ignored by you. You suggested it was time to leave. She was shocked and hurt. Who could blame her? You didn't care. You just wanted to go home, alone. The whole evening had been a bad mistake as far as you were concerned.

About an hour after she was almost shoved into a cab by you, my telephone rang again, this time waking me up.

"It's me," you murmured.

"What's wrong?"

"I miss you so much," you said, and then you apologized and told me to go back to sleep and hung up.

I was as confused as you sounded. I couldn't fall back asleep. I kept hearing your voice in my head. I missed you too.

I was just dozing, when the sound of a ringing doorbell woke me. I stumbled from my bed to the front door and looked through the peephole. I fumbled with the lock and finally opened the door. You walked in and put your arms around me and held me for the longest sweetest time, and I surrendered to what we felt, which was more powerful than any outside forces. We loved each other.

෨ 28 ෬

Another year had gone by for us, and we were doing really well. You seemed to have lost all interest in seeing the pretty young things, and whenever we did run into someone you knew you actually introduced me to them as "your girl." You said it so naturally that I had begun to believe we were a real couple.

You started to do unexpected but lovely things for me. One night, we were lying in your bed when you jumped up and ran into the other room. You came back holding a large box. "Open it," you said with a look of excitement on your face. You had never given me anything before and it was just as exciting to me. I couldn't imagine what I'd find, and when I opened the box I found a beautiful blouse. I looked at you in amazement. It was truly gorgeous. You explained that you had been walking down the street when you saw a beautiful woman wearing the blouse, and you had followed her into Saks Fifth Avenue. You stopped her and told her that you thought your girlfriend would look beautiful in the blouse, and could she please tell you where she bought it. She thought it was so great of you that of course she told you. I wonder what she would have thought if she knew your girlfriend was probably years older than she was. It was the most precious gift I have ever received.

You had even given me a key to your apartment. I would never show up unexpectedly, but it felt wonderful to know you wanted me to have it.

I have a confession. I did something really awful. You were going to Los Angeles on a business trip with Peter. You thought it would be fun for me to spend a few days living in the city. Your apartment was much closer to the office and it somehow lent a sense of reality to our relationship. I loved the idea and packed a weekend bag and moved in. I fussed around the apartment and tidied it up and began to feel as though it were ours. Late at night, you'd call me and we'd talk and talk and you'd tell me how much you loved me, how much you missed me, how you hated being so far away from me and what it was you were fantasying about. It was perfect. But a little part of me was always looking to spoil it all. I could never really defeat the awful jealousy that possessed me. It would lay in remission for months on time and then raise its ugly head. One night after I had finished talking to you I felt very restless and began wandering through the apartment. I opened drawers and looked through everything in them. At the beginning my mission was just to feel you near me and, by touching your things, it brought you closer.

Then I just became really nosey. Eventually if one looks one finds. I found a letter from Drue buried in a drawer. The letter had been written the day after the party on the houseboat years earlier. The letter confirmed all I had believed. You had slept with her that day, and she described each touch, each embrace, vividly. I know it was stupid on my part to react to something that had happened so long ago and way before we had ever acknowledged our feelings for one another. But why did you keep it? I couldn't help wondering how many more times the two of you had been together. When she touched you in the office, as she did very often, was that to rile me or because she had the right to touch you? You knew how I felt about her. You had watched her and listened to her when she tried to taunt me. How could you sleep with her? The thought of it was unimaginable to me. If you loved me as you proclaimed, I couldn't believe you would still be sleeping with her.

I couldn't ask you about this, since I had done something far worse, I had snooped. I knew I had to put it out of my mind.

I did for a time, because we were very happy together. Yet it always seemed to come back to haunt me.

෨ 29 ෩

Peter had wanted to throw a party at his home to celebrate his latest successful movie. I had been given the responsibility of planning the entire evening. On the night of the party, everything looked beautiful in the majestic living room on the second floor of Peter's penthouse. The floral arrangements perfectly complimented his magnificent antiques. A brilliant fire in the huge marble fireplace added a welcoming glow to the fabulous room. The guests were all recognizable film people; each dressed more beautifully than the other. This was before it was fashionable to wear jeans to parties and premieres. The waiter and waitresses quietly passed their trays. A quartet of musicians with stringed instruments had been placed in the adjoining library, and their heavenly music floated throughout the house.

Peter had walked over to me to thank me for having accomplished an outstanding job in planning and executing the party. I felt so proud of myself. It had been stressful. Yet it was fun working with all the vendors, making up the guest list, hiring the music and seeing it all come together so beautifully.

As he stood talking to me I caught your eyes and they were smiling at me with pride. Just then one of the guests, who had been a very famous actress in her day, came over to us. She told Peter how much she had enjoyed his film and then, pointing to you, asked Peter who you were, remarking on how attractive she thought you were. Peter gave her a strange look that said to me that he found it repulsive that an older woman would find a younger man attractive.

For an instant I felt hurt. How quickly people assume things, I thought. An older woman asks about a younger man and immediately there is some form of snide reaction. "Oh Peter," I thought, "if you only knew how much in love this little 'Doris Day' of yours is with a younger man, you'd die of shock."

I smiled at her and took her arm. "Let me introduce you to him Sally, he's Matthew McKenzie, an up and coming writer. Peter has high hopes for him."

I pulled her across the room and introduced her to you. You were so excited to meet her in person. You had actually seen most of her films and she was entranced with you. I left the two of you talking, and circulated.

Pat came over to me bringing me a glass of wine. "Hi friend, you look like you could use this right now."

"Is everything going okay?" I nervously asked her. She gave me a big grin and assured me everything was perfect. "Look who is coming over," she said. I turned and saw you working your way to me. Pat walked off just as you got to me. You bent down and kissed me on the cheek.

"You look beautiful tonight."

I laughed. "So do you."

We stood side-by-side just watching everyone. To me this was all unbelievable. It was so hard to imagine that just a few short years ago my life had been filled with constant turmoil and fear. In my wildest dreams I never could have imagined being at a party filled with famous people, which I personally had arranged, standing next to a beautiful young man that I adored and who loved me equally.

"Peter asked me to take Sally home," he told me. "Do you mind?"

I didn't and told you so.

"I'll see you back at my place later. I shouldn't be very long. Is that okay?"

"It's fine."

I looked up and groaned.

"What?"

Before I could answer, our dear friend Drue was upon us. Rather upon you, since she ignored me.

She was all-aglow as she put her arms around you and kissed you. Suddenly, Peter appeared at our side. He looked at the two of you and seemed pleased, as though the idea of you two being a couple appealed to him. You, always thinking ahead, finished the illusion by running your hand up and down her arm.

Peter was soon joined by some friends and left our happy little group.

You continued rubbing her arm and I was getting angrier by the minute and forcing myself not to show my feelings. I had become an accomplished actress.

I sweetly asked the bitch where Tony was and all I got from her was a shrug, meaning, "who cares."

I then turned to you, my hero, and reminded you that you had to leave soon.

You saw the look in my eyes and your hand dropped as though you had just touched a burning fire. You'd had no idea what you were doing until that moment. You really hadn't.

Of course Drue wasn't going to take defeat easily. She wanted to dance with you. She couldn't believe you would leave the party so early.

I had to speak for you since you seemed incapable of getting out of the mess you had just put yourself into.

"He's taking Sally Barnes home," I told her. "Isn't that right dear?" I said with daggers in my eyes.

With that, you were off and running. You managed to peck us each on the check as you rushed off to find Sally.

Drue wasn't finished with me. "Don't you just love him?" she sighed. "I just don't know what to do about him."

I could be as sickeningly sweet and phony as she was.

"In what way do you mean dear?" I asked. I'm nauseous just remembering I did that.

"Well, he's always so physical with me. He's always touching me. I don't mind in private, but you know in public it's a little embarrassing."

Oh God how I wanted to kill her. I bit my tongue and continued with my sweet voice as I tried to assure her that you were just a very physical person. "He loves women my dear, it's not personal with you. I wouldn't be embarrassed. We all know how he is."

I thought she'd kill me. Then the bitch laughed at me. "But of course you wouldn't understand. I mean you love him like a mother." She went on and on. She thought it was so wonderful of me to be so helpful to you all the time. She knew how appreciative you were of all my help. Wasn't that sweet of her?

I finally lost it. "Darling," I said in the most condescending voice imaginable. "You have a vivid imagination, but rest assured I have no more maternal feelings towards him than you do." That said, I turned and walked away from her.

What I didn't see was what happened next since I got out of Peter's apartment as fast as I could and raced home.

Drue was furious by my response and would have left the party as well but she noticed Peter standing by himself. She made an instant decision that would eventually cost her heavily. She took a deep breath and forced a radiant smile on her face as she sauntered up to him. Without saying anything she pulled him on to the dance floor. It took just moments for Peter for recognize what she had in mind and he did nothing to discourage her. He was in the mood to get laid, and here it was being offered to him on a silver platter.

I, on the other hand, reached home and threw myself on my bed to wait for the phone to ring. You were true to form and called.

"What?" I answered. How sweet was I?

"Where are you? I thought you'd be here. What's wrong? " I could almost see your face filled with innocence, as you asked all the questions you've asked me so many other times when you had upset me. Particularly, "What did I do?"

"Leave me alone," was my response.

Then you got angry. "Stop it. What the hell did I do?"

"Why did you have to stroke her like a little kitten, and in front of me? You know how I feel about her."

"It was nothing. I wasn't thinking. I didn't mean anything."

"Nothing," I cried. "You couldn't keep your hands off of her. And then you left and you know what that bitch said to me? 'Don't you just love Matt? He's so physical.' I could have killed her and you with her."

You couldn't help but laugh, particularly at my imitation of Drue.

"I don't see anything funny about this, Matt."

"I love when you get jealous. You're so cute."

How could I stay mad at you? You always knew how to worm your way out of things. By now we were both laughing.

I apologized to you, because I had let her spoil my evening and our evening as well. "I'm sorry," I said. "I can be a real pain in the ass sometimes."

"And what an ass," was your response.

I loved when you talked to me that way, but I had a point I had to make. "Matt, please promise me something. I've never asked you to promise me anything before, but…"

You interrupted by saying, "Anything you want babe, just tell me what you want."

That was so beautiful of you to say.

I didn't know how you'd answer what I had to say, but I had to try. "You don't understand, but I'd die if I thought you were sleeping with her. I can handle you sleeping with someone I don't know, but promise me you'll never sleep with Drue. I couldn't stand it if you were."

You were quiet for what seemed like forever, and I didn't know what to make of it. "Forget it," I told you. "I have no right to stop you or dictate who you may or may not sleep with." I could feel myself choking up.

"You have every right,' you answered. "I promise you I will not sleep with her. You didn't have to ask. I have no desire to ever sleep with her or anyone else."

"Truly?" I asked you like a little girl.

"Truly," you said and I could visualize you smiling at me.

"Thank you." I murmured.

"You have nothing to thank me for. I love you, you fool."

To this day I can still hear those words as you said them to me on the phone. I know people say I love you to each other over and over again, but I knew these were not idle words; these were words from the heart. They have always sustained me, and even during the years to come, when you surely didn't always think this love still existed, I knew it did. And I was right.

ಬಿ 30 ಛ

One night we decided to go out to dinner to a new restaurant that had opened in your neighborhood. It was rare for us to spend much money on dinners, but you had a lot on your mind and needed the change of scenery. We had spent the last few days talking about your future. You had reached the point in your life where you felt working for Peter was not going to give you the career you had dreamed about and, by now having worked for Peter for almost five years, I knew him well enough to know you were right. He hired young struggling, talented people at low wages and made promises he didn't always fulfill. If during the course of their tenure they decided to jump ship, he rarely cared because there were an abundance of new ones dying to have the opportunity to work for him.

You had written a wonderful new script on your own time and knew if you gave it to him he'd either hire a famous person to rework it so it never looked or sounded like anything you had written, or he'd dump it into a drawer where it would sit gathering dust as your others had.

We were still talking about it when you mentioned the idea of moving to Los Angeles. I shouldn't have been shocked, but you saw my face and quickly told me it was just a thought. I knew you were right. Los Angeles was where you were meant to be. I knew at that moment that our time together would soon come to an end.

You suggested the dinner, so I wouldn't look at you as though I had lost my best friend, which of course was exactly what was going to happen to me.

We had just sat down when I said "Oh no!"

"What?"

"Shush," I whispered. "Oh my, don't look up, but at the table to the right are Fran and Milton."

Of course you immediately looked up. I kicked you under the table and you said "ouch," really loudly. You could be such a pain when you set your mind to it. They hadn't noticed me as yet.

"Which one is she?" you asked.

"Guess."

"I can't tell, they all have so much jewelry on."

I couldn't help laughing because you were right. There were two other couples at the table, and the other women were as bedecked in jewels as Fran.

"Lower your voice," I said. "They'll hear you."

"Why, are you ashamed of me? Is that why I've never met your friends?"

I knew you were joking and I started to laugh aloud and took your hand. To me you were so beautiful and I adored you. You bent down to kiss my hand and at that exact moment Fran turned and saw us. Her face was unbelievable. It registered in one moment shock, horror and envy. She looked you up and down. You kept my hand in your mouth and began nibbling my fingers. I waved my free hand at Fran and mumbled "Hi."

Fran shook Milton's shoulder until he looked up. He looked equally aghast and tried to cover it by smiling weakly.

You mumbled in between nibbling "Do you think she approves?"

"She's probably dying of jealousy. Please, when we leave can we stop at their table and let me introduce you? This is really fun."

You loved the idea. I had almost forgotten how sad I had been when we had arrived at the restaurant.

When we finished eating and had paid our bill, we got up and you grabbed my hand and led me to their table.

I smiled brightly at my friends. Milton, always the gentleman stood up to shake your hand. The physical difference between the two of you was awesome. Poor Fran; she had little old Milton and I had you. She quickly introduced us to her other friends. You put your arm around me during the introduction and since Fran had only said that I was her friend Ann, you clarified the situation by adding "and I'm Matt, her boyfriend."

Fran, not to be outdone by my handsome younger man quickly announced that they were celebrating their wedding anniversary. She shoved her newly minted diamond bracelet wrist in our faces. She didn't understand that all the diamonds in the world could never make me feel the way you did. I didn't need jewels to feel loved and happy.

I could sense your desire to run so I sweetly said good night to them. As we walked away I heard Fran say to Milton "God, he's gorgeous."

You turned to me the second we were out of earshot. "Was I good?" you asked.

"You were perfect. What time do you think she'll call me tomorrow?"

You stopped and looked at me with the biggest grin.

"What?" I asked.

"Do you realize that we're finally able to laugh at ourselves?"

We headed back to your apartment and we barely made it through the door and into the apartment before most of our clothing landed on the floor. We had reached a moment so filled with need and lust that made every second we had shared before seem mild and pristine. Our bodies were on fire and we responded to each other fiercely and divinely. We were one.

ɞ 31 CȜ

Since our talk about your discontent with Peter, you hadn't mentioned Los Angeles again. I had not opened the subject up either because I couldn't stand to think about it. Each day I hoped that something wonderful would happen for you in New York that would make you want to stay.

In the meantime, months went by. Peter had asked you to renew your contract and you had told him you preferred to continue on a month-to-month basis. He hadn't argued with you and had allowed you to stay on for as long as you wished.

My kids were growing up and suddenly I had one daughter who had graduated college and was looking for her own apartment in the city. She had found a job, albeit lowly, at *Vogue* magazine and was very excited. Jennifer had always been interested in fashion and this was a wonderful start for her.

Liz was still at George Washington University in DC. She, too, would soon be off again, leaving me.

Jennifer finally found a small but charming studio apartment in Chelsea that one of the girls at work was vacating. Liz and I met her at the apartment. Although it was a third floor walkup, the building was well kept. The security system in the lobby looked good and the apartment was immaculate. Liz and I walked through it as Jennifer stood watching us. "Well?" she finally said.

I told her I thought it was terrific. She was so excited.

"Can I take it?"

"I can't see why not, if you're really sure you can handle the rent and you really like it."

"I love it mom and I can handle the rent."

Liz interjected with "I love the bars on the windows." And we all laughed.

"I was only teasing," Liz said. "Well old lady, what are you going to do without us?"

I tried to be light hearted. "Time sure does fly. I was just putting you in your cribs and now," I paused for effect. "And now your brave mother will handle this with much dignity. One must let one's children grow up." I stopped playacting. "Oh shit I care a lot. This is really hard. I'm going to miss you both so much but I'm so proud of the two of you and I wouldn't have it any other way."

With that said, the three of us starting tearing up. We hugged each other and as I held them in my arms I knew how lucky I was to have raised two such lovely daughters and I knew it was right for them to begin living their own lives.

The next weeks were filled with packing cartons and helping Jennifer move into her little apartment. She was finally settled and then it was Liz's turn to leave. She, at least, would be coming home on holidays and long weekends.

Once the girls left, you and I spent more and more time together. Very often I'd wait in my office until you were ready to leave and then we'd walk out together. I was careful never to let Peter see us together. However, one night after Peter had left, I walked down to your office to wait for you. You were sitting at your desk and I leaned over to kiss your neck. You put your free arm around my waist. We were in this position when I felt your arm drop as the door opened. I turned and there was Peter, glaring at us. His first question was to me. He wanted to know why I was still in the office.

"I'm waiting for someone," I mumbled. I turned and walked out.

You then asked him what he wanted to talk about, assuming he'd come in to your office to talk about something.

He gave you a dirty look and told you to wait for him, that he'd be right back.

I had gone back to my office to put everything away. Peter walked in and without saying anything simply sat down in one of my guest chairs and stared at me as though he had never seen me before. Indeed he never had. He had just lost his "Doris Day," the perennial virgin.

He finally spoke with total contempt in his voice. "I can't believe it."

"What?" I asked.

"You, him, he's just a mother fucker."

I couldn't believe what he had said. I got furious. I remember I shouted "What did you call him? I don't think it's any of your damn business. Who are you to judge me or him?"

"So I'm right. You are fucking him, you of all people." He kept shaking his head in bewilderment. "You of all people, I respected you. I trusted you. You don't do things like that."

I didn't know whether to laugh or cry. "What in the world does respect and trust have to do with this? I haven't done anything to you."

"He's a kid for God's sake. I had great plans for you. I thought you were one of the few women I knew with her head on straight, and you pick on a lousy kid."

"What are those things you parade through my office week after week, grandmothers?" I cried.

"That's different."

"I don't believe this," I shouted again. "Oh why, tell me, why is it okay for you?"

"It just is."

"And that's an answer. 'It just is?'"

"You're not like that."

"Like what? You don't even know me. You see what you want to see. I'm a person, a real one not a figment of your imagination. Why do people expect so much from me? For once in my life I did what I wanted to do, for me. Is that such a crime? Who have I hurt?"

I could sense Peter's hostility diminishing. He was listening to me. "But why him?" he asked in total bewilderment; "why him?"

I tried to find the right words. "He doesn't expect perfection. He's the only person I've ever known who allows me my faults. He lets me scream, act like a baby, laugh, cry, everything and he still loves me. He knows me inside and out." I had seen Peter's face react to the word love. "Yes, Peter, he does love me and I love him. It's that simple."

I stopped talking. There wasn't anything else I could say.

We were both sat in silence for what seemed like hours. I finally looked up at him and told him that if he found our relationship so offensive I'd leave.

"I can't work for someone who's going to sit in constant judgment of me."

He got nervous when I got up and started packing a few of my belongings.

"Calm down. I just have to get used to the idea that you're a woman."

I just shook my head in helplessness.

He kept looking at me as though he'd never seen me before, and indeed he never had. Then he smiled.

"Friends," he finally said. And of course I smiled back. He walked to me and hugged me. "I'm sorry. You're right I shouldn't have judged you."

He turned to leave and then hesitated.

"One more thing, I want you to fire Drue. She's a pain in the ass. I made a big mistake with her and now I can't get her off my back."

I looked shocked.

"Fire her, she's a stupid cow."

"What do I tell her? I've never fired anyone. Why me? Let Pat take care of it."

"I would think you'd want to see her go. I've seen her with Matt. She's always on him too. I'm sure Tony won't care; he's had enough of her as well. Just get rid of her."

I had no idea what had prompted this outburst. What had she done? I wondered. As soon as Peter left the office I picked up the phone and called Pat at home. It was Pat who was Peter's confidant when it came to his personal life. That's when I found out what had happened the night of the party. Drue had not only slept with Peter, but had tried to use the incident to have him promote her and dump me. Peter had met hundreds of Drues in his lifetime and wasn't about to have "some little cunt" use one night for her rise in the movie business. Perhaps if he had found her remarkable, who knew what might have happened? But to him, she was just another little tramp. Men like Peter have very strange values. They'll sleep with almost any attractive woman, but in their hearts they want a pure and innocent woman as their wife or mistress.

When you came to get me that evening and I told you what had transpired between Peter and I, you were as amazed as I was. But you were glad to be out in the open regarding us. Whatever decision you were to make regarding your future with Peter would not be based on our love affair and that was important to both of us.

I'd never fired anyone in my life. Of all people for me to experiment on, the person I disliked the most was given to me on a silver platter, and I didn't want to do it. This wasn't how I envisioned getting back at her. I stalled for about a week until Peter reminded me that he meant business. I was to get rid of her "now."

I called her on the phone and asked her to come to my office. She wasn't at her desk and one of the girls that answered her phone told me she'd give her the message. About two hours later she sauntered into my office. I looked up at her and found her annoyed face peering at me.

"I'm off to a client meeting," she said. "What do you need me for?"

I thought "what client," but didn't say anything.

I pointed to a chair in front of my desk and she looked at me as though I had all the nerve in the world asking her to sit and face me. I kept staring at her until she finally sat down, and I couldn't help noticing a pink ribbon holding her hair as she began fiddling with it with her fingers.

I got up from my desk and walked to the door to close it.

"What's going on? What's so important? I'm in a hurry."

After all the mean things she'd done to me, I still felt awful. I didn't know how to begin. Somehow I blurted it out. Somehow I must have told her she was fired, because I know I heard her screaming at me as she ran from my office. She called me a bitch and accused me of influencing Peter. "You're just jealous because Matt and I are sleeping together bitch. Did you really think he'd ever want to make it with you, you fool? I see you drooling over him. Why don't you look in the mirror, you dirty old woman?"

My door slammed and she was gone. I was totally drained. After all the things she had screamed at me, I was glad to see her go. I hoped I'd never see or hear about her again. I realized what a mean sick girl she was and I didn't believe a word she said about you Matt. You had promised me you weren't sleeping with her and I believed you.

ജ 32 ൽ

Months went by without any further news about Drue. We had all begun to forget about her. You were still talking about the possibility of going to Los Angeles and I sensed the day for decisions was not too far off. I tried not to think about it.

Roz, who'd recently joined a country club, invited me to spend the day with her. I desperately needed a day of R&R and said yes. While we were having a really nice day playing tennis, lunching on the patio with other women and swimming in the pool, you were facing your own dilemma.

For months, you had been receiving calls from Drue. When they first started, you'd said you were busy and couldn't talk to her. She would start screaming, sounding totally irrational: "You owe me Mr. You must know the bitch fired me. Don't you wonder why Peter is so good to her? He's been promising her producer credits. He must like old women in bed."

You had been furious and called her a pig. You'd started to hang up, but she'd stopped you. "You have to convince her to make Peter take me back. I'm coming over to your house and you're going to help me."

"I won't be home," you had said.

"I'll ruin you and her. I'll make sure she knows you slept with me. I'll tell Peter that you and she are lovers"

You told her she was crazy and had hung up. For weeks, she'd continued calling over and over again. Her threats became unnerving. Now she was threatening to ruin your career by implying that you had copied someone else's script and sent it off as your own. She "would prove it," she screamed, as she slammed down the phone. She didn't let up. You didn't want to tell me, or Peter for that matter. When I was with you, you never answered your phone, and you kept your machine off as well. You didn't' want me to hear her threats which had become so frightening.

I knew nothing about any of this at the time. In your attempt to protect me, I almost destroyed us forever.

Roz and I were driving home from her club. I thanked her for a really great day. It had been so nice to just relax and allow myself to be spoiled.

"You know, you could have all this if you'd think about meeting men with careers and financial stability."

I burst out laughing and she looked upset. "I'm sorry but you just sounded like Fran."

Even she laughed at that. When she asked me if I would stay and have dinner with her and Stan, I told her I was seeing you.

"You're crazy you know," she said.

"Why are you so uptight about this? I love him. Is that so hard to understand?"

"Oh Ann, when will you grow up? Love is for children. We're adults."

"I don't believe that."

"I understood at the beginning. You deserved to be happy. You'd had so little for so long. But this has been going on for years now. If you love each other so much why don't you live together and get it over with? "

I was quiet for a moment or so. It wasn't as though I hadn't thought about what she just said many times. "I can't," I finally answered. "My kids, people."

"The kids are out of the house. They're just excuses that don't wash."

She was right of course. I finally confessed that I was afraid I'd lose you someday to some young thing.

"If you really believe that, then end it now," she implored.

"Not yet. I'm not ready. I can't."

"Maybe it could really work. Maybe you should gamble if you love him so."

I wanted to hug her but she was driving. "Do you really think it could? Can the age difference really be ignored? People are so cruel."

She smiled her kind smile and wisely said, "You'll never know if you don't try."

I felt resolute, and when we got to her apartment I went upstairs to use her phone to call you. You answered after about five rings and sounded upset.

"Wow! Some hello," I said.

"Hi! I'm sorry. My mind was on something," you assured me.

"What time do you want me to come over? " I asked.

"Something's come up."

'Oh. Should I not come over?"

"No, no. I just have to do something. Can you meet me here at eight?" you asked.

You sounded funny, but I thought you were probably working on your script and agreed to see you later.

What I didn't know when I hung up the phone was that at that moment, a fully clothed but out-of-it Drue, was sprawled across your bed. She was partially drunk and had taken some unknown drugs.

This time she hadn't called you before showing up at your apartment. You hadn't wanted to open the door, but she had pounded so hard that neighbors had opened their doors and you finally had no choice but to let her in. Nothing you could say or do could get her to leave. She had raved and ranted and cursed both of us, then collapsed on your bed. You had been trying to get her up when I'd phoned. Once I hung up, you tried to pull her up again and, when you finally had gotten her on her feet she became sick. Somehow she made it to your bathroom, where she became violently ill. As soon as she stopped vomiting, you wiped her face with a cold cloth and struggled to get her out the door and, finally, into a cab. You were afraid to send her off alone, so you went along to make sure she got home safely.

I arrived at eight. When you didn't answer the door, I pulled out my key and entered the apartment. It was summer, but it had started to get dark and no lights were on. I turned them on as I walked through the living room. I put my bag down and went into the bathroom to wash my face, which had gotten sweaty during the ride from Roz's apartment to yours. I reached for a towel, and it was then that I saw a pink ribbon on the toilet tank. I knew at once to whom it belonged, as I picked it up and held it in my hand. I have never felt such defeat, such disappointment, or such hurt. I had believed in you. "You can't do this to me," I thought, as I felt my hands trembling, and I dropped the ribbon on the floor. I slowly walked into your tiny bedroom and all the proof I needed was in front of me; the messed up sheets and a towel crumpled on the floor. I covered my eyes for a moment and when I opened them everything was still there for me to see and know. I walked back in to the living room and reached into my bag and pulled out your keys. I placed them on your desk, and walked to the entrance hall, when I heard the sound of a key in the door. I stood motionless as you entered. You noticed nothing as you kissed me lightly on the cheek and walked further into the apartment.

I heard you complaining about the heat. I heard you go into that same bathroom to wash up. You had stripped into your jockey shorts, ready to take a quick shower. You must have picked up the ribbon exactly at the same time as the sound of the slamming door announced my departure. You knew, as you raced through the apartment and pulled the door open. You saw me standing waiting for the elevator, and just as it arrived you reached me and pulled me by my arm back into your apartment, slamming the door behind us. You pushed me down on to the couch, trying to calm me. But I was hysterical by this time. I jumped up and began pounding your chest, crying all the while, "why, why? How could you?"

You stupidly asked, "What did I do?"

Of course that made me more hysterical. I ran into the bathroom, found the damn pink ribbon and threw it at you. "You bastard," I cried. "You knew I was coming here, but you couldn't even hide it. You had to throw it in my face."

"Let me explain," you said, as you tried to put your arms around me. You were trying so hard to calm me down.

"Keep your filthy hands off of me," I screamed. "Why, why did you do it like this?"

"I swear, I didn't sleep with her. Please let me explain," you begged.

I wouldn't listen to you. I called you a liar, a whore and anything else I could think of. I was totally ballistic and so unfair to you.

You once again pulled me to you, wanting to calm me, to reason with me, to explain. But I couldn't hear anything. All I could do was feel.

"I can't deal with pink satin ribbons anymore," I cried. "I can't deal with someone else's perfume and your lousy scum on a towel. You promised me you wouldn't sleep with her. You promised."

"I didn't sleep with her. I don't sleep with anyone but you. She was furious because you fired her. She came here to beg me to ask you to do something, and she threatened to tell you we once, do you hear me Ann, *once* slept together, years ago. She made all kinds of threats; she's been calling and threatening for months. She was going to tell people I plagiarized my latest script. I didn't want you to know. She was drunk and on something and I couldn't get rid of her, and then she got sick and made a mess. It was all meaningless."

It didn't matter anymore. My stomach ached, and my heart ached because it had to end. "Too many things are meaningless to you, but never to me," I said. "It's over. Can't you see? I can't stand the idea of you being with someone else, no matter who she might be. I can't pretend any more. It all hurts too much. It's all too hard."

Again you tried to hold me, but I pushed you away.

"I can't believe I came here tonight believing we could be together, we could have a life and that the age difference didn't matter. And now I feel so disgusted with myself. I feel so stupid, and so dirty. A sick old woman getting her kicks with a boy young enough to be her son."

"You don't know what you're saying," you cried.

"Oh I do. I finally do." I felt so weary and I picked up my bag and walked away from you.

ಞ 33 ಛ

The next few months are barely memorable. I know you suddenly disappeared from our office. One day Peter announced to everyone at a staff meeting that you had come in to talk to him and had told him you were leaving. You gave him no further information, and knowing Peter he probably felt anger. He was used to being the one to dismiss you, not you him. To his credit, he never discussed or asked me about you.

One evening, after everyone else had gone home, I walked into your now empty office. I sat at your empty desk and ran my hand across it and touched the empty pencil holder. I opened a drawer where only left over paper clips and rubber bands remained. I put my head down on the desk and felt your presence and smelt your smell. How silly can a person be? And once again I cried. I cried for what could have been, but had been an impossible dream. I cried for all I had lost. I went home to an empty house that night. I took the shirt I'd had from our first night together and breathed in your being. I longed for you as I've never longed for any living soul.

A few nights later, my phone rang at about ten o'clock. When I answered it, I got a hang up. I hated things like that. I picked up a book and tried to read but couldn't concentrate, and then I heard my doorbell ring. I jumped up and walked to the front door. I asked, "who is it?" but couldn't make out the mumbling from outside. I looked through the peephole and it was you. My hands trembled as I unlocked the door. You looked awful. You needed a shave, you had dark circles under your eyes and you looked so sad. I stood aside as you walked towards the living room.

I followed you and stood looking up at you. I opened my mouth to say something but you stopped me.

"Don't talk," you said. "This time I want you to listen to me. Promise me you won't open your mouth until I'm finished."

I shook my head yes and sat down on the couch.

You walked back and forth choosing your words.

You turned back to me, your eyes blazing. "How could you degrade yourself by saying those things? I could kill you for ever thinking you were disgusting." You looked at me with such urgency as you continued talking. "I love you so much. I never meant to hurt you. She was there, but not by invitation, and I swear I didn't sleep with her. The only time I ever slept with her was years ago, that day we were all on the boat and she ran after me. And that day I wanted you, but didn't think that could ever happen, so I slept with her. I was young and stupid."

I knew you were telling me the truth and my eyes were brimming with tears as you kept talking. "You believe me, don't you?"

I shook my head yes.

You sat down next to me and took my hand. "You've been the most important thing in my life. You probably always will be."

By this time I was crying softly.

You got up and began pacing the room.

"I'm leaving," you blurted out.

"No," I cried. "You can't leave, not now."

You came back to me and sat down again. You pulled me to you and held me and stroked my hair and let me cry. I touched your face and felt your own tears.

You tried to say something, but I stopped you. I just wanted your arms around me. I couldn't listen to anything you had to say that would take away this moment. I had known in my heart that the day would come when you'd leave, but I wasn't ready. You had just come back to me when I had believed we were beyond another beginning. I had been sure I had lost you forever. I don't think I really understood how much I loved you until I had opened my door to you this night. I felt a love indescribable in words. I felt a love that overpowered all sensibilities. It was pure and total with no explainable reason. It just was. I needed a little more time to acknowledge it and protect it from the years that will come, so that nothing and no one could ever take it from me.

I don't know how long we sat that way, but you waited until I was ready to talk. I finally looked up at you and asked when you were leaving.

You couldn't look at me. You stood up and once again began to pace. "I sold my script." You finally said.

I jumped up from the couch and rushed to hold you, but you held back and I saw your eyes and knew there was more.

"I'm going to Los Angeles. I have a new agent and it looks good." You looked at me for a sign and I had to give it to you. This was your time; your moment and I wanted all it might bring you as much as you did.

I put my arms around you and held you and finally got the courage to look up at you and smile.

"I'm so proud of you," I said, controlling the sobs that were aching to burst from my lungs. "When are you leaving?"

"Tonight."

You saw my face and knew I needed time to absorb the news.

"Can we get out of here? Let's take a walk."

We put on our jackets and left the house. You put your arm around my shoulder and pulled me close to you as we walked quietly and aimlessly for several blocks. We passed an old deserted house with a big porch. You took my hand and pulled me up the steps and on to the floor. No one walking by in the street could see us. We sat hidden from the world just holding each other. You put your hands through my hair as you studied my face from the light of the street below.

"You're the only thing I'll miss," you whispered.

"What will I do without you?" I cried, as I pulled you to me.

You tried to make light of it by humoring me. "Yeah! What will you do?"

"I don't know."

We threw our arms around each other and I can still feel those kisses. They were filled with more love than I had ever known or given.

We finally pulled away and you grabbed my arm and pulled me up. We brushed our pants and climbed down the steps and began walking the streets again.

I stopped in the middle of a silent street to tell you how happy you had made me. "These have been the happiest years of my life. I wouldn't have traded what we had for anything."

You laughed in your special way. "Even with all the fights?" you said.

I laughed too. "We sure knew how to fight, didn't we?"

You looked down at me with a sadness I'd never seen and said the most beautiful thing you had ever said to me. "I wish we could have had a kid. I bet it would have been gorgeous."

At that the tears poured from my eyes.

"Don't cry," you said as you once again pulled me towards you, and we continued walking aimlessly, neither one of us ready to say goodbye. As I walked I looked down on the ground and saw our shadows; you so tall and me so petite.

"What a nice couple we make."

You looked down at the shadows. "I was just thinking the same thing. We had something really special, didn't we?"

I took your hand as we kept walking.

"You were a little girl when I met you. Now you're all grown up."

"That's what no one ever understood but you."

"Come with me!"

"We couldn't."

"Listen to me. I love you. We love each other. We belong together. Let me take care of you. Let me grow old with you. Please."

I wanted to say yes so badly. I wanted to be as brave as you thought I was, but I couldn't, I wasn't. I answered you with the first things that came out of my mind. "I can't give you children. I'll soon be going through menopause, my hair will turn grey. I'll be a grandmother and you'll still be young. People will make fun of you. They'll never understand why you'd want to be with an older woman."

"I thought you were a strong woman," you argued; "someone who's not afraid, who is a survivor. Can't you gamble on my love? I'm not some stupid vain kid. I'm a man and you are the only woman I've ever wanted." You paused for a moment to catch your breath. You were so full of energy and belief in what you were saying. "At worst, wouldn't a couple of good years be worth something? How many people ever get that?"

We stood on the dimly lit corner of the street outside of my apartment building holding one another. We were desperate not to let go of what we had realized, more that night than any other time in our relationship -- how much we deeply loved one another. It hurt too much to think of the moment our bodies would part, because we both knew it was goodbye. No matter how much we might dream of a life together, it wasn't going to happen. We held on to one another, just allowing the feelings that overwhelmed us to remain. You looked down at my face and almost cried as you pulled me even closer. You had seen in that one glance such love and at the same time such pain. You could hardly stand the thought of leaving me. You felt so protective. You had never before wanted to take care of anyone as you did me and now you were walking away.

For a brief moment, we had dared to dream of a life together. It had been so unbelievably tempting. Perhaps we could have put it together, but I knew it could not last and I'd rather forever love you in my heart than have it end with bitterness or dislike, disappointment or hatred. Maybe a relationship like ours could work in other worlds, but in our world time would be the enemy. I could cry all I wanted about the unfairness of it all. Why was it so acceptable for an older man to fall in love with a beautiful young woman and marry her and everyone thought it was so great? If an older woman married a young man, most people would say "look at her, isn't she disgusting, and look at him, he must be sick. Why would he want a woman almost old enough to be his mother?" I couldn't change the world and I didn't have the courage to try.

I turned in your arms and looked up at you, at the same moment you chose to once again look down at me. I couldn't stand the pain and the exquisite beauty I felt at that moment.

Oh my darling if only I'd had the courage to listen to you that day. You were so right. I would have given my life for the couple of good years we would have had.

But in the end I told you I couldn't leave. In my heart I knew you needed the freedom to build a life, build a career and not have the responsibility of me. No matter what we each would have said, you would have felt you had to take care of me and you were in no position to do that. You needed to take care of you.

We started walking again and finally stopped in front of a little orange Volkswagen bug filled with all your worldly possessions.

You looked at me as if to beg me to squeeze in besides you and share your adventure.

"I can't," I told you, helplessly.

You pulled me toward you and held me not wanting to let go, and this time it was your tears I felt. Finally you pulled away and got into the car. I stood watching you. You rolled down the window and I put my head inside the car and kissed you. I pulled my head out and whispered "go." You put the key in the ignition and started the motor. You gave me one last look and again I said, "go."

The car pulled out, the motor roaring. I stood on the sidewalk alone my arms wrapped around myself and watched you disappear.

"Oh Matt," I cried, "Oh Matt." I don't know how long I stood in the silent street, the only sound my sobbing when a tap on my shoulder frightened me and I turned.

"Want a ride lady?" you asked.

I threw my arms around you breathing your essence, holding you and never wanting to let go. For just a moment, I almost said yes. But once again I sent you off, and this time you didn't come back. This night would be the end of one part of our love affair that would sustain me throughout the rest of my life. In the years to come we would have our special moments, but nothing could ever be what these years had been, what they had given to me as a woman.

You called me almost every day as you drove to Los Angeles. I lived for your calls. You would tell me how much you missed me, and how you hated being so many miles away from me. I would try to sound upbeat when you called, and every time you had second thoughts about what you were doing, I encouraged you to go on. I knew in my heart that Los Angeles was where you belonged.

I worried about where you were going to live once you got there. Your script had been optioned, but you had used most of that money to pay off all your debts before you left town. Your new agent had promised he'd find you more work as soon as you got out there, and the producers who had optioned your script were already working on raising the money for development and production. Hopefully, all of these things would kick in fast and you'd be in good shape financially. But for now things were not going to be easy. You had one credit card of your own with a very small credit limit, and I had forced you to take one of mine "in case of an emergency" I pleaded.

Your cousin Jon lived in Los Angeles, with his wife and two kids. When you called him and said you were moving out to Los Angeles he told you that you might be able to stay in a small house he owned in the Hills for a month. He had leased it to a young actress who was going on location for a month. She could use some extra money, so she had agreed to meet you when you got into town, and if she liked what she saw, you could use her place while she was away, and she could save the month's rent. In the meantime, if she didn't agree, you could stay in their house with them for a couple of weeks while you looked for your own place.

You arrived in Los Angeles five days after we had waved goodbye. You had driven for almost eighteen hours some days, and very often slept on the side of the road. You were just anxious to get there and see what life would bring you. You pulled into your cousin's driveway one late afternoon looking disheveled and in desperate need of a shower and shave. Jon took one look at you and burst out laughing. You were a total mess. He grabbed you and gave you a big hug. He hadn't seen you in over five years and was very happy to see you. He looked at your little car and all the contents you'd stuffed into it and just shook he head in amazement.

His wife Dawn, and Ali and Beth, his two little girls, were warm and welcoming, and you began to feel better about your decision. It hadn't been easy for you to leave New York, particular leaving me. You loved me more than you believed it was possible for you to love anyone, and that had been a shock to you. It had never occurred to you before meeting me that you would ever really love anyone so much that you'd want to spend the rest of your life with her. And now you'd left that one person who really mattered. Throughout your five-day road trip, you had questioned your decision over and over. This was the first moment when you felt you had been right. The next day would be your second moment of assurance, when Jon introduced you to Jeramie King.

After an uncomfortable night's sleep on Jon's couch, you knew you had to find a place of your own. You had left all your belongings in your car except for your backpack, which had your toothbrush, shaving cream, razor and things that you absolutely needed. After breakfast with the family you called me and filled me in on your possible temporary housing and, along with you, I hoped it would turn out well.

Around noon, Jon had you follow him in your car and he took you to the house he rented to Jeramie. She was standing outside when you arrived, and that was your first look at the woman who in time would become a vital part of your life.

The rest of this story is so much more yours than mine, my dear. You lived it from your perspective and so much of it was never mine to live or share. So many days, months, years will be lost in the telling. Fragments were all that were to come to me. You were capable of splitting yourself in half, without the awareness that others were hurting in the process. I truly believe you never meant to hurt anyone, not me, not her.

Of course she liked what she saw, and who wouldn't. You were and still are extraordinarily attractive, probably more now than then. Woman constantly turn to stare, and would regardless of who or what you were. She took you in to look at the little house, and as far as you were concerned it was perfect. You ignored her freshly washed bras and panties hanging from the rod in the bathtub and which she hadn't bothered to remove. In a way, it was a sign of the comfort she had with men. A deal was struck between you almost immediately. She told you she was leaving the next morning, but if you wanted to unpack your car and move in that morning it was fine with her. She even offered to let you spend the night sleeping in the small screened-in porch, which had a sofa bed. You were thrilled and agreed.

Jon helped you unload your car and then left the two of you. You offered to take her to lunch and she accepted. You didn't know your way around, so she drove both of you in her car to a local coffee shop, and it was over lunch that you got to know more about one another. She had been raised in a wealthy family. It was obvious she was well educated, as she spoke several languages. She had been married briefly, but it hadn't worked out. No details given. She had come to Los Angeles to try her hand at acting and she'd been getting some work, but she had discovered that she found the behind the scenes aspects of film more interesting than the acting. She was trying to get a job working on a film where she could really learn more about producing. She knew she could be good at raising money. She was bright, had a good personality and was pretty. She was positive she could learn quickly. For now she took whatever acting jobs came along. It paid the rent.

You were very impressed, particularly by her confidence. You called me later to tell me all about your new digs and the girl who was leaving in the morning. It sounded great to me.

During that month that followed, you started making good contacts. Your agent also found you a job writing a "movie of the week" for television, and your own script was now in the process of casting; on the first day of filming you'd get a decent check. Things were going good. You sounded so much happier, and I tried to sound upbeat for you.

You told me you were looking at apartments, since you only had the house for a month. I expected you'd find something and didn't really think about it.

I wanted everything to work out for you. I truly wanted you to become a huge success and reap all that comes with it, but I also wanted to be able to share all that was to come, and every time I realized I never would it was very hard to accept.

ೞ 35 ೞ

The months went by. You casually mentioned that the girl had come back from her trip. You still hadn't told me her name. You also hadn't found a place of your own, but she was letting you use the second bedroom until you found something. Of course I believed you, and had no idea there wasn't a second bedroom. You still called me every day and still told me how much you loved me. You really did then, and even when I wondered about the girl that lived in the same house as you, I didn't believe she meant anything to you. It had always been very easy for you to get comfortable with someone very quickly. And again, what could I have said or done? I had waved goodbye to you. I had no claim on you.

I buried myself in my work. With both girls now away from the house and you gone, the job was even more important to me than it had been before. Peter had accepted the new me, and started to treat me in what I would call a more grown-up fashion. He actually started taking me to meetings, when he thought it appropriate and when he considered the meeting a good learning experience for me.

He sat down in my office one night after a very long day and started to just chat. It was really refreshing to have a normal conversation with him, one where I didn't have to choose my words carefully. It was probably the most I had ever really been comfortable with him in the years I'd known him, and he realized that he, too, was enjoying the talk. I think we actually became friends that night. He simply no longer intimidated me, and I felt free with him. To his credit, he never mentioned you to me. He knew it was out of bounds and he kept it that way.

I was coming into my own career-wise. I knew that I had a good eye for materials that were, not only commercial, but meaningful. I just didn't appreciate fluff over substance. I had shown two scripts to Peter that I thought were really good and he had encouraged me to negotiate the optioning of both of them. In what seemed like overnight, I was no longer a secretary but the Vice President of Development. He had discussed this with Pat before telling me, and she had been thrilled. She had seen the potential in giving me scripts to read almost from day one, and she was very proud of her protégé. When he told me about my promotion, I was overwhelmed. Not only did I get a bigger office and a much bigger salary, I got an expense account and got to hire someone to be Peter's secretary. It was all so exciting and wonderful.

The night I got the promotion, I called you to tell you my good news. Jeramie answered the phone. You were still living in her house a year after you had arrived in Los Angeles. and you no longer mentioned looking for your own place. She was very pleasant to me. You were in another room and I heard her call "your friend Ann's on the phone." From the way she said it, I could tell she knew nothing about our relationship, and it was at that moment that I realized I hadn't been paying attention, and I didn't know enough about your relationship with her. I still didn't know her name was Jeramie.

You got on the phone and you were, as always, warm and loving and very happy for me. I had left the best part for last. I was coming out to Los Angeles in a week to meet with an agent and would be staying for four days. You sounded as happy and excited as I, and we made plans for my visit. I'm going to be staying at the Beverly Hills Hotel, all expenses paid, I told you.

"Wow! That's great."

To me it was thrilling, and the thought of us together in a hotel was all I could think of during the next week.

I spent one afternoon literally buying out Saks' lingerie department. I wanted to look beautiful for you. This was the first time we would see each other since you had left New York.

I called you when I landed in LAX. I had hoped you would be at the airport to meet me, and when I realized you weren't, I was disappointed. I tried the house but there was no answer, and those were the days before cell phones so I had no way of reaching you.

I took a cab to the hotel. As I got out of the cab in front of the hotel I felt a strong pair of arms grab me from behind and twirl me around. I looked into your eyes and all was well with the world. I threw my arms around you and held on unable to let go of you. We must have made quite a scene at the bottom of the steps of the hotel, blocking cars from moving and the bellman from taking my bags. We finally pulled apart and I followed you into the hotel.

I know I checked in, and I know we rode up in the elevator, and I thought the bellboy would never leave as he turned on the air conditioner, insisting on showing me how to input a code in the safe, and how to order room service. Finally, the door closed shut. We looked at each other and smiled. We moved towards each other, at first touching each other timidly, and then we looked at each once more as we literally pulled our clothes from one another. We fell to the bed, all the while you were kissing my face, my lips, my eyes, my neck; whispering how much you'd missed me. I was trembling with excitement and lust. We were insatiable. We had always found each other desirable. We had never needed to pretend. That day we were beyond anything we had thought possible between two people. It was, and still is in my mind, indescribable.

What I learned in the years that would follow was that we were able to repeat those feelings, those passionate moments many, many times over. Maybe it had something to do with our constant absence from one another, but I think, had we spent our lives under the same roof, we would have still had these feelings forever. We would ignite at the sight of one another. Who can explain? Not I.

We finally emerged from my room at dinnertime. By this time, you were familiar with Los Angeles and you drove me to a tiny Italian restaurant where we drank some wine and I let you order my dinner. We sat grinning at each other like two kids and it was pure heaven. We talked about your work and about mine and about everyone we knew in common. I told you about my meeting scheduled the next day and you gave me some good pointers for my negotiation. We were planning my strategy like a team. It felt so right.

The trip was perfect and the subject of Jeramie didn't seem necessary, so I never asked about her. You stayed with me each night at the hotel, so I believed that indeed you were just roommates. What I didn't know was that it wasn't hard for you not to go home because she was once again out of town.

I don't mean to sound as though you were a cad, my darling. At that time, you really didn't love her. She was pretty, she was good company, she was convenient and obviously okay in bed. You had always had a woman; it was your lot in life. You didn't have to love one to be with one. You loved me. Loving me was enough love, but I wasn't living in Los Angeles and she was.

೧ 36 ೮

The years seem to fly by since you had moved to Los Angeles. Your film had been made, but it hadn't been a huge financial success, and work wasn't always easy to find. Yet you loved living out there. You had found your comfort zone. You were still living with Jeramie, but I never asked about your living arrangement anymore. I had no right to tell you whom you should or shouldn't live with. I had been the one to say "no" to going to Los Angeles with you. I still knew I had been right in my decision, but it would hurt me too much to know the truth about your living situation.

Jeramie had given up acting and had gotten a job with a talent agency. She was now a junior agent. She loved the work, and she seemed to be a natural. Her bosses were crazy about her, and she was trying to talk you into taking an acting class. You were considering it. That bit of news amazed me, since you had never shown any interest in acting.

I was coming out to Los Angeles in a few weeks, and this time I was staying with a new friend at her home in Marina del Rey. I had met Anita during one of her trips to New York. She represented a company that booked actors for commercials either on camera or as background voices. She had pursued Richard Stewart who, although still famous, was getting older and not getting the lead parts he had always been famous for. She adored him, and finally had met him in Peter's office where both Peter and she convinced him to lend his voice to a car commercial. The fee was really big and he finally acquiesced. She was in heaven. It was through that meeting in Peter's office that she and I became friendly, and as time went on we discovered we had a great deal in common. We were both pretty much the same age, both raised in New York, both had two daughters and both loved younger men. I had confessed my love for you when she introduced me to Willis, her young boyfriend, who had accompanied her to New York. He was real fun, cute, smart and adored her. Best of all I loved him because he showed no reticence in expressing his feelings for her. She had begged me to visit her on my next vacation and promised me all the privacy I would want, plus a beautiful room and bath and a view of the Marina. In her youth, she, unlike me, had married a very successful man. When he fell in love with his young secretary it cost him a very heavy settlement to lose Anita. She took her settlement and moved to California, where she'd built a good life for herself. She was so much fun, and never took herself seriously. Everyone who met her loved her. She was one of the most comfortable people one could be with. I really adored her and miss her terribly. If there's a heaven I hope we find each other.

I flew out for a two-week stay. This was my first real vacation in years. I had taken a day or so since I started working for Peter, but never had I gone away for two weeks. I felt tired. It had been a very cold winter in New York, and my body ached for sunshine and some pampering.

Anita was at the airport to meet me. I wanted to rent a car, but she assured me it wasn't necessary; she had two cars and I could use one anytime I needed to.

The weather was glorious and it didn't take too long before we pulled up to her house. Willis was waiting and grabbed my bags as I just looked around at the Marina and breathed in the air. It was so great, and I saw boats just lined up from one end of the Marina to the other. People were shouting and calling to each other and everyone just seemed so happy.

I put on a pair of shorts and a top and joined them on her patio. Willis had cooked lunch for us, and we sipped our wine while he served wonderful crab salads and yummy croissants. I kept thinking to myself how much I would love to live like this. Suddenly New York City seemed so dark and dismal. I wondered if it was possible. My thoughts were running rampart. "We could open an office here," I thought. "I could buy a condo here with enough room for my girls when they wanted to visit. They could be just as happy here as in New York," I thought.

I closed my eyes and felt the sun on my face, and for a moment I really thought I could do it.

You called me later that day. You had been working on a new script and hadn't realized the time. "Did Anita pick you up?" you asked. I assured you it was fine, she had met me. I hadn't expected to see you until the evening, so I wasn't upset. When you told me you had to work and we couldn't get together, I understood how important your work was to you. Although this was the first time since you had left New York that you hadn't rushed to my side the day I arrived in Los Angeles, I didn't dwell on it. It didn't register as anything I had to be concerned about. Since Anita and Willis were happy to take me to a party they were going to, on one of the boats anchored in the Marina, I didn't feel too bad.

We agreed that you'd pick me up around noon the next day and we'd spend the day together. As an afterthought, you mentioned that Jeramie wanted to finally meet me, as you'd talked about me so often. Would I mind if she joined us for lunch? She had to get back to work after lunch, so it was just for lunch. We'll be together for the rest of the day you assured me. Of course I said yes. I wanted to finally see her as well.

At noon you pulled into Anita's driveway. I ran out the moment I saw your car, and you barely cut the engine when you jumped out and grabbed me and hugged me as you always had, and it was if time has stood still. Our reunions have always been that way. You looked so good, and you told me I did too. I had tried on five different outfits until I decided on what I thought would turn you on the most. It seemed to work. Anita and Willis had gone out. They didn't want to make you uncomfortable when you showed up. They were so thoughtful and kind. I showed you around, but we couldn't stay because we had to pick up Jeramie. We got into the car and as you drove your hand roamed up and down my leg until I was breathless. I held your hand against me and if we hadn't had an appointment I think we would have headed right back to my room at Anita's. But we were going to get Jeramie.

It's really hard for me to be objective about Jeramie. People have always called her beautiful, yet I never thought she was. I'm very sticky on the words "beautiful," "pretty" and "attractive." To me they all say very different things. "Beautiful" is someone that you can't stop looking at. Someone that men swoon over and women wish they looked like. "Pretty" is the Prom Queen. She's got perfect features but something important is missing from the whole picture. "Attractive" is someone who's noticed and who works very hard to take what they've been given by God and make it look the best it can be. Jeramie to me was in between Prom Queen and Attractive.

On that day, at least to me, she looked ordinary. She had on a blazer and slacks. Her hair was light brown, and long and wavy. Through the ensuing years I've seen her change the color and length of her hair, and her cheap blazer to Armani. Her eyes were brown then and still are. I will say she photographs as far more beautiful than she is in person. Maybe what I saw that day was a woman who, even twenty-odd years ago, knew what she wanted out of life and how to get it. To me, her inner being took away the outer beauty. I guess I still can't be objective when it comes to her, but then I'm sure the feeling is mutual. Let's get back to my feelings on that first meeting.

I almost breathed a sigh of relief when I first saw her, because I didn't think she was half as pretty as all the girls you used to take up with in New York. So much for my gut feelings. She greeted me warmly, and I knew at once that she had no idea that you and I had been and were still lovers, albeit long distance ones. She just assumed by looking at me that we were only friends. I would have to think that had to do with, not just my age but, whatever you had led her to believe. She would eventually learn never to assume anything, as would I. I had believed you until that day; why wouldn't she?

I could have been an actress, as I greeted her with a big smile. We got into her car and drove to a nearby restaurant for lunch. We all had a friendly meal, and you seemed very happy that we were getting along. When she excused herself to go to the ladies room, you turned to me and said with great joy and no warning, "Isn't she great?"

I looked at you and knew then I had lost a part of you. It wasn't your fault. It was your destiny to build a life. I know I had told you to go without me. I should have known I would be replaced. I tried to smile. What did you expect me to say? Before I could answer you took my hand and said, "Can you understand if I tell you that I feel like I have both sides of the coin?" You had no doubt that I would understand. You felt so blessed. You had two women in your life, and between us you were complete. I have never forgotten that moment, although I would guess you have. You were so right you know; you've always had both sides of the coin; how lucky you were. I couldn't answer you. You had thrown this at me without an inkling of preparation. I felt as though I had been brutally beaten. I fought for control of my emotions and was grateful she returned to the table, leaving no time for any response from me. There weren't any words I could have said. I don't know how I kept up the charade of cheerfulness, but somehow I did. Hurt would be too simple a word for what I was feeling.

Before leaving the restaurant you excused yourself, and now it was her turn. She wanted to ask me something. She wondered if I thought it mattered that she was a year older than you. Can you believe? I had to sit next to her and with a straight face and tell her than I didn't think it could possibly matter. God! Can you imagine what she must have thought when she finally found out about us? If that wasn't enough she went on to assure me that if you walked out tomorrow, she wasn't so invested in the relationship that she couldn't deal with losing you. Well goodie for her. This was the woman who was the other side of your coin! I wish I could have felt that way about you. It would have been so much easier to leave that table and never care again. You know better don't you? I think it was her attitude and words about losing you that helped me to never once, in all the years that followed, have a guilty conscience about my relationship with you.

When she got back to her office, we got out of her car and walked back to yours. "Where do you want to go?" you asked me.

"Take me back to Anita's please."

"What's wrong?"

"Please Matt, just take me back. I can't be with you today. I need to think," I said. I fought so hard not to cry.

"What did I do?" you asked me with total innocence. I wanted to hit you. I wanted to physically hurt you. I wanted to scream. There was so much I wanted to say to you. I wanted to ask you if you had any idea how I felt, how much I hurt. Didn't you think that perhaps you could have picked a different setting to tell me she was more to you, not use the two minutes she had gone to the ladies room? Couldn't you have let me believe you were still roommates for a while longer? How quickly you'd found your other half. To equate me with her was not fair to me. It was too soon to absorb that there was another woman's presence in your life that was as important to you as I was. Realistically, I should have been prepared to turn you over to another woman. I know that sounds so self-important on my part. I never was and have never been realistic about you, and at that time I still believed that what we had was so unique nothing could equal it for either one of us. It never did, but you weren't looking for equal; you didn't need it. You had it all. So what if it took two of us to make you complete? For you it worked.

I didn't answer you.

When we reached Anita's house you begged me not to leave. "Please let's talk."

"Do you love her?" I finally asked.

"It's very hard to explain. I need you both. She's a very strong woman, and very sure of herself. She could never love me, or anyone, the way you do. You're so full of love, and you're so nurturing. You'd do anything for me because you love me. Even in lovemaking you give me everything. You'd never question anything I would ask of you. It would always be from the heart. You give me life, but she gives me the right to be weak. I think she prefers the part of me that's weak. It feeds her strength. She had a strong father, and a strong husband and it was counter to her own needs. She's going to be very successful someday. I can share the ride. At least for now we're satisfied with the way we are. But Annie, it doesn't have anything to do with you."

"How can you say that? If you're with her, than that's where you belong. There's no room for me. I don't see you as weak, and why would you want to believe that of yourself? I couldn't love you if I thought that of you."

You smiled at me as though I were a child. You pulled me to you and held me as we sat in that tiny car. I began to cry. I had tried so hard not to, but I couldn't stop myself. The thought of losing you to someone else was more than I could deal with. When you were in New York it was never a particular person I feared, just the knowledge that it could happen. Now it was real, it had happened and I had seen the person.

I finally stopped crying and moved to get out of the car. You just looked at me but didn't try to stop me. I pulled the door open and just ran.

Anita was aghast when she found me hours later curled up in my bed. I looked like hell and felt like hell. She sat down on the chair next to me and waited for me to talk and finally I told her everything.

"Oh honey," she said holding me like a child. "He doesn't mean to hurt you. I haven't met him but I really believe he loves you. But he's smart. You're not here and he has to get on with his life. Remember, he did ask you to come out here with him and you said no. It was your decision."

"Yes," I interrupted, "but it didn't take him more than a few weeks to get involved with her. "How much could he have ever loved me? What if I had said yes, and had come along believing we could make it. How long would it have taken for him to find himself a 'Jeramie' and leave me?"

"You don't know that. If you had gone with him you would have made him feel safe and secure and he wouldn't have needed her or any other woman. Don't do this to yourself Ann. It's not true."

I didn't know what to think or say. Maybe she was right, but part of me believed I was, and that's what upset me so much. More than anything, I would never know what might have happened had I come along with you. I would never know if, tested that way, if our love would have withstood a long term, day to day relationship. I've never stopped wondering, even now.

Yet, when you called me the next day, I said yes when you asked to see me. I couldn't give you up. No matter how hurt I got, living without you in my life would be worse. Throughout the years that would follow, I tried so many times to say to myself "enough" and then one word from you, one look, one touch and all was right with the world. And if I sound the fool as I sit here talking to this stupid machine, I know that for me, loving you was always right. I never needed both sides of the coin. I had it all in you.

ೂ 38 ೞ

Time flew by. In New York, my life was full. I had become accustomed to your relationship with Jeramie. I flew out to Los Angeles periodically on business, often staying with Anita, other times staying at a hotel.

You and I always managed to spend at least a day together. There were always plausible reasons not to see each other every day throughout my trips, and it became easier for me to accept. Wasn't it amazing, my dearest, how in those years, no matter what our lives were like apart from each other, the moment we saw each other everything was as it had been for us at the beginning? A first glance was all we needed and the passion was reignited. We could make a day enough to feed us both for months.

In the early years Jeramie believed we were just friends. There were times we all dined together and had a really nice time. I had developed the ability to be with the two of you and remove myself from the equation. You were a couple and I the friend.

During one of my trips, and on one of my days with you, we were riding in your new car; a second hand convertible, with the top down. As we stopped for a light, a woman in another car waved to you. You waved back and gave her a big smile. When we pulled away you told me that you and Jeramie were thinking of buying a house and that she was your realtor. That was the first I had heard about a "house." We had spent hours together that day, and you never mentioned buying a house until that woman had seen us. Once said, you couldn't wait to show me the house in question. I sat quietly while we drove up in to the hills and you parked outside of a little house. We couldn't go inside, because you had only put a bid on it, so I had to visualize the inside then. Eventually, I would see the inside.

"I always want you to know where I am," you told me.

And I have. I can visualize you at this moment in your latest home, and on weekends in the one in Malibu. I can see you as clearly as if I'm there. It has always helped me to stay connected. Oh Lord, how sick I would sound if anyone other than you heard me saying all this!

You told me Jeramie wanted a house, and since she was now earning really good money, you didn't have much say in the matter. I just looked at you. I could tell you were excited about the house, and now you were trying to blame her. You didn't want me to know how happy this new experience was making you. This was just the beginning of how you would tell me the next important event in your life. You wouldn't. You would leave it to her. We spent the rest of that day together, having so much fun that I didn't allow myself to think about the house and what it represented.

I had parked my car in your driveway that morning. We drove back to your rental house so that I could pick it up. As we pulled into the driveway, you noticed Jeramie's car and realized she was home. It was about seven o'clock and it would have been wrong for me not to say hello, particularly since until that moment I still believed she thought of me as your "friend." We went inside and we greeted each other warmly.

"Ah", she said. "Now I know who that beautiful woman was that you had in your car." We both looked at her surprised.

She explained that the real estate broker had called her about the house, and then proceeded to tell her that she had seen you riding with some beautiful woman.

I laughed and we all dropped the subject. I think that was the day she began to wonder about us.

ೞ 39 ೮ഠ

About six months later, I once again arrived in Los Angeles. As always, I was filled with excitement. I was staying with Anita and Willis this trip and planned on spending an extra week for some R&R.

I called you as soon as I arrived at Anita's house. You sounded really happy. You told me how much you had missed me.

You and Jeramie were now living in your new house and you couldn't wait to show it to me. I actually took the news well. I was getting on with my life. My feelings for you would never change, but I was able to live with your new life and understand that it was good for you. I accepted that fact that I couldn't in any way change anything. I had made my decision the night you left New York, and looking back wouldn't change anything. Life had to go on.

You told me you were having dinner that night with a group of Jeramie's business friends at a Thai restaurant and you wanted me to meet you there.

"Are you sure? I mean they're all her friends and yours. I won't fit in. We can see each other tomorrow."

You begged me to come. "I can't wait another day to see you, and they're all movie people so you'll fit right in," you assured me.

How could I say no? I had missed you so much. You hadn't understood that, when I said I wouldn't fit in, I had meant that they were probably all so much younger than I was. But, bless you; it never crossed your mind.

I hadn't rented a car yet, since Willis had been kind enough to pick me up at the airport. He and Anita were in the room while I was talking to you and, romantics that they were, immediately offered to drive me to the restaurant that night. You assured me you would drive me back to the Marina after dinner.

You were waiting in front of the restaurant when we arrived. I had barely closed the door to their car when you grabbed me and held me. I have never needed more than your arms around me to feel whole. When we moved apart, we were met by Jeramie, who had been inside the restaurant and had come out to see if I'd arrived. She had witnessed our reunion. To her credit she pretended all was well, but anyone witnessing our greeting would have known we were more than friends.

We went into the restaurant and the rest is a blur. I vaguely remember you introducing me to six people whose names I didn't hear, whose faces I would never recall. Somehow I was sitting at a table, and you were sitting to the right of me. Jeramie had ended up at the other side of the table next to another couple. Until that evening I had believed that our attraction for one another had always reached peaks beyond the heights of description. Simply said, I have never been in your presence when I haven't had the desire to devour you. But that night, sitting next to you in a room full of strangers I had a meal I never ate, I had a conversation with people I never had, I smiled and answered questions and all I can remember is the feeling of your hand on my leg, moving upward and caressing me while I tried to look anywhere but at Jeramie, for surely she could see the burning desire in my face. I didn't dare look at you. I have never to this day, my darling, felt anything to equal the emotions that scorched my body as I sat at that dinner table trying to make small talk.

Finally, dinner was over. As we all got up from the table I feebly said goodbye to all the other guests. You announced that you were driving me back to the Marina. Jeramie at once offered to go with us. You sweetly but firmly assured her that it was silly for her to go so far when it was late and she had to be up early the next morning. Whoever it was that had sat next to her during the meal lived right near your house and would drive her home. She was forced to smile and acquiesce. I could have kissed that other person.

I will not here say aloud what transpired between us in the car as you drove me to the Marina. I know you remember that ride as I do. By the time we reached Anita's house we were still in heat and almost crawled to my room where we released all that remained of our desire. It was like nothing we had ever experienced before. I say that a lot I know, but it was always true. You'd barely caught your breath when you realized you had to get home as fast as you could or you'd been unable to account for your time. I let you go, almost hoping you'd show some sign of our last hour and she'd throw you out. She didn't.

However, she never again let you knowingly be alone with me if she could help it. And you never told me what happened when you got back to your house.

I walked into the house believing Jeramie was asleep, as all the lights were out. I quietly undressed and crawled into our bed.

"Don't ever, ever do that to me again," she said in a voice that was frightening.

I tried to pretend I didn't know what she meant.

"Matt, I'm not a fool. Only a blind person would have missed what was going on between the two of you. The two of you were on fire. It was humiliating. What an ass I've been. I really believed she was just your "friend from New York." Is she that good? She must be to get you so crazed. You've never been that way with me."

I tried to deny that anything had happened.

"If I ever find out you're sleeping with her again, you're out of here, and I mean it." With that she turned her back on me, and that was the last of the conversation.

I was glad she had, because what could I have said? Could I have told her that sex with her was just a release and never anything more? She just didn't feel the way you did. With you it's pure love, pure lust, and pure abandon. We just fit so perfectly and I didn't think I could ever give that up -- not for her or any other woman.

I couldn't sleep that night. Having you one moment and quickly watching you leave to sleep in another woman's bed tore me to pieces. This wasn't what I had ever envisioned for myself. I was a decent person who had fallen in love and had let this love take over her life. I simply couldn't exist without you, and yet sharing you was so very painful. Yet, I couldn't give you up, and the only way I could imagine giving you up would be at your request. So far that hadn't happened.

❧ 40 ☙

Months had passed since my last trip to Los Angeles, and our eventful dinner at the Thai restaurant that included the trip back to Anita's house.

Once again I was back on Los Angeles for a meeting. You had never told me about Jeramie's ultimatum and, when you called me at the hotel, you asked me to please meet you at the house, so I could get to see the inside as well as the spectacular view from the terrace. I said okay. And so I found myself cautiously driving from Beverly Hills across a canyon to your new home. I never enjoyed driving, and this trip made me really nervous, but I managed to get there in one piece. You came running out the moment I pulled into the driveway. You were so proud as you showed me a pretty little house with a spectacular view of the hills. Things were picking up for you. You had met a fellow writer who had the rights to a best-selling book. Together, you had written a very good script and had found a company to produce it. It was a very exciting time for you. I realized, listening to all your news and looking at your new house, that you had been the wise one in our relationship. You had realized almost at once that you had found a woman who would be able to allow you to pursue your creative dreams without the pressure of a steady income. It is a dream come true for any creative person, and you were indeed lucky. She was pretty, smart and supportive. You had what you needed and you seemed really happy. I no longer felt I had made a mistake by saying no to joining you on your journey. I knew I had been right. It still hurt every time I saw you, knowing I would soon be saying goodbye. But I could not have financially been able to support your dreams, and eventually I would have felt that history was repeating itself for me. I would have equated you with Charlie and that would have been unfair to you. Or you would have given up your dreams to make our life more comfortable and you would have lost 'you'.

What I didn't take into the equation was that you did lose 'you,' only in a different way. As the years went on, you became someone else; but then who knows what kind of person you would have been had we shared your life. Time changes us all as we grow and learn. I certainly changed. I became more protective of myself in relationship to the rest of the world. I expended so much emotion on our relationship, albeit absentee most of the time, that I had little energy for allowing myself to feel too much in regard to the rest of the world other than, of course, my family.

Both Sides of the Coin

I loved a young man who eventually would no longer exist. Would I be as much in love with the man you would become? You know the answer. In the end it didn't matter.

You had errands that day and I was free to be with you and just watch you do your thing. You wanted to buy a new car, and wanted to know if I minded going along with you. Of course I didn't, because to me that was sharing, and all I ever wanted to do was share whatever little part of you was offered. We drove to a road that had one car dealership after another, and finally settled on the one you wanted. I have no recollection of the name of the car, but hours and many documents later you were the owner of the car, which you could pick up in a week.

We stopped for a bite to eat and before we knew it early evening had arrived and it was time to head home. It had been a great day. We both felt so happy in each other's company. When we got to your house, it was obvious Jeramie was home by all the lights burning inside. I had no choice but to go inside with you. Again, I had no idea she knew we were more than friends. I also didn't know that she had known we were spending the day together and had made it very clear to you that you had to be home by dark and that you had to bring me into the house.

All I thought of was that my car was parked on the side of your house and she surely had seen it. If I hadn't gone in, it would have looked strange.

We greeted each other in a friendly manner. In fact she seemed overly friendly. After a few moments of complimenting her on her taste in furnishing the house and saying whatever one says to sound enthusiastic, I said I had to leave soon as I hated driving when it was dark. She asked me to wait a moment while she showed me something. I said sure and waited while she went into the other room.

She came back not carrying anything, and then smiling brightly put her left hand in front of me and sweetly said "look what Matthew's given me. It's an antique engagement ring. Isn't it beautiful?"

Oh Matthew, that was one of the cruelest things you've ever done to me. How could you spend an entire day with me and never tell me you were getting married? How could you let me be put in this kind of position? Do you have any idea what it took for me to smile as broadly as humanly possible, and cry with joy for her and hug her, and hug you too, and look at the damn ring as though it was the most gorgeous thing I'd ever seen? "I'm just so happy for you both," I kept saying. "When's the wedding?" I finally managed to spit out.

"In six weeks," she replied. "Didn't Matthew tell you?"

You jumped in right away, explaining that you knew she'd want to tell me. "It's a girl thing," you said.

"You shit head," I wanted to scream. "You coward," I cried to myself.

I somehow managed to stay another fifteen minutes before reminding you that I didn't want to drive at night, and I was allowed to leave, but not before she invited me to the wedding. I somehow managed to explain that I couldn't get away but I'd be thinking of you both. She had accomplished her mission, so she couldn't have cared less when I left.

You said you'd walk me to my car, which was all of ten feet away from the front door. We walked out of the house, and as the door slammed shut you had the audacity to put your arm around my waste and then drop it to my butt. I would have knocked you out cold if I had the strength, but all I could do was push you away and hiss at you. "How could you?" I cried over and over. Out of her sight, the tears were uncontrollable.

I couldn't open the damn door to the car. My hands were shaking and I was close to hysteria. You came near me to help and I just pushed you away. You said something about not knowing how to tell me, but I didn't want to hear anything you had to say. I have never hated anyone as much as I did you at that moment. How could you hurt me like this? How could you, who professed to love me, inflict such pain. And what was wrong with me that I allowed you to do this to me. I finally got in the car, and with tears pouring down my face I drove through the damn canyon back to Beverly Hills; I couldn't have cared less if I had gone off the mountain.

For the rest of that trip, I wouldn't take your calls; I just couldn't talk to you. I needed time to think about us -- what we were and what we were not. I had somehow never given much thought to what our lives would be like once you had married someone other than myself. You had been with Jeramie for over three years and obviously she cared enough to want to go to the next step, and obviously so did you. It was natural and right for both of you. Her obvious dislike for me was understandable. If I had been her I would have hated me. No woman wants to think her man cares for someone else, and in our case she knew you had cared for me a lot. Yet all my rationalizing didn't take away the hurt, the envy of the life she would have with the man that I loved so very much. And how much could you really love me if you were able to commit to marriage with another woman. I hadn't done that to you. Ah, but that was my choice, not yours.

I cut my trip as short as I could and went home, back to work and friends.

Oh Ann, I just didn't know how to tell you. I spent the whole day trying to find the right moment but there wasn't one. I knew it would hurt you and if I'd thought for one moment you would have said something that could change our lives, if you had said "don't marry her, marry me," I would have grabbed you and ran as fast as I could. But I knew you wouldn't have done that, and honestly when you weren't with me I was happy with her. She made it easy for me. I couldn't take the chance and have her walk out. I wasn't ready to be the man you would have wanted. But I was the kind of man she wanted.

ॐ 41 ॐ

Peter had become a friend, as well as my boss. It was so strange, really, because we were from two different worlds. He had been brought up in a life of privilege and, although he had built his own empire, he was still so much a rich man's son. He had gone to all the right schools, had lived on Park Avenue and had spent his summers in Martha's Vineyard at the family home. It wasn't until the late eighties that he'd bought a beautiful beachfront house on Further Lane in East Hampton. Years later he would sell it to a famous comedian for a fortune. He had been married to a beautiful French woman, Jeanine, the mother of Louise, his only child. Although he hadn't been an angel during their marriage, when he'd found her with another man he hadn't been able to forgive her. Their marriage had quickly disintegrated. Jeanine had gone back to Paris and quickly married a very rich investment banker. Her picture often appeared in the fashion magazines, where she was seen attending many charity affairs as well as sitting in the front row seat of the fashion shows of the like of Yves St Laurent, Armani and Jean Paul Gautier.

Amazingly, we had come to really like one another. There were times, if he wasn't dating anyone at the time and needed a woman at his side, when I actually went to screenings and premieres with him. I had gained confidence in myself. A good haircut and highlights didn't hurt and neither did the nicer wardrobe; Peter had given me a clothing allowance, because he felt my job warranted a better look than the one I had originally appeared in. Who was I to argue? It was fun to shop now, because I was being encouraged to look nice. What a treat. Peter confessed that he found me to be the only sensible person he knew, and when he had a problem he trusted my common sense to solve it. I think in most cases I probably was that sensible person. You were the only person who really had been able to unleash a part of me that knew no bounds. Other than not following you to Los Angeles, nothing about my feelings and actions towards you have ever been sensible. I'm so glad.

Peter and I enjoyed each other's company and he had given me more and more responsibilities. We had never crossed the line of being more than friends. He had so many women to fulfill his sexual needs, and I had no desire to become another one of those women. I think in his own mind he still liked to visualize me as his little Doris Day, but with a little more spice.

He rarely asked me about you, and when he did it was more about your career than about us. He had forgiven me for you, my dear, or at best pretended he had imagined the whole thing.

Pat and I were in the process of co-producing our first film with his blessing and expertise, and it was a very exciting time for us. It was all so new and I had to pinch myself to believe all this was happening to me.

We could never have pulled it off if we hadn't had Peter behind us, making the important calls to money people, lining up the distribution deal and going over all the contracts. We were his students and he was enjoying the challenge of teaching us. We were so lucky, and I in particular for having fallen into this unbelievable opportunity after a lifetime of unhappiness.

I made a lot of trips to Los Angeles during that time, but for over a year I never let you know that I was in your town. I knew you had married. I read it in the trades. I couldn't take the chance of facing you and Jeramie, knowing I would betray my feelings, and above all not wanting her to see the hurt and envy in my eyes.

You kept calling me at odd times, and on the occasions that I picked up my phone without letting it go to voicemail I would hear your "Hi" and not have the courage to hang up. The sound of your voice was all I needed and I was undone, and so I'd talk to you, at first as carefully and with as much control as possible. After a while, I'd forget about Jeramie and we'd be talking as we always had.

Had a stranger overheard our phone calls they would have believed in our love, and never would have imagined a third party existed in this relationship.

I needed to hear your voice, then and always. But seeing you would be more than I could take.

And then one day, about a year after your wedding, you called me on a Saturday morning. "What are you doing for dinner?" you asked.

All pretext of not seeing you vanished. "You're here?" I cried. I couldn't believe it. You hadn't been to New York since the day you pulled away from my house.

You had meetings lined up for the next week. The movie you had just written was going to be filmed in New York. You and your new partner had insisted on working very closely with the producer and director on this one. You both wanted to learn everything you could, including looking at possible sites for the film. He couldn't make the trip, so you were on your own.

Honey Seltzer

You were so excited about it all and your excitement was contagious.

"Pick a restaurant," you told me. "It's been so long since I've been here I don't know where anything is anymore."

I thought fast, and since we both loved Chinese food I suggested Shun Lee, the best Chinese food in New York. I chose it more for the side-by-side seating than the food. At that moment all I could think of was sitting besides you, and feeling some part of you. I really didn't allow myself to think beyond that. You were married and it would be wrong, I told myself. I knew how strongly we were attracted to one another, and I didn't want you to do something you might later regret. I personally had given myself permission to make love to you, telling myself I had you first and I had given you to her. What nerve to presume I could hand you over to someone. You had gone to her on your own volition not because of my generosity. You were in control of your life, not me, not Jeramie. It's amazing what one can convince ones self of.

You were seated at a table when I arrived, and as I approached all I could think of was how handsome you were. I've never known any man that looked as gorgeous as you. You were wearing a stunning Armani jacket over a black sweater and chinos. Gone were your perennial sneakers, replaced by Gucci loafers. You looked so elegant, so successful, and yet so casual. You jumped up when you saw me and ignored all the diners as you pulled me in your arms to hug me. I could feel my face burning and my legs trembling when you finally released me and we sat down. This had been the longest we had been apart since the day we'd met, and yet it seemed as though we had seen each other yesterday.

All I could think of when I saw you walking towards me was how much I had missed you, how beautiful you looked and how much I loved you. I wanted to grab your hand and race off with you to my hotel. No talking, no eating dinner, no being civil; all so unnecessary as far as I was concerned. You were so wondrous my darling, then and always. You will never know the constant confusion I faced each day. You were my first and only real love. I would find myself consumed with guilt when Jeramie pushed me for a love I couldn't give her. I did all I could to make her happy. She has been what I've needed in a wife. She has always needed to be the one in control of our marriage and it was easy for me during the early years when I wasn't making any money and wasn't sure of what it was I was looking for in a career. I had obviously chosen the motion picture industry, but what talent did I really have? Was I really a good writer, did I enjoy the loneliness of writing? Did I want to produce? I was never a financial person. Did I want to direct? I think I knew then that was the direction best to follow, but I had

157

no experience, no one was going to hire me so it was for me to follow a very slow road in the business I had chosen, and finally after ten or more years I could begin to reap the benefits. For now, my benefits were courtesy of my wife who was making more money than I had ever imagined any woman would make, and loving her work tremendously. She had started to build her reputation in the agency and was now representing some actors who were becoming big stars. The more money she negotiated for them, the more she made for the agency and herself.

We did eat and talk, and you told me all about your work and I told you about mine. And I was the happiest I had been in a year. I felt your leg against mine and knew all my honorable thoughts were not going to last. I loved you and wanted you too much to be sensible or kind to a woman I cared nothing for. You never once mentioned her during dinner and that was fine with me. If you asked me to go with you to your hotel, I knew I would.

We left the restaurant holding hands and we began walking up Park Avenue. Walking with you always made me so happy. When you put your arm around me as we walked, I felt so tiny, so protected and so loved. It was always the place where our age difference disappeared. You were my hero, my protector. It was to me pure heaven. We got to the Regency Hotel and rode up to your room. We didn't have to say anything. We had no choice. Jeramie did not exist.

﷽ 42 ﷽

My phone rang one day in the office and it was you. I was as always happy when I heard your voice. Then I noticed something in your tone that made me question you. I thought you sounded upset.

You cleared you voice a few times and I finally realized you had something to tell me that wasn't easy for you to say. I wasn't prepared, I will admit, maybe because in the past you never had the courage to break bad news to me. You let someone else tell me. This time it was your turn and you didn't know how to spit it out, which is really what I finally said to you after, a lot of hemming and hawing on your part.

"Matt please just tell me whatever it is you're trying to say."

"Annie please don't be too upset."

I waited for what seemed an endless amount of time and finally heard you say, "Jeramie's pregnant. We're having a baby."

The moment you said the words, your voice changed. You were happy, so very happy about becoming a father. You couldn't control your joy, and why should you? But you were trying to be kind to me and there was no way to be kind.

My world came crashing down. Once again, oh foolish woman that I was, the tears came rushing out. I couldn't stop them. I couldn't talk. Someone else would have those beautiful children you had dreamed about, not I. I felt such a deep emptiness. I knew I was acting like a fool, but emotions have no reasoning. I just couldn't deal with the thought of another woman having your baby.

You tried so hard to console me. You wanted me to understand that we were soul mates, and that you truly believed that, during the course of our many lifetimes together, we'd had children together. This just wasn't one of the lifetimes we would have children, you told me. You really believed all this and wanted me to as well.

I wasn't in the mood to hear any of this. Where did all this come from, I wondered? My heart was broken. I didn't want to hear about past lives. I couldn't listen to all this. I finally stopped crying, and you were grateful to get off the phone.

By the time Luca was born, I had gotten past the hurt and sadness of another lost dream of my own. There wasn't anything I could do to change

matters. I should have finally closed the book on us, but I never could. I sent a gift, congratulated his mother, and as the years passed couldn't help but fall in love with a little boy that looked just like his father.

ഇ 43 രു

Pat and I continued under Peter's tutelage, but she was beginning to get frustrated. Although Peter had encouraged us to find projects and develop them, in the end he had never let us finalize anything. We would get ready to go into production, and suddenly he would become actively involved. Our roles became minimal and each film became another Peter Simmons Production.

I didn't care that much. I enjoyed finding the projects, and beating other producers out of obtaining the rights. I loved working with writers and often reworked some of the scripts, because I seemed to have a way with dialogue that was meant for film. But I didn't enjoy budget planning, or pampering stars or starlets or their agents. I was just happy to be involved in the making of a film, and so grateful to be a part of the excitement. Peter paid me very well, and even provided both Pat and I with a percentage of the profits. Whatever he asked me to do seemed appropriate. I was content.

Pat was younger than me, very smart and very beautiful. She had also worked a lot longer than I had in the business and was very ambitious. She had been approached many times by other producers to join their companies, but had until now been totally loyal to Peter. She had never wanted to leave New York, because she was involved with a married man for over ten years, and he had promised time and time again that he would divorce his wife when the children were in college. His last child had gone off to college the year before, and he still hadn't made a move to divorce his wife. Pat had finally accepted the fact that he was never going to marry her. In her own way, she, too, was a hopeless romantic.

"I've got to change my life," she told me. "I need to get away from Thomas and New York. I've been asked to join Lotus Films as a Vice President in charge of Business Affairs."

"But you hate Reid Augustine."

"He's been very nice to me. We had dinner last night and he offered me a great deal, Ann. I can't turn it down. I want to take the chance, and it's in Los Angeles and I said yes."

I knew she was right, but I felt sick at the thought of losing my closest friend to Los Angeles. She'd been the one who had given me this opportunity to start a new life, to meet you my darling, to support myself and my children, and to find a sense of value I never had before. She'd taught me so much, not just about work, but about life, about theatre, about museums, about art, and about clothes. She had made a real lady out of me. She had been my Henry Higgins.

I wish I could shake you as you tell this to me. You were a real lady long before you walked into Peter's office and Pat hired you. Only a real lady could have done what you were forced to do during your marriage and those first years at Peter's. Sure, she showed you how to dress a little better, but you would have known that yourself if you'd had money before you met her. You have always given her too much credit.

She was the one who gave me the courage to love you and not care what people thought.

You would have loved me no matter what she did. It was our destiny.

I asked her when she was going to tell Peter. She had just told him, and he was surprisingly very understanding and promised she could call on him for any help at any time. He had actually worried that I might be going with her.

"I wish I could," I said.

"Anytime you want Ann, there will be a place for you".

"I can't live there. I can't share Matthew's life out there and I couldn't stand to watch from the sidelines. I'm much better off here in New York."

"What happened when you told Thomas?"

"I don't think he believes me. He's so used to this Geisha girl always being available to him, that it doesn't occur to him I might ever finally say 'enough'."

"I'm so proud of you," I said. "He's never appreciated you and he's lied to you so many times. You could have almost any man you set your mind to and you still have plenty of time to find someone who'll give you a real life."

"So could you, you know."

I just shook my head no. I wasn't Pat. I found the life I needed, even the part that seemed absurd to my friends and family were enough. I could never expect to feel anything remotely resembling what I felt for you in another person, and I would never again allow myself to settle for less.

Right now Pat's main thoughts were on her new job and finding a place to live. I suggested calling Anita, who knew everything that was going on in

Los Angeles and probably could send her to an honorable realtor, but Peter had recommended JoAnne Benson, a woman he had had an affair with years earlier, who was one of the biggest realtors out there. Bless Peter, he always managed to stay friends with ex-girlfriends as well as his ex wife. JoAnne had been happy to hear from Pat and had already sent her a list of apartments and houses to look over.

It suddenly sounded so exciting, and for a moment I so wanted to go with her. She could sense my excitement and asked me if I could at least take a week off and fly out with her to look at some of the places JoAnne had faxed to her.

My schedule was really light, and I wanted to go. I told her I'd check with Peter and, if it was okay with him, I'd love to go with her.

Once I assured him that I had no intention of leaving my job or New York, he was happy to let me go off with her. I promised him I'd only be gone for a week.

Two weeks later, Pat and I flew out to Los Angeles. I hadn't told you I was coming out.

When I called to tell you I was in town and about Pat's planned move, you got all excited. You thought the move included me as well. I hated to disappoint you, because you sounded so happy thinking I might be moving out to Los Angeles, but I had to explain that it was only Pat. You tried to convince me it would be really wonderful for me to make the move. I didn't want to talk about my reasons on the phone and told you we'd talk more when we saw each other.

We made plans to have dinner the next evening. Jeramie was out of town and you had a lot to tell me. You wanted me to meet you at your house so I could see Luca who was now over a year old. You had become the perfect stay-at-home dad, and together with a combination nanny/housekeeper he was doing very well. The house was very organized, and Jeramie was hard at work and rarely home. She had little patience for her child and was happy to leave him either in your capable and loving hands or in the Nanny's hands as well.

I had a car drive me to your house so I could see Luca. You told me you would be able to bring me back to my hotel after dinner. Jeramie wasn't home and I didn't know about her rules regarding me, which included never driving me home. Obviously you planned on violating that one. There were other ones that I would find out about as time went on.

I visited with your beautiful son until his bedtime, and when I held him in my arms and hugged him goodnight, the beginning of a love affair began. I never again felt anything but absolute love for Luca.

We drove off to a tiny Italian restaurant away from your neighborhood, where no one knew you, and we spent the next three hours eating and talking. You filled me in on all that had happened to you the past year, since our phone calls had become less frequent. When we did speak, you were often rushed. She had also put her foot down on phone calls to me. They were taboo, unless she was in the room and could hear what you were saying to me. You managed to occasionally slip in personal calls away from her presence, but never on your phone because she checked the phone bill. You had never told me about all her rules, so I had believed you just didn't feel the need to talk to me as often as you had in the past, and I had tried not to make a big deal of it.

During our dinner you finally explained that, once Jeramie had realized we had been lovers not friends, she had demanded you cut me off. You refused, but promised that our relationship would never again be more than that of friends.

I thought of our encounter when you had been in New York but didn't mention it.

"We'll try to honor her request."

"She's my wife."

You looked so serious and sad. I loved you so much and I would do anything for you, or almost anything. I left it up to you. I told you that as long as we could still talk and see each other occasionally, I would be content. You smiled at me with such gratitude, but I knew that we were fooling ourselves.

You had become very frustrated with the movie business. The last film you had worked on didn't do very well financially. You had thought it was great and it hadn't been. Since then you had found writing a chore you weren't enjoying. The only thing that seemed to pick your spirits up these days was Luca.

Jeramie had finally noticed your lack of new written matter, and when she questioned you, you claimed writer's block. Her first solution was a visit to her shrink. She had personally taken to going weekly. She now encouraged you to go as well. She thought that might help with your writer's block.

You found that, after a while, the doctor actually helped you, and you did start writing again, but could get nothing finished. You had about three started scripts and you just weren't sure about any of them.

You also needed someone to talk to about your insecurities, your feelings about your marriage and your feelings about me. There was a great deal of confusion in your life, and you needed someone who wasn't emotionally involved to talk to and allow you to unburden yourself.

I asked you if I couldn't help, but you shook your head no. You took my hand and looked at me and I saw such sadness in your eyes. I wanted to help you so much, but you shut me out.

"It's for me to figure out Annie. I'm a mess." And then you forced a smile.

I squeezed your hand and held it tightly. I wanted all my love for you to somehow flow from my hand to your heart.

Then you told me about Jeramie's other idea. "Granted you're writing again, but there's no guarantee you'll ever write a movie that will become a major film. So why not take some acting classes?" she'd told you.

At first you'd thought she was crazy. You had never thought of acting. You couldn't imagine yourself pretending to be someone you weren't, and particularly in front of a camera. She had had answers for every negative comment you came up with, and then had continued to prod you by telling you how attractive you were and how women would probably go crazy seeing you on the screen.

I have to hand it to her, she was a great agent and motivator. She had gotten you going to classes.

You waited for my response.

At first I didn't know what to say. I had never thought of you as an actor. But you were in Hollywood. Anyone could be an actor out there. Physically, I could imagine females loving you, but I had no idea if you could act. But then I thought of all the actors who depended totally on their looks and were making fortunes; why not you?

I looked you up and down as though I had never seen you before, and then I grinned at you. "I for one will swoon over you when I see you on the screen."

You laughed, and then you confessed that you were enjoying the classes. They were a distraction from your real life, and maybe that was what you needed.

Annie darling, it was so hard to admit to you that I felt like a total failure. I had begun to realize that I wasn't a great writer, and I was living with a woman who was supporting me. It wasn't that she threw it in my face, because she really didn't. But everything I had was hers, not mine. My credit cards were in her name, the house was in her name, the car you had helped me pick out was in her name. I had been in Los Angeles for over five years and had so little to show for it other than my son. You had always had such high hopes for me, and I felt I was disappointing you as well as Jeramie and myself. Just having you sit with me that night and look at me with the love you always showed me, made me feel guilty. I didn't deserve such love. I hadn't done anything to earn it and I suddenly felt that I was cheating you out of a life. I wasn't worth you spending your life loving me. You deserved someone who could give you something.

I felt something I couldn't explain. I felt a deep sense of loss and didn't know what to do. For the first time in our relationship, I couldn't help you.

We finally left the restaurant and you asked me to come with you. You had something you wanted to show me before taking me back to my hotel. You seemed to perk up as we drove on to the Pacific Coast Highway and into Malibu. You pulled off the highway and parked the car, then got out and signaled for me to follow. It was dark, and except for the stars to light our way, I almost tripped as I walked behind you. You put your fingers to your lips to mean that I should be quiet and as we reached the sand of the beach in front of us I took off my shoes. You pulled me down on to the sand and pointed above us to a tiny house that stood on wooden stilts. All I could see was a screened porch. The house wasn't lit.

"Jeremie's buying this. It's very small, but look at the view. Can you imagine living with the ocean at my door? I really love it."

Oh Matthew, I wanted you to be happy, but your happiness only brought me new unhappiness. Once again I couldn't share a part of your life. We lay on the sand looking up at the stars and you turned to me and said with so much feeling, "Someday Annie I'm going to buy you a house on the beach, I promise you."

I turned my face so you wouldn't see the tears welling in my eyes. I got up and brushed my skirt and told you it was time we went back.

We got to my hotel and you let me leave you with a simple kiss and hug. I held on to you so tightly, because in my heart I knew that I had lost a part of us. I felt helpless in that knowledge. I knew we had to let our lives fall into place. Sometimes loving someone is not enough.

☙ 45 ❧

As you developed your skills in acting, your wife, the agent, had all the right people in the business come see anything you were performing in.

The amazing thing about all of this was that you were a natural. You were born to act. It was the right thing for you. There was something about you, beyond your good looks, that made the camera fall in love with you. There was a special quality that spoke volumes of the man you were, and the man you could be. You were sexy but vulnerable, and tough but kind. You were a man that both women and men could admire and love.

Ah, eventually they all did fall in love with you.

But that was a little later on.

We continued to occasionally speak on the phone. We were now more friends than the lovers we had been. It was almost easy to transition into this new form of relationship, because we weren't in the same room with one another. I assumed, based on our last evening together, that you no longer felt the physical attraction that had originally drawn us together. I didn't really believe your conscience had a part in the withdrawal.

One day you called me sounding very excited. You had wonderful news to tell me. You had gotten the lead in a new TV series. It was to begin filming in a month and you were coming to New York, because some of the exterior scenes would be filmed here. The other scenes would be done at the studio in Los Angeles. It was an exciting detective series and you were on screen most of the time. If it was as good as everyone expected, it could run for years and you could finally be financially independent.

I was so happy for you, and couldn't wait to see you. It had been almost two years since the night we had sat in a tiny Italian restaurant and talked; the night we had walked on the beach and I had felt a loss.

I had been out to Los Angeles on numerous business trips during those two years, but I hadn't once called you. It didn't feel right. Had you once said something to me on the phone that made me feel a visit from me was what you longed for, I would have phoned in a moment. But you never did.

Oh Matthew, we were on a constant merry-go-round for so many years. We were up and we were down. We couldn't make it together and we couldn't let go.

I knew when you were there. Pat always told me. I was trying so hard to make my marriage work. I wanted to be fair to Jeramie. She had done so much for me. It wasn't her fault that I could never feel for her what I felt for you.

One afternoon, you suddenly appeared at my office, more to impress Peter than anything. I understood that, and found it cute. You looked fabulous. You held me in your arms to hug me, and all resolve was gone. Everything I had ever felt for you jumped back into my being within seconds.

Peter was shocked when he saw you. He remembered the slightly disheveled young man in jeans, sneakers and long dark curly hair. He looked at the handsome man who was now in his mid-thirties, and was astonished. He looked at me and seemed to finally understand what it was I had seen almost ten years earlier. I felt so proud walking out with you. I had been vindicated. Sounds so stupid as I tell this, but its how I felt. I had fallen in love with a young man who had captivated me, who had understood me totally and who had loved me equally. Now he was all grown up and I still loved him, and I thought, based on the way he was looking at me, in his own way he still loved me.

We left the office. You had made dinner reservations, but you needed to go back to your hotel to drop off some papers you had been carrying. I followed you through the streets of New York oblivious of the crowds, only focusing on you. We reached your hotel, and until we walked through the door of your room I hadn't thought about what might happen. I had believed until that day we would never sleep together again, and I had promised myself I would never do anything to encourage a breech in this belief.

We had no more control than two animals in heat. Do you remember how fast we reached for one another? You smothered me with kisses and I you. We lost all thought of anyone other than each other. Nothing could have kept us from ending up in your bed. We were incapable of thinking, only feeling the need to touch, to feel and to love.

When we were finally able to stop, you looked at me, holding my face in your hands, and you told me how much you loved me and how hard you had tried not to.

I felt tears well in my eyes as you bent down and kissed them.

"Don't cry, my Annie, please don't cry."

"I thought I'd lost you."

"You'll never lose me. I promise you."

"Don't say that Matthew. You have a life that doesn't include me. It's going to get even richer now with success."

"None of that will ever make a difference in how I feel about you. You are my first, my special love. You were the first person I ever cared about more than myself, and I have always treasured that feeling. I will always love you. I hope I don't hurt you as I know I have."

I threw my arms around you and held you and for that night felt the luckiest woman alive.

When we were together we were so special, but all those times between were not always so special.

You know Matthew, I have realized just recently, probably when I got the news of my illness and began reflecting on "us," that all we've really had since the day you drove off to California in your little orange bug were a series of montages -- click, click, click. As in any script you've read, you know only too well when it says "Cut to: Montage," we watch our hero and heroine race through brief but important moments in building their relationship, thus saving us from all the nitty-gritty details. That's been us, remembering the key elements of our brief times together, moments that have somehow been so important to us that we've sustained them for over twenty-five years. I see us meet. I see the recognition of what we may be feeling over a late dinner. I see us dancing on the deck of a silly houseboat that never left the harbor. I see us making love that first time, not sure but so desperate to find out if we both feel the same way. I see me crying as I race out of a cab, as you call my name, not understanding why I ran from you. I see us at the beach house making love. I see all our fights and all our reconciliations. I see us sitting on the stoop of a deserted house, and I see you driving away. I see you barely able to contain yourself in a restaurant in California while Jeramie looks on from the other end of the table and reads our faces. I see us spending a lovely day in California and returning to your home to find out from Jeramie that you're getting married. I can never wipe out the look of victory reflected on her face. I see us sneaking up to look at the tiny beach house you have bought. I feel my hurt and loss. I visualize you touching her stomach that holds your child and see the pure joy on your face. All this and many more little moments comprise our montage. What was it in me that made this enough? It was never enough for you.

Annie, Annie we were so much more. I failed you my dearest. I should have been with you and only you all those years. I should have had enough courage for both of us.

The next few years are an almost-blur in my life. You went back to your life and your new career. Your series became an unbelievable success and you were every woman's fantasy.

I rarely heard from you. You worked very long hours, and the time difference made it difficult to have phone contact. Ah, but something new had entered all of our lives; now we had email. How simple and quick to send a little note expressing love or the latest expression of affection "xoxoxox". That was supposed to be sufficient. That became our new way of communication.

When I think about it, Matthew, I was really pathetic. I actually took pleasure in knowing I had been the woman who had slept with you before fame reared its ugly head. I had been the real love of your life, or convinced myself I had been. When I saw your face in magazines and read articles about you, I wanted to shout from the rooftops "hey world look at me, I'm the one who meant something important to him, not that woman being photographed alongside of him." I cannot believe that I had allowed you to become my life.

I think it was the night you won an Emmy that finally brought me out of my long sleep. I sat propped up by pillows in my bed, watching Joan Rivers interviewing all the important people she could grab before the Awards, and I strained my eyes looking for you. Suddenly you appeared. You looked so absolutely wonderful, and Joan gushed over you accordingly. She barely paid attention to Jeramie, which was typical of her treatment of wives, but you made a point of introducing Jeramie "my beautiful wife," and Joan was forced to tell her how exquisite she looked and asked the standard question, "whose gown are you wearing?" She was quick to answer that it was a Balenciaga, made especially for her.

I looked at your face and saw your pride in your wife. When you accepted the award, I waited breathlessly for a hint that you were thinking of me. You thanked everyone who had helped you in your career, but most importantly your wife Jeramie. Of course you hadn't mentioned me, why would you? What could you have said that could have been acceptable to your wife, and did you even think about what you might have said if you could. You hadn't even given me the little special signal we spoke about so many years earlier, which I would have understood and which would have helped. I had finally and totally lost you. The sadness was overwhelming. I vowed at that moment to live my life without you. We had had something very special, but I didn't believe it existed any longer for you. I had to let it go. I had lingered too long. I felt an utter fool.

Oh Annie, I was proud of her. She's an amazing businesswoman and she had created me as an actor. On my own, I would never have thought to pursue acting. Without her pushing me I wouldn't have had the series that started all of my successes. I did owe her and I did care for her. I just never loved her the way I loved you. Weeks before the Emmy's I had thought about how I could acknowledge you and all I felt for you, but I honestly couldn't think of a way of doing it that would have been right. I'm so sorry I hurt you so badly. I should have talked to you about it. Since you never said anything, I thought it was okay.

❧ 47 ❧

From that day onward, I began sending my assistant to Los Angeles on many of the trips that I would normally take. I just didn't want to be tempted to call you or see you. I never told you about my decision, and since you rarely phoned any more it was easy to answer your emails with a cryptic response. You were so involved in your career, you didn't even notice. You were now, during hiatus, making your first feature film where you had the starring role. I read that you had been paid eight million dollars to do this movie. If it became a box office hit, your price would skyrocket. You had never told me about it. In the past we would have had long talks about the pros and cons. No more talks, no more sharing. Eight words or so in an email was our communication.

I kept busy at work and the years flew by. I had finally agreed to become more social, and let it be known that I would not say no if an agreeable man asked me out. Unfortunately, I didn't find most of the men I encountered very agreeable. Either they were totally boring or only interested in arm candy and a quick roll in the hay. I was never going to be a quick roll in the hay, although sometimes I wished I could be. I just wanted to forget you, and then maybe I could fall in love again.

One night, Peter and I had just finished a long day, and as I started to put everything away in my desk he walked into my office and sat down. He had a bottle of wine and two glasses, and poured some wine for both of us.

"Are you in a rush?" he asked.

"No," I said, taking a glass from him "What a good idea."

He smiled and sat back in one of my chairs.

"I had a better idea today. I think we all need a vacation, especially you. I know I do too. So I had Travel rent a villa in St. Bart's for a two-week stay. It's very big, plenty of bedrooms and private baths. It's very beautiful and has all the amenities, including being on the beach, a swimming pool, servants, etc. etc. etc. I've asked Richard and his wife, Louis and his partner, and Tony and his new wife to stay. I'd like you to join us."

I didn't know how to answer him. I thought it was the sweetest, kindest thing for him to include me. I hadn't been good at hiding my unhappiness, and although I never talked to him about you, he knew more than I realized.

It seems that he kept in touch with Pat and he plied her with questions. He meant no harm, he really cared about me; far more than I realized.

He waited for me to answer and finally said, "Well?"

"Oh my goodness, I'd love to. This is so fabulous and so sweet of you. I'm overwhelmed."

I got very excited as I said yes. I hadn't had a real vacation in years, and this sounded so glamorous and exciting. "When are we going? I have to shop. I have to get new bathing suits. I could go to Saks now. They're open late on Thursday." I said as I looked at my watch.

He burst out laughing. "You don't have to go shopping now. I give you permission to spend all day tomorrow doing whatever ladies have to do get ready, because we are leaving Saturday morning."

I ran to him and hugged him. "You're the best. Thank you so much."

"You're the best. You never take anything for granted. You're a very special woman my dear."

I felt myself blushing at his words. We so rarely ever got this personal. I didn't know what to say.

He laughed. "Before we get too emotional, go home Annie."

He got up, took his wine and went back into his office.

The next two weeks were magical. Peter had arranged everything. We all met at a private airport in Westchester, where we boarded a private plane. This was a first for me. Despite working for Peter for almost fifteen years, I had never been self-indulgent. True when I traveled on business, I usually was booked on first class seats, and stayed at the best hotels, but it was never at my own request. The travel department took care of these things; my travel was always for business. This was actually the first trip I was taking that was for pleasure and it was exciting and made me think of what else I might do in the future.

I now certainly had much more financial security. I had been able to help my children finish their educations and begin their new lives as young women, without too much of a struggle. Jennifer was now a senior editor at a fashion magazine and had married a serious young man who, ironically, worked in motion pictures. Liz was now a lawyer at a prestigious law firm in Los Angeles. She had chosen to move to Los Angeles when she fell in love with a young man she had met in law school. This had all recently happened, and if it weren't that I couldn't chance the possibility of facing you, Matthew, I probably would have moved there as well.

I rarely did special things for myself. True, I dressed very well, and my hair was styled and even highlighted, but this was all for work; to meet and greet clients and future clients. Oh sure, I went to the best restaurants both in New York and Los Angeles, but again this was all for business. Not to say I didn't love it all, because I did. I was so grateful for the life I had been given after believing I'd never find happiness.

As we flew off that morning, I realized that I had to start making changes in my life, and one of the first would be to move to a new apartment. All these years, I had stayed in the home that I had shared with Charlie and my girls. I had to let go of so many things.

My daughters had their own lives and I was very proud and happy for them. The apartment definitely had to go, I told myself. It was time for me to move to the city. I don't know why I had waited so long. The idea filled me with excitement.

We landed in St. Barts. Four young men met us with four jeeps to carry us and all our luggage to the villa. As we began our drive, the beauty that surrounded me overwhelmed me. I hadn't realized how magnificent this island would be. On one hand, I saw gorgeous mountains, and then, the blue, unbelievably beautiful waters of the Caribbean. It took my breath away. In moments, all the confusion I had been feeling for years just left me. I felt as though I had recovered from a very long illness. I felt such hope for the possibilities of new happiness. I knew I had so much to be grateful for and I felt so sure that there was more in the offering.

Peter turned to me, and said, "well, what do you think?"

"Oh, it's beyond beautiful. It just takes my breath away. Thank you so much for asking me along."

He just gave me a big smile.

After a wild drive down winding narrow roads with no guardrails, we turned off the road and reached our beautiful villa. Hidden beyond bougainvillea bushes, the sea appeared. I got out of the jeep and stood mesmerized. A young native woman came running out of the house to greet us. Her name was Usula and she was to be our housekeeper during our stay. Following her came two other young women who were introduced as Sarina and Tomara. They were the cook and maid. We later found out there was also a laundress who arrived each morning and left each evening. Her name was Bettina. I hoped I'd remember everyone's name.

We were taken into the house and shown our rooms. All of the bedrooms were painted in various pastel shades. Each of them had a private bathroom, and all of them faced the sea. I had a large room painted pale tangerine. A big four-poster bed, enclosed with sheer white curtains, was in the center of the room and faced a wall of windows that revealed the sea in the distance. The linens on the bed were of the finest cotton, and a soft, lightweight comforter, also in white, rested on the foot of the bed. A beautiful bleached wood armoire stood in a corner, and a breathtaking multicolored area rug was resting on the polished wooden floor. On the wicker sofa, which had been placed under the windows, were assorted pillows of varying colors. Sheer white curtains covered the windows, but had been pulled back to allow the glorious view to be seen. I then walked into the adjoining bathroom and could not believe my eyes. I found a huge claw-legged tub as well as a separate shower. I looked at all kinds of soaps, shampoos, body lotions, and bubble baths lined up in bottles, together with a soft robe; I couldn't wait to take a bath. I couldn't think of a thing that was missing. As I looked further, I found make up remover, hair rollers, hair clips, make up to suit almost anyone's coloring. It was all absolutely unbelievable. Everything I could possibly need for the next two weeks were sitting in front of me. I felt totally spoiled and we'd just arrived.

A knock at the door took me out of my stupor and I went to open it. One of the young men who had met us at the airport had my luggage. Followed by him was Tomara. She had been instructed to unpack my things and if anything needed ironing or refreshing, she told me she would have Bettina do it immediately. I didn't know what to say. I tried to tell her I could unpack myself, but she wouldn't hear of it. I finally left her to her work and walked back into the house, where I found everyone else. At that moment, Usula walked in and announced that lunch would be served on the patio. We all followed her outside where a table had been set with local colorful pottery on a beautiful embroidered tablecloth. Peter opened the first of many bottles of wine and we all toasted what was to be an unbelievable two-week stay at, what I later learned, was to be called "St. Barths," not "St. Barts."

Sometimes an episode occurs in your life that is the substance of all future deeds. The trip to St. Barths had a profound effect on the years that followed. There was something about that island that made me long for the dreams of my youth. All I had ever wanted was to love someone deeply and to have them love me back equally. When we rode through the island that first night on our way to dinner at a restaurant, I breathed in the fragrant air, and as I looked at the star filled sky, the mountains, the sea and the total beauty of this tiny island I wanted so much to share this with you. It is such a perfect place for love, for the rekindling of lost love or the formation of a new one. I longed for you more than I ever had, and knowing we would never share this moment made me want to cry. I needed to share all the love within me, and I came to the realization that no matter how much I loved you I couldn't spend the rest of my life living on a love that only existed on old memories. I wanted new memories, and if not with you it was time to start again.

I shook my head clear of you and looked around at what life had blessed me with and told myself I was an idiot. I wasn't going to spoil this fabulous trip by feeling sad and sorry for myself. It was too special to ruin for feelings that were best left to history.

That evening we all ate, laughed and got a little drunk and it was great. It was the beginning of having fun, relaxing and all of us getting to know each other on a more personal level. Even Tony, who had married a lovely girl, Julie, was now so much nicer to me. The days when he had let Drue almost destroy me had long since gone.

We'd been on the island for about four days; each day filled with new and exciting experiences. One day we spent the day sailing, something I had never dreamed of doing. I absolutely fell in love with sailing and Peter, who owned a boat that he kept in Sag Harbor, promised me that in the summer he would teach me how to sail. He seemed to get a kick out of my excitement. When he suggested we go snorkeling I almost chickened out. Much as I adored looking at the water, and now sailing, I'd never liked having my head under the water. As a child I had been pulled out to the ocean in an undertow at Coney Island, and as I tumbled through the water, thinking I'd never come up and terrified that I was drowning, I developed a serious fear of the strength of the waves. Peter assured me he'd watch out for me, as did the teacher, and if I got frightened, the lesson would end immediately. I couldn't believe how much fun I had. I took to it like a duck takes to water, and had the time of my life. I couldn't wait to go down under again.

Everything I did just seemed to make me happier. The Island was magical, and one night it turned even magical. We had all said goodnight and I had gone to my room. I found I wasn't sleepy and decided to go outside and sit on a chair and look at the twinkling lights from boats that were anchored far out in the sea, and to listen to the sound of the crashing waves. I had carried out a glass of wine and felt relaxed and content when I felt a light kiss on the top of my head and a touch of a hand on my shoulder. I looked up to find Peter smiling at me.

"I thought that was you. I couldn't sleep either. It's such a glorious night."

We smiled at each other.

"Let's walk for a while, shall we?"

I put my glass down and got up to walk with him, and he very naturally put his arm around my waist as we walked. It was the most comfortable feeling. As we walked and quietly talked, we stopped to look at a falling star. We stood quietly looking into the sky and we then turned to one another, about to speak, when Peter moved towards me and took me in his arms. He looked at me quizzically for a moment, and my eyes said yes. I wanted him to kiss me as much as he did. When we breathlessly pulled apart, I think we were both in shock. We had known each other for so long and neither one of us had ever encouraged -- or thought of encouraging -- the other to be anything more than what we were; boss and employee. At least I certainly hadn't.

"What are you feeling?" he asked me.

I sat down in the sand. I was so surprised by it all I didn't know how to answer him.

He sat down next to me and took my hand. "It was only a kiss Ann." He looked at me very seriously before he continued. "I'd like it to be more, but only if you're sure."

I suddenly knew that I did want it to be more. Every part of my body yearned to be loved by someone who truly cared for me, and who I felt I also cared for. I had always admired him; I thought he was amazing, charming, brilliant and way beyond the likes of me. In the midst of this unexpected, but most welcome moment, I remembered my friend Fran saying something in a demeaning way to me all those years earlier, she "hoped I didn't think someone like my boss would want me." I don't know why she came to mind at that moment, because I hadn't set out to prove her wrong, but in so many ways I had. Yes my boss did want me, but the irony was I wanted him as well.

I moved close to Peter and this time I initiated the kiss. He took me in his arms again and on the sand away from every one, and with only the lights of distant boats, which seemed to glow for us, we made love for the first time.

We never went to sleep that night. We sat on the beach and talked and talked and talked. It seemed we had never really spoken to one another before as two equal mature people, and we had much more in common than we had ever realized. He hadn't been in love with anyone in many years. He admitted that most of the women I had seen him with were mostly arm candy or short-term sexual relationships. He knew about you and asked me if I still loved you. I tried to explain my feelings about you. I didn't want to lie. He stopped me before I could say too much. "There's always one special love in everyone's life. If there isn't then I feel sorry for them. I've had mine as well. Don't worry about it Ann. You don't have to explain. I know I was a real jerk to you when I first found out, and for that I'm sorry. You were right to follow your heart. I think that's one of the first things I found so appealing about you. And you've continued to add things to your appeal throughout the years."

"You did, you have?" I was shocked to hear him say this, and even more shocked to think he had seen me in a way I had never visualized, and for much longer than I would have ever believed possible.

He ruffled my hair and pulled me to him. "I've been crazy about you for ages but I didn't think you were ready to know."

"Why now? How did you know I was ready now?"

"I guess I know you pretty well."

He pulled me up from the sand and we silently walked back to the house, holding hands. It felt good and it felt right. It just felt so comfortable. We were good together. We hardly had to say anything to know that in one night we had entered into a committed relationship. A walk on the beach had changed our lives drastically and I will forever be grateful for that moment in time.

The rest of our trip was amazing and the others immediately noticed the changed dynamics of our interaction. We tried to be discreet and kept our own rooms, but Peter found his way to my bed most nights and I never tired of him, nor he of me.

Both Sides of the Coin

On our last night on the Island all of us gathered for dinner on the patio. The cook had made a wonderful meal for us, and we had opened and had finished drinking several bottles of wine when Peter asked for champagne. When the glasses were filled he stood up to make a toast. I had no idea what he was going to say and I thought it would be some cute thing about the end of a great trip. He caught me and the others totally off guard when he turned to me and began to speak. "I would like to toast the lovely Ann who I have admired for a very long time and who has finally come to see my many virtues." Everyone started to laugh, but he stopped them. "I'm not finished, please people. I know you all think I'm smug, conceited, so very sure of myself, but I'm not always. Right now I want to ask Ann a very important question and I'm too much of a coward to do it in private, because she might say no, so Ann, in front of my friends I ask you if you would consider being my wife."

Silence prevailed. They were shocked, but more importantly, I was shocked. We hadn't talked of marriage and it had never occurred to me that Peter would want to marry. He had had a disastrous marriage as had I. He could have married some of the most beautiful woman in the world and he hadn't.

I looked at his handsome face, and at the moment he looked like a little boy, a boy I had never known and I felt a rush of affection and love for him. Not the kind I've had for you Matthew, but a decent and sincere love.

My face was burning, but I knew my answer and I got up from my seat and walked to his side and said, "Yes, of course I will," for all to hear.

Everyone started shouting and then kissing and hugging and it was all so wonderful until Peter said, "Wait."

We all stopped. I thought, "it's all a joke and he's not really asking me to marry him."

"Annie, I had hoped with all my heart you were going to say yes, and I took a chance and did a little shopping while you were resting this afternoon. I hope you like this and I hope it fits." He put his hand into his pocket and took out a box that I knew, by its very shape, had to contain a ring. He opened the box and took out the most beautiful ring I had ever seen and placed it on my finger. It was a perfect fit.

With that, of course, I started to cry. It was so much more that I could have dreamed. I couldn't believe this was happening to me. I had gone on this trip filled with loneliness and sadness, and in just a short time my life was changing drastically.

Realization finally set in when I arrived home. Suddenly the fairytale had become real life and it frightened me. Did I really fit into the new life being offered me? I felt totally inadequate in becoming Peter's wife. Away from the magic of the island and the romantic beauty of it all, I saw myself so far removed from the kind of woman that I believed was Peter's due.

I was ordinary. I had believed this most of my life. Even my love for you Matthew, and your love of me, had never convinced me otherwise. But we never had to live in the real world. I had made sure of that. We never felt very much criticism or skepticism because so few people knew about our relationship.

With Peter it was different. I didn't come from wealth. My education never included the finest boarding schools, or the most prestigious universities; a city college had been my campus.

True, the last years working at Peter's company had shown me a new world. I had been able to converse with many people in this dynamic atmosphere, but deep down I always remembered who I was and where I came from.

What would they expect from Peter's wife?

For a man who could sometimes be curt, unfeeling, and blunt he came to me one day, and in moments removed all my self-doubt. He had known, without me saying a word, that I was frightened and insecure. He looked at me with those blazing blue eyes and convinced me of his deep love for me. He had no doubt whatsoever that we would be good together, and I was to believe him. He didn't want to marry any other woman. Had he, it would have happened and it hadn't.

"Trust me, sweetheart, we're going to be great and you're going to knock 'em dead."

I believed him and let him get on with our wedding plans, but not before promising me that it would be a small and simple wedding.

My daughters were thrilled and surprisingly not shocked. Jennifer told me she had always had a feeling about us, and Liz wanted to shout the news to the rooftops. She thought it was the greatest thing that could have happened to her mother. She had never adjusted to you and me, and was grateful it was finally over.

Even Louise, who now lived in Paris with her new husband, was pleased. Fortunately she had always liked me.

I knew that I had to be the one to tell you, before Peter announced the news, and so I called you. I was told by your assistant that you were out of the country and he would pass a message on to you. I tried emailing you, asking you to call me, but I didn't say why I needed to speak to you. It took two days for you to call, and the moment I picked up the phone and heard your voice I could tell you knew.

You sounded awful. "You can't do this," were your first words. "I'm at the airport in Rome and I'm leaving for New York in an hour. I've got to see you. I've got to talk to you."

"Matthew please, don't do this. I'm marrying Peter. He loves me."

"What about you? Do you love him? You know you don't."

"That's not fair. You don't know how I feel. If you knew me at all you'd know I wouldn't be marrying him if I didn't care for him."

"Annie, I said love, not care. Tell me you love him and I won't get on the plane."

I was trembling and wanted to cry out to you and tell you that I'd never love anyone the way I've loved you, but what good had that done me?

"I love him Matthew. Don't get on the plane."

There was total silence on the phone and I imagined your face and how you were feeling and I couldn't deal with it so I hung up the phone.

You have no idea what I was feeling. I had never thought about you marrying someone else. How selfish was I? I hadn't really thought about your feelings when I married Jeramie. I thought that as long as you knew I loved you more, everything would be fine with you. How arrogant was I that, when I told you I had both sides of the coin, I expected you to rejoice for me? How stupid, spoiled and naive was I? And these past years, I'd ignored you so much, just when I had finally gained some success, and again I thought you'd understand. You had been the first to believe in me, and I had just ignored you. You, who deserved to join me in my ride to riches, I had left behind. I thought you knew that, no matter how little we spoke, my love was always there for you. I thought you knew all that was happening in my life by osmosis, without me having to tell you. What was wrong with me, that I would take your love so for granted that I did nothing to assure it? Oh Annie, you have no idea what I felt at that moment.

As promised Peter made all the arrangements for our not-so-small, but beautiful wedding. He had tried to keep it limited to fifty people, but in the end that had been impossible. I gave him a list of my family and friends that I wanted to invite and left the rest to him and his secretary. All I had to do was buy my dress, and show up on schedule at the magnificent brownstone house he said he had rented for the occasion. Thanks to my daughter Jennifer, who knew everyone in fashion, Vera Wang herself designed my simple but exquisite dress that befitted a movie star, and made my future husband's face light up in pure joy as I walked down the aisle to join him.

I had invited my childhood friends Fran and Roz with their husbands. Although slightly bewildered by being in the presence of people whose names they had only read about or seen on the screen, they were beside themselves with happiness for me.

Peter hadn't told me where we going on our honeymoon. He kept telling me it was a surprise, and that I didn't have to pack anything because everything I needed would be taken care of. He seemed to love surprising me, and I found him so endearing and loving. I sometimes had to pinch myself to believe this was all happening to me.

We finally said goodbye to the last guest, and I turned to my husband with a look of "what now?"

He smiled and took me by the hand and led me up the stairs. We walked to a door and he opened it and I found myself inside a huge bedroom. The first thing I saw was a lit fireplace burning brightly as though welcoming us into its fold. A huge four-poster bed enclosed in soft panels of fabric faced the fireplace. I didn't have time to look at the rest of the furnishings as he took my hand and walked me to the bed.

"You like?" he asked.

"It's so beautiful. Whose house is this?"

"It's yours, darling. I bought this for you as a wedding present."

I was so overcome with emotion I couldn't speak at first. The tears began before I could say more than, "Oh Peter."

He put his arms around me and held me and I felt so safe and protected. The knowledge that this man would always be there for me struck a cord that was indescribable. I could not believe I was so blessed, nor did I believe I deserved it.

‮ఴ‬ 51 ‮ఴ‬

Peter and I had been married almost five years and I loved him more as each day went on. We were so in synch and, as promised, I had proven to be as good a wife as he had assured me I'd be. His friends and associates had accepted our marriage almost from day one, which had made it so much easier for me. With their acceptance, I began to relax and enjoy my life as Mrs. Peter Simmons.

He hadn't wanted me to continue working, but I needed to be busy. We had completely redone the house during the past few years, mostly with the help of a decorator. Although she certainly listened to me when I expressed my desires, she was so good that I hadn't been needed very much. Now that the work was completed, and with a staff of household help, there wasn't very much that needed my attention.

I liked going off with him in the morning. He'd go to his office and I'd go to mine. Very often, if we didn't have an outside luncheon scheduled, we'd order lunch in, and sit in one of the conference rooms watching a film we were working on. We were able to share our work in a very compatible way. If we disagreed on something, we rarely raised our voices, which was actually funny since Peter had very often been guilty of raising his voice to people, He claimed I had brought a sense of calmness to his life.

During the years since our wedding Peter had made a lot of trips to Los Angeles, but I had always found a reason not to accompany him. It was now the time of the Academy Awards and I had no way out. One of Peter's movies had received numerous nominations including Best Picture. He was very excited and of course so was I, not just for him, but also for all the people who had worked so hard to make this film so great. I knew our paths would probably cross yours, and I tried to prepare myself for the inevitable. I had managed not to think of you too often, and had hopefully put our love in the past, where it belonged. I knew I would always love you, but I had vowed that this love was never going to intrude on my new life.

We arrived in Los Angeles a week before the awards, and were staying at a Bungalow at the legendary Chateau Marmont. The hotel was beyond anything I had thought possible; a world onto itself. Our private veranda offered us a spectacular view of the city and at night, after an evening of being out, I would change into my sweats and sit outside waiting for Peter to join me with a glass of wine. There we would sit quietly enjoying the stillness and beauty of the lights of the city.

Then the day of the awards arrived. I had to prepare for the main event of the motion picture industry. I had watched the award show from the time I could remember, first on my parent's television set, and then on mine and Charlie's. Like millions of others around the world, I loved the excitement of the night. I loved watching all the celebrities walk down the red carpet, and I would pick out which gown was my favorite of the night and rehash it the next day with my girlfriends. It was all such fantasy, such excitement and beauty. To actually attend this event was a dream come true; and to be attending it with a man who was nominated for one of the highest awards, my very own husband, was beyond fantasy. No dream of mine ever came to such high expectations.

Los Angeles of course is three hours earlier than the East Coast, and I wasn't mentally prepared to be ready in full make up and gown at three PM for a four PM arrival. Somehow, a person unknown to me until that morning, arrived at our cottage at ten AM, and I found myself being sprayed from head to toe with an instant suntan. When finally dry, I was allowed to put on a robe and await, first the hair person and then the makeup person. I had never had my makeup done professionally before. I had told Peter this was all unnecessary. "I'm not a star," I kept protesting. He laughed and walked into another room. I shrugged in helplessness and let everyone do their work.

When my nails were done, my hair and makeup both finished, I was finally allowed to look in the mirror. I barely recognized myself. I for the first time in my life found myself thinking that I was beautiful, and it was an exciting, unbelievable feeling. My black gown, designed especially for me by Georgio Armani, was simple but elegant. The bodice of black Chantilly lace covered one shoulder, leaving the other bare. The flowing chiffon skirt had a small train that made me feel like a Queen. I loved the gown. It was everything I could have ever fantasized about wearing to the Academy Awards. Peter had given me a stunning diamond pin, which I had placed on the shoulder that was covered in lace. My earrings were beautiful diamond drops, also a gift from my generous husband. When the ladies attending me had put the finishing touches to my lipstick, they lead me in to show Peter.

The look of pleasure on his face was all I needed to give me courage for the evening. He didn't stop telling me how beautiful I looked. He looked so handsome in his Armani tux. I was determined to make him proud that night.

He had also arranged for our limo to pick up first my daughters and their husbands, and then us. He had made all the arrangements for Jennifer and Cole to fly in from New York. He had also booked hotel rooms for the four of them, even though Liz and Jonathan lived in Los Angeles. He thought they'd enjoy being together in the same place, where they could all be spoiled courtesy of Peter. He had had them choose their gowns and the bills were sent to him. He had spared no expense so that my family could share this night with us. Louise wasn't able to fly in from Paris, as she was awaiting the arrival of a baby she was adopting from China. We were going to fly to Paris as soon as the baby arrived. So many good things were happening for us.

My daughters looked so beautiful, and they thought their mom looked pretty good too. We all carefully got into the limo and rode to the theatre. Peter had an assistant waiting to meet our car, and my daughters and their husbands were escorted into the theatre and to their seats. We, because Peter was a nominee, had to walk the red carpet. It was bedlam. The stands were filled with screaming fans. I would turn my head when the screaming became very loud, because I too wanted to see who was arriving. A part of me had never really grown up. A part of me didn't believe I was a participant of all of this glamour and excitement, but rather an observer as were the fans in the stands. We stopped for an interview with the infamous Joan Rivers, and I stood back so Peter could answer her ridiculous questions, when I felt a hand on my shoulder. I didn't have to turn to know it was your hand, Matthew, my body's reaction told me so.

To love someone as I have loved you is equal to a debilitating illness. I knew before I felt your touch that our meeting that day would occur, and I had told myself that I would be calm, I would not react, I would be friendly, and I would do nothing to hurt Peter. Once I had taken the necessary short breaths I needed, I turned to you and was prepared to smile as though you were an old acquaintance. Our eyes held and said all the words we did not. Jeramie had been standing several feet behind you talking to another woman, and until that moment hadn't seen me. Peter finished talking to Joan Rivers and turned to me. I was about to say hello to you, as it would have seemed strange if I didn't, when Joan saw you Matthew, and pulled you -- or rather her handlers pulled you -- towards her for an interview. Jeramie, seeing you were on camera, rushed to your side. Peter simply nodded to you took my arm and off we walked. You and I hadn't spoken, we hadn't needed to. Our eyes had.

"Are you okay?" Peter asked me.

I squeezed his hand and smiled brightly. "Of course I am. This is such a special night."

The cast of the movie Peter had been nominated for soon surrounded us, and Peter once again was in front of a camera being interviewed by someone else. The hour flew by and we were finally in our seats. I was so grateful to sit down, and when the lights came down, I momentarily closed my eyes in an effort to relax. The wonderful night I had so looked forward to had changed like a sudden fall hurricane; warning signs that only I could read were all around me, and I was petrified. I needed to be very strong that night and I knew it. Sitting in the dark I prayed I wouldn't disappoint Peter.

I never moved my head away from watching the stage throughout the evening. I had no idea where you were sitting and I didn't want to know. You hadn't been nominated so I knew you couldn't be sitting that close to us, and I knew you wouldn't be going up to get an award. What I hadn't thought of was that you might be a presenter. When you walked out on stage with Doreen Blair, a young and beautiful star, to present the award for Best Supporting Actress, I was caught unprepared. I could feel the heat rise to my face, and at the same time I could feel Peter staring at me. I knew he'd expect me to look at him and I turned to him and looked into his eyes and whispered "isn't she beautiful?" He took my hand and held it and I put my fingers through his and smiled contentedly. He seemed satisfied.

"This is taking so long," I whispered. "Are you okay? Are you nervous?" I asked him.

"I'm fine. There's nothing to be nervous about. If I win, I win. If not it doesn't matter. I am the winner Annie, I have you."

I looked at my dear, sweet and generous husband and I felt tears well.

He bent over and kissed my cheek. "No crying, you look so beautiful. I don't want you to spoil your eyes."

Someone had won the award and I hadn't even heard who she was. I looked up and saw you and Doreen walking off the stage. I was grateful the moment had passed.

Finally, the last award of the evening came, and as always it was for Best Picture. When they announced Peter's name and Peter's film, the audience broke out in huge applause. He pulled me into his arms and kissed me and made me go up the aisle with him. I tried to pull away and whispered for him to go. "It's your night," I cried.

"We're partners, Annie; it's your night too." He literally pulled me up the stairs on to the stage. Behind us were our co-producers, the director, the writer and other people who had brought the movie to the screen.

He took the Oscar in his hands and it was such a thrill for me to see him holding it. He had scribbled a note to himself which he took out of his pocket and began reading. It was a list that had the names of all the people he wanted to thank. He had been adamant when he told me about his list. If he did win, he didn't want to forget any one who had helped you. When he had finished reading his list he turned to me. I had been quietly standing at his side. He took my hand, as he told the audience and heaven knows how many millions of people watching us on television how grateful he was to have me, the woman he loved by his side and how much I had helped him in earning the award.

Oh Annie, as I watched Peter looking at you with so much love and such pride in you, I felt as though I were so little a man. I knew then that I didn't deserve the love we had had. I don't think I would ever have had the courage to tell the world of my love for you, even under the right circumstances. I would have thanked my wife if I'd won an Oscar and she was sitting in the audience, as most winners do. No one ever knows if they mean it or not, but it's the thing to do. Watching Peter, I knew he would never have thought that would have been enough for you. It was such an awakening of what kind of man I really was, and it wasn't pretty. I needed desperately to tell you how I felt. I needed to tell you how sorry I was for never having the guts to keep you and honor you.

After the awards, and after dozens of people had run up to Peter to congratulate him, we finally made it to our car. My daughters were beyond thrilled. To them, the evening was a dream come true. We were all giddy with excitement as we drove to the first of several parties.

My daughters and their husbands were dancing and Peter and I were talking to friends. Suddenly I saw Jeramie coming towards me. She had a big smile on her face, and one would have thought she was my best friend as she grabbed me and hugged me. I felt my body freeze.

"Ann, it's just so good to see you after all these years. How exciting this must be for you. Who would have thought?"

"Thought what?"

She never got a chance to answer me. Peter knew who she was, because she had during the years as an agent tried to cast some of her clients in some of his films. She also handled directors, and Peter had worked with one of hers just a couple of years back. He certainly knew who she was married to.

As soon as he saw her talking to me, he quickly finished his conversation. Putting his arm around my waist he turned to her.

She immediately began gushing about his award and how thrilled he must be. She hoped she could do business with him in the future she told him. He was polite and suggested she have her office calls ours when we got back to New York. "Tonight's for partying Jeramie, so let's not talk business. Where's that handsome husband of yours?" he asked.

She got flustered, which was amazing for the Jeramie I had known, and I loved it.

"We're actually separated," she said. Then she looked at me. "Didn't you know?"

Once again she had put me in a position of hiding any emotions I might feel. "I hadn't known." I said very surprised and calmly. "I haven't seen anything in the trades. Is this something new?" I wanted to say that I'd seen the two of you standing outside on the red carpet together, but I didn't want to acknowledge that I'd seen you or had paid any attention to the both of you. "You've been married for such a long time. I'm shocked it would end. I always thought you two were such a happy couple." I continued.

"I would have thought you'd be the first to know," she said with malice.

I wasn't going to let her get to me.

"I'm sorry to disappoint you Jeramie, but it's been years since we've been in touch. If I recall you were the one who didn't approve of our friendship? You really should have kept up-to-date with your husband."

She realized she had started something she shouldn't have, particularly since just a few minutes earlier she had been hell bent on getting some of Peter's business. It was obvious she would always hate me, even now after so many years.

Peter turned to her and said, "you'll excuse us but I would very much like to dance with my beautiful wife." With that we walked away from her.

"She really has it in for you, doesn't she?"

"She's never tried to hide it," I said. "I'm sorry."

"You don't have anything to be sorry about sweetheart. I don't know how he ever got involved with her."

"He loved her," I answered.

For the rest of the evening we danced, dined, laughed, and I pretended to have a marvelous time. I couldn't vouch for Peter either way. He, too, could act when called upon. I hoped that he believed I was happy that night. It was his night and I had so wanted it to be perfect for him. I felt so guilty for allowing you to intrude on my thoughts, my feelings and my love. But you had from the moment you had rested your arm on my shoulder, and now even more so because of the knowledge that you and Jeramie had parted. Or had you? She was so mean-spirited when it came to me that she could have said that to see my reaction.

೫ 52 ೫

We'd been back from Los Angeles for six months and life had resumed its normal pattern. I had managed to block you out of my daily thoughts and Peter and I were doing fine.

Soon after returning from Los Angeles, we had flown to Paris to visit with Louise and her little boy. This was Peter's first grandchild. I had never expected him to be so good with a baby, and I was amazed at his ability and his desire to be a real grandfather. Louise had told her father she wanted to name him Peter, and needless to say my husband was thrilled. Little Peter at that early stage wasn't really very beautiful, but you couldn't dare tell his grandfather that. It was a joy to see his face when he took the little guy's finger in his big hand. Looking at him during those moments, I so wished we could have had children together. I imagined a happy home with happy children. I knew it was foolish to think about such things. I was very blessed to have my daughters and my life with Peter.

ಙ 53 ೞ

In the years since winning the Academy Award, our office was busier than ever. I had been receiving more scripts than I could possibly read, and we were developing more properties than we had ever done in the past. We had expanded our development department and added on several readers. We had always had young people who were film students at NYU as interns, and we had nurtured a few who were particularly talented. Upon graduation we had hired several of them and they had proven us right. We had built quite a company of bright, ambitious and talented young people.

Peter had been asked to address a graduating class at UCLA and had accepted. He was going out to Los Angeles a week beforehand to have some meetings with Reid Augustine, Pat's boss. They were thinking of doing a film together, which would be a first since neither man usually worked with another producer. It was a huge film, with a huge budget. It had the potential, if it became as successful as both men felt it to be, of becoming the start of a franchise that could earn a fortune for years to come.

I would have loved to go with him, since I hadn't seen Pat in ages, but we were so busy in New York I couldn't get away. After the trip to the Academy Awards, I had realized I could handle going to Los Angeles more often, and was disappointed not to be able to join Peter.

I hadn't heard anything about the separation of you and Jeramie. I hadn't spoken to you on the phone. I saw nothing in the trades, heard nothing on television shows like *Entertainment Tonight*, and began to wonder if I had been right and she had lied just to see my reaction. By now you were a pretty big name in movies and it seemed unlikely that your marriage -- or end of marriage -- wouldn't have made the news. Sometimes I'd see a picture of you next to a pretty star, but they seemed contrived and strictly for publicity. I heard no gossip at all.

Peter called me when he landed in Los Angeles and promised to call me every morning and every night. "I miss you already Annie."

"Me too. Try to enjoy yourself and don't work too hard."

"You too."

I was used to having him travel, and usually my days were so filled at work that by the time I got home all I wanted to do was take a long hot bath and have a light dinner, read a script and go to bed.

I did that the first couple of days after Peter had left. I planned on doing it again, when a friend of mine who was a literary agent in theatre phoned me. She wanted me to attend a reading of a new play that she thought was fabulous, by one of the writers she represented. "I want you to have first crack at possibly optioning the movie rights," she told me. Serena had an uncanny sense of when a play would be a good movie. More often than not, theatre did not transpose to film very well. When she got this enthusiastic, I knew I had to attend the reading. Since the reading was being held in a loft on Green Street, we agreed to meet for dinner in a small restaurant in Soho. When Peter called me in the office that afternoon, I told him about my plans for the evening. He was happy that I was doing something other than going home. I told him I'd fill him in about the play when I got home; based on the time difference, it wouldn't be too late to call him. He was having dinner with Reid and Pat, he told me, so if I couldn't reach him, he'd call me after the dinner. He sounded excited about the possible project.

When I couldn't get a cab, I took the subway downtown from the office. It just made more sense to me, and I hadn't become so spoiled that I didn't remember how to ride the subway system. It was a pretty misty night and it looked like it might rain any moment. I didn't care really. I had on an old raincoat, carried an umbrella and wasn't wearing anything that would bother me if it got wet. I got out on West Broadway and began walking towards the restaurant. As I walked a yellow cab passed me, and then I heard it screech to a stop. Of course I stopped to look at it, hoping no one had been hurt, and then the back door of the cab opened and out you jumped.

I stood there staring at you, unable to move, unable to think. In one second so many moments of the past flashed through my head, and in that moment my legs found their way to your open arms. We stood there just holding one another, oblivious to the world around us. I was lost in another world; one I had tried so hard to obliterate, as I breathed in the essence of you. All of this couldn't have lasted more than a minute when I felt myself pushing you away. What had I done? What was I doing? No, no, I cried to myself.

You read my mind as you had always done in the years gone by. "It's okay, Annie."

I stood there crying, "it's not okay, it's not, Matthew." The rain had begun and I hadn't even noticed. You pulled me under a canopy of a small unassuming restaurant, and ran back to pay the driver of the cab who had come out looking very irate.

After you had obviously tipped him handsomely, he had gone off and you returned to my side. I was trembling and you put your arm around me but I threw it off. "No, Matthew, you can't. Please."

"Let's go inside. You're chilled. We'll just have a glass of wine and talk. I promise you that's all we'll do."

I felt so disoriented. I suddenly looked at my watch realizing I had to meet Serena. "I can't. I'm meeting someone for dinner in a few minutes."

"Can't you call and say you'll be late?"

Oh God how I wanted to stay with you Matthew. "But we're going to a reading of a play afterwards."

"What play? That's where I'm going. Is it by Brandon Ames?"

"Yes. How did you know about it?"

"Come inside with me. Who are you having dinner with? Can't you call and say you'll meet them at the reading?"

I let you walk me through the door of the restaurant. I sat down at the table you led me to and let you take off my raincoat. You sat down opposite me and we just sat looking at each other. I suddenly jumped up. "Where are you going?" you asked me.

"I'm going to call Serena and I'll tell her to meet me at the reading. I'll tell her I got stuck at the office." As I said this to you, I thought, "lie number one. What am I doing?" I ran to the ladies room to make the call.

I phoned the restaurant we were to meet at and left a message for her. She hadn't arrived as yet. I didn't call her cell phone. It was easier to lie to someone I didn't know than someone I knew.

By the time I returned to our table you had ordered our wine and it had arrived together with a bowl of snacks.

My hand shook so I could hardly hold my glass. Of course you noticed. You noticed everything. You always did.

You reached across and took the glass out of my hand and put it down.

You picked up my hand and held it in yours and I let you. I didn't want you to let go. I needed to feel your touch so badly and I knew it was wrong. I knew how Peter would feel if he saw me sitting across from you like this, and I couldn't do anything about it.

We each had so much to say to one another, and yet we hardly spoke. In the end we didn't need the words. I knew, and you knew, it was never going to end for us.

You were the one who realized when the time came for us to leave and go to the reading. I found out it had been Jeramie who had told you about the play. You had been approached; or rather she had been approached, about the possibility of you appearing in a Broadway play. This new Brandon Ames play might be your entrance to Broadway. I had to ask you about your marriage. When I told you what she had said the night of the Academy Awards you were amazed. She had been taunting me. They had never even talked about separating.

"You see Annie the game for her was over. You appeared to have won a bigger prize than me, something that upset her terribly. I realize now she had wanted to marry me the moment she realized you and I had been lovers. It was impossible for her to imagine that I had loved you. You were older than her, and another obstacle for her to overcome. She couldn't let you win."

"But didn't she understand that I had been the one to send you away? Didn't she understand that I wasn't an obstacle? I never would have broken up your relationship."

"Oh Annie, of course you were an obstacle. She knew I loved you. She saw how we were that night in the restaurant and she never put that out of her mind."

I thought about what you were saying. I'd always known how she felt towards me, but as I listened to you I felt a moment of sadness for Jeramie. "I know that if I thought the man I lived with or was married to felt so strongly about another woman, I'd have been as upset as she had been. I would have hated her as well. I had been as guilty as you in that I never let her have you completely."

"Don't feel sorry for her. She has what she wants. We did have some good years Annie, and we have Luca. We share a lot of the same interests and, before her career took off so brilliantly, she was so much softer and almost sweet most of the time. It was when she got more successful that she changed a lot."

I didn't know what to say. In reality it didn't change anything for us, whether or not you were married to her or not. I hadn't gotten in your little orange bug and married you almost twenty years ago for a very good reason; I was sixteen years older than you, and that hasn't changed. If anything it seemed to me it was more important now. You were still so vital, and so attractive. I was so definitely now an older woman. Twenty years ago I wasn't really old and we could have gone unnoticed by society for a while. By now, the difference in age would be more distinct. But even if that weren't the case, I had a husband, a wonderful man who I loved. My love for Peter was genuine and his for me was more than any woman could expect to have. I would never hurt him, never.

What I felt for you was more than love; it was the other half of me. We were one and would be that way until we left this world. What we had was indescribable. There was no name that fit our feelings for one another. You knew it as I did, but we were not meant to be joined in our lifetime. We would always be on the outside of a real life together. I think even you finally understood that.

We both looked at our watches and realized we had to leave. We walked together as we had all those years before with your arm around my waist and our hips touching in synch. We didn't have to say a word, and in my heart I wanted this walk to go on forever. When we reached the corner of Greene Street, I left you and walked to the building by myself. As I climbed the steps to the loft, I willed myself to take control of my emotions. I entered the loft and immediately found Serena who had saved a seat for me alongside herself.

"I'm so sorry I couldn't meet you for dinner. I hope you're not angry."

"No, no. I was fine. Actually I bunked into Jo Dennison eating alone and so we sat together."

"Oh that's great. How is she?"

I just wanted to have any kind of conversation at that moment so that I wouldn't be looking at the door waiting for you to walk into the room. It was Serena who saw you first.

"Oh my goodness!" she exclaimed.

"What? What's the matter?"

"Look who just walked in."

I turned everywhere but where you were standing, so I wouldn't be obvious.

"Over there", Serena pointed. "It's Matt McKenzie"

I realized that Serena had no idea we knew each other.

You looked towards me and you smiled at me with a look of surprise.

"You know him?"

"I knew him when he was a young, starving writer. He worked for Peter years ago. It's been ages since we've seen him."

You walked to us.

"Hi Ann, how nice to see you. What a lovely surprise." I got up from my seat and hugged you. It seemed an appropriate gesture. "Matthew, what a surprise. What are you doing in New York?"

"I'm here on business and my agent asked me to come to this reading while I'm in town. You look great Annie. It's been such a long time. How's Peter?"

"Oh he's wonderful. He's in Los Angeles right now or he would have been here tonight. Oh Matthew, this is my friend Serena. Serena is Brandon Ames' literary agent. Brandon wrote the play they're reading tonight."

You shook her hand and gave her a big smile. She looked as though she was going to swoon. It was amazing to watch someone else's reaction to you.

"Is this seat empty?" you asked. You didn't wait for an answer and sat down next to me.

I can't really remember most of the evening. I tried so hard to listen to the reading, because I knew Peter would ask me about it. He'd want to know if I thought we should option it and I didn't think I could give him an honest answer. I finally asked Serena if she had a copy of the play, that I might read. Fortunately, she did and she gave it to me.

The three of us left the loft together. Serena lived on Twenty-Third Street, I lived on Sixty-Fourth Street off Park Avenue, and you were staying at the Regency Hotel on Sixty-First Street and Park Avenue. You offered to get a cab and drop each of us off, and there was no way I could say no when Serena immediately said yes. We were lucky, and in minutes found ourselves in a cab on the way uptown. We said goodnight to Serena as she got out of the cab. I promised to read the play that night and to call her in the morning. The second she left us you took my hand and moved close to me.

"Did you like the play?" I asked you. "Do you think it's something you'd want to do?"

"I'd be in New York if I ended up doing it."

"Matthew don't do it if that's your only reason. Please. I can't handle it. I know that now. Please don't put me through this."

"I love you, Annie. I can't have you out of my life again. I'll do anything you ask but let me stay in your life some way."

"How? I won't sleep with you. You understand that I can't. I can never do that to Peter. I couldn't live with myself and I'd hate you afterwards."

"I promise you I will live up to anything you ask. I will never make you unhappy, and I will never put you in a position where you cannot live with yourself. I have loved you from the first day you came out to the reception area in Peter's office and brought me in to meet him. I looked at you that day and knew you were my real and only love. I will love you always on any terms you chose. I've hurt you more times that I meant to, but I won't again. I promise."

I felt totally wiped out. I looked at you, and you will never know how much I wanted you that night. With all my words of protest, if you had pushed me I would have probably followed you to your hotel room and hated myself forever. You believed me thank goodness, and dropped me off at my house, asking only if you could call me later. I said yes, and gave you my number. You kissed me on the cheek and I got out of the cab.

I had only been home about fifteen minutes when the phone rang. I thought it would be Peter and I planned on telling him I had met you at the reading. It was you.

"What are you doing?'

I couldn't help but laugh. It was so reminiscent of years gone by. The years when we were so involved, so emotional, so crazy in love.

"I just got in and I'm trying to get undressed so I can climb into my tub and relax".

"Ummmm."

"Don't start Matthew."

"I can dream can't I?"

You knew I was enjoying this because we'd done this before long ago, and it was a replay of happier times in our relationship.

"I'm going to say goodnight right now. In addition to my bath, I have to read a play I seemed to have missed hearing tonight."

You laughed and finally said, "goodnight."

I started to undress when the phone rang again, and I almost said your name, but before I could, I heard Peter's voice saying "Hi darling," and the reality of who I was and what I had been doing sickened me.

I swallowed hard and forced the brightness to my voice. Peter thought I sounded tired. "Has it been along day for you? You sound exhausted."

"I was just getting ready to get into the tub. It's raining and chilly out and I am tired."

"How was the play?"

"I didn't enjoy the actors who did the reading so I took a copy of it home, and plan to read it when I get out of the tub. Do you know who I met there? Matthew, of all people."

"Matt McKenzie? What was he doing there?"

"He's a fan of Brandon Ames and he's interested in working on Broadway. He came to the reading to make his decision."

"And, did he make his decision?"

"I honestly don't know. He didn't really say. He was kind enough to drop Serena and myself off, but I didn't feel it was my place to question him. I personally can't see him doing theatre, but maybe I'm wrong. Anyway, I'll read the play tonight and I'll let you know what I think."

I wanted to change the subject. I had told him about you, and that was my way of easing my conscience. I asked him how his dinner had gone, and it was then that I realized he had probably just arrived at dinner since it was only eight o'clock in Los Angeles.

"I'll call you later, will you still be up?"

"You can wake me, I won't mind. I'm really dying to know what you decide. Oh, and give my love to Pat."

I knew by the shortness of our conversation that Peter was upset. I became annoyed with him, in defense of myself. What was I supposed to do? He had been in the company of ex-lovers during the past years and I hadn't cared. Couldn't he understand that it didn't mean our marriage was in jeopardy, just because we had met? You and I worked in the same business and it had been amazing we hadn't crossed paths before other than that brief look on the red carpet. Our meeting one another was inevitable. He had no right to make me feel guilty based on an unplanned meeting. What I had felt, what we had spoken about was not his business. I hadn't hidden the fact that we met, but I had a right to my feelings, feelings that were relentless in causing me turmoil. It was my turmoil and I would deal with it. I couldn't share this with him. He should have enough faith in me as his wife, and as a woman to not treat me as though I had done something wrong, and his voice had conveyed his feelings by unsaid words.

I got into the warm bath and thought about the evening. I tried so hard to put you out of my mind. I questioned my sanity. How could I have such strong feelings for someone who I rarely saw, who had built a life that hadn't included me, and who in his own way if truth be known had run hot and cold in his feelings towards me for years. Oh yes, when you loved me, you loved me completely. But, Matthew, there had been many times throughout the years that I'd known you when you hadn't loved me. I could always sense those moments and anguished over them. I'd let time go by and then I'd do some little thing that awakened the dormant feelings and you were mine again. I couldn't let 'us' rest. I reeled you in, as any excellent fisherman would do. I needed your love so desperately. It was I who never had one day in those years where you weren't the first thing I thought of upon awakening and the last before sleep overtook me.

It was the idea of your love that kept me alive. I, who never believed in games, had played you as much as you had played me. We were both willing participants in our game of love. Sometimes I would be strong and I could let you go for months, even years, on end, but then one day some little thing would stir within me and the need for you would begin again.

But this time I couldn't allow the game to begin. I had fallen into it so easily tonight, and I had to take the bait off the hook and leave the shore. Life cannot always be a game and I had too much to lose.

I didn't see you during the remainder of your stay in New York. I had spoken to you the morning after seeing you, and you knew from my voice that I meant it when I said I couldn't see you.

You tried to convince me otherwise but I stood my ground. I didn't lie to you Matthew, I never did, I have never tried to. Yes there were the games, but never did I lie. You did often, but I knew when and why.

One of the most important things in our relationship throughout the many years has been that I have always been able to tell you how I felt about you without feeling fear of rejection or ridicule. I have never had to hide my love for you. It was probably the healthiest aspect of 'us'.

You called to say goodbye and told me you had agreed to do the show. You'd signed a contract for a six-month commitment and would be back for rehearsals when they were ready for you. You had even found a new apartment and had instructed your business manager to buy it for you. You didn't want to stay in a hotel when you came back to New York.

When you told me you were going to do the show, I prayed for the strength to not cave when you returned. You were making it so hard on me, but I was determined to be all I could be to Peter. I loved him, and he loved me. I also passed on optioning the film rights. I didn't want to be involved with the project, and I knew without asking him that neither would Peter. I think Serena was upset by my decision, but I assured her there would be other projects we would work together on in the future.

ಐ 54 ಛ

Peter returned from his trip in a very good mood and never asked me about you or our meeting. He was very excited about the project he and Reid Augustine had agreed to co –produce. Reid was coming to New York with Pat the next week, and I was very happy. I hadn't seen her since the Awards and, ironically I had never met Reid. I immediately called Pat and invited her to stay with us. She loved the idea and she couldn't wait to see our house. She had been at the wedding, but since then the house had been totally redone and I knew she'd love it. We had so much room for guests that I wondered if we should also invite Reid, but she explained that he had an apartment in one of the hotels that had recently been built in the Financial District and he wouldn't need to stay with us.

I couldn't wait to see her. She was the only person I would ever feel free to talk to about you and how I felt about you. She had been there at the beginning, and she had been the one who had given me the courage to go after my heart and not listen to my head. Now I needed her to give me the strength to do the opposite.

She breezed in as only she could, with a rashness that on someone else would be obnoxious but on her was exciting.

I met her at our front door and immediately she was gushing over the beauty of the house. She charged through all the rooms screaming with delight, with me following behind her. I finally caught up with her in time to usher her into the room I had prepared for her. She threw herself on the bed and grinned at me.

"Oh Annie, I'm so proud of you. Look what you've done. This house is magnificent."

I sat down beside her and she raised her eyes, questioning me with a look.

"What?" she said. "Something's wrong, I can see it in your face."

I couldn't answer her.

"Oh God, don't tell me it's Matthew?"

I felt my face burning.

"I should have known. Does it never end for you? "

She shook her head, but in sympathy. "My poor dumb friend. Tell me what happened. I was so sure you were cured of this disease. I thought you had found real happiness."

"I have," I cried. "I really have. I love Peter and I have a wonderful life with him. I never believed I would have all this. He's so good to me, Pat. He loves me very much. No one has ever taken care of me as he does."

"But he's not Matthew, right?"

"What's wrong with me? I see him for one night and I'm back to square one. I can't get him out of my mind, no matter how hard I try. I've told him I won't see him and I haven't, but I don't trust myself to keep saying no. He's going to be staring in a play in New York in a few months. How am I going to ignore him? I even begged him not to take the part, but he wouldn't listen to me. He promised he'd honor my wishes, but he's as bad as I am. There are months and even years when we've managed to live without one another. He's had his life, his career, and so many things I've never been a part of. I don't know his day-to-day existence any more than he knows mine. I don't know his friends, his acquaintances, if he has had other women other than Jeramie; none of these things, and yet when we find each other again it's as though time has stood still for both of us."

"I would hate for you to lose Peter but I don't think you can ever be content without Matthew in your life."

"What are you saying? You think I should leave Peter?"

"No, I didn't mean that. He's the real substance that you need, and I'm not talking about money. He's real Ann, and Matthew's more a fantasy. He came into your life when you needed a fantasy so badly and he gave you back your youth, and your vitality and zest for life. He made you feel like the woman you had hidden, and of course you can't forget him. And now he's even more exciting, he's a big movie star, every woman's fantasy of a lover."

"I don't think being an actor has anything to do with how I feel. It's just him. We are so connected. Oh I hate that expression, it's so New Age. But it's true. I feel a bond that's so powerful it's beyond description. In all the years before Peter and I discovered our feelings for one another, I was content living on the memories that Matthew and I had stored. When he first married Jeramie, I felt torn and broken into hundreds of pieces. I still needed him in my life so badly that I took whatever crumbs I could get. That sounds so terrible, but for years they sustained me. His calls, although sometimes very infrequent, were enough to fulfill me for days. Pat, if I saw his name on an email, my day became joyful. They filled my needs, they gave me life, they enriched me as a woman and on the occasions that I felt sadness and wished there was more, I learned to live with that too. He still always made me feel that I wasn't alone, and that I was truly understood by the one person that mattered in my life."

"Have an affair with him Ann if you must. You will, you know. It's inevitable. Just don't throw away the good that you have with Peter. Please think about all this very carefully."

"You don't understand, it's so much more than sleeping with him. We haven't slept together in years and we still yearn for each other. It's the being together that's so compelling. Just to touch him, and have him put his arm on my shoulder takes my breath away."

Our conversation was interrupted when we heard Peter's voice coming towards us. He had come home early to welcome Pat, and he had brought Reid with him so that I could finally meet him.

I jumped off the bed and ran to meet him. He didn't notice anything on my face because he was focused on greeting Pat, and I was so grateful for the chance to pull myself together.

A tall, grey-haired and very attractive man walked in behind Peter. He gave me a broad smile and then hugged me.

"You're Ann; it's so great to finally meet you."

He was absolutely charming and his arrival took my mind off you, as I assumed the part of the perfect hostess.

We all went down into the library where Peter offered drinks, and we spent about an hour getting acquainted. I felt very good about this man and knew that Peter was making a wise decision in partnering with him. I was happy to see that Pat had made such a wise choice as well, and enjoyed watching the two of them and their easy banter. I had a feeling there were things between them that my friend had yet to tell me, but then I had monopolized our entire conversation. I hadn't given her a chance to tell me about her own life. I'd been so busy crying over you.

Peter had made arrangements for the four of us to go out to dinner. Pat and I left the guys talking and went upstairs to change our clothes and freshen up. I stopped her before she went into her room.

"Is there something you haven't told me about you and Reid?" I said and felt myself grinning.

"Yes." She laughed. "I'll tell you later. I'm glad to see you smiling. Keep it that way, sugar, promise?"

I couldn't help but smile back. She could always bring out the best in me.

We had a lovely dinner at a charming restaurant called Chanterelle. The food was exquisite and the service impeccable. Pat and Reid were tired, as they had flown in that day, and so we ended the evening fairly early. We all agreed to meet him the next morning at eight-thirty for breakfast. Several of our investors were meeting us as well. He had suggested Windows on the World on the top of the World Trade Center. He'd heard the view was spectacular. None of us had ever been there, so we all agreed it would be fun and he quickly made a call to his secretary to set it up with the restaurant and the other people involved.

In the morning Peter realized he needed some papers that he left at the office. I volunteered to pick them up because I had previously scheduled a seven-thirty morning meeting with a writer and I hadn't been able to cancel. I promised to cut the meeting short, pick up the papers and meet them at the restaurant.

I left Pat with Peter sipping their wake-up coffee, which they both always needed to function, and their secret cigarettes that they both thought I didn't know they still on occasion smoked. I kissed my husband goodbye and waved to Pat as I closed the door. She winked at me as if to say "good girl."

❧ 55 ☙

What can I say that could ever describe what I saw that morning or more importantly what I felt. I had gotten into a cab and was almost at my destination when a scene that only one would expect in a movie was unfolding in front of my eyes.

It was September 11th and at approximately eight-forty five AM that morning, two minutes before I arrived, a plane had flown into the North Tower of the World Trade Center. My car had stopped at the sight of people running and screaming. Everyone riding in a car had stopped, got out and looked to see what was happening. I too got out and looked up, and then I screamed with all the others. I started to run towards the building and was held back by the driver of my car. I tore free of him but he pulled me back.

"You can't go there. You'll get hurt. We have to get away from here fast."

He pulled my arm as I cried out "my husband's up there, my best friend is up there, and I'm supposed to be up there. I'm supposed to be meeting them."

I heard one siren after another, and looking up and seeing the flames shooting out of the side of the tower I knew without a doubt that this was going to cause many deaths, but in my wildest dreams I would never have believed how many and in what horrible circumstances.

My driver kept dragging me down the street, and if not for him, I have no idea if I too would have perished. I was as crazed as most of the people running alongside of us.

What had caused this people, kept asking? One person said they had seen a plane hit the building. It had been a terrible accident, he thought. And then an unbelievable sight occurred. We heard an airplane flying above and we all seemed to stop in our tracks and look up into the sky, unable to move or think as it made its way into the South Tower.

The sounds and sight of that morning will never leave me. What seemed like tons of ashes fell towards everyone and I felt myself being dragged further down the streets, having no concept where I was being pulled. I found myself unable to see, and thought I was blind. I fell to the ground unable to walk another step, and began crying. All I could think of was Peter, and Pat and Reid and all the people in those buildings. Would they get out safely? I convinced myself that, knowing Pat and Peter, they'd make it. They were strong and determined people. They'd find a way out of this mess.

Ironically the crying cleared my eyes. They were burning badly, but I could see; and then I wished I couldn't, because when I looked up I saw people jumping from windows. It seemed impossible. I covered my eyes with my hands. I couldn't look.

I didn't know what to do. Police and fireman were ushering us further and further away from the horrors of the burning buildings that ultimately collapsed within the next two hours, killing thousands of people.

I was so paralyzed with fear that I hadn't been able to think clearly. I hadn't thought of trying to call Peter on his cell phone. I was amazed to see I still had my purse hanging from my shoulder and reached in to find my phone. My hand was shaking so badly that it took me three tries until I dialed the right number, but when it rang it went immediately to voice mail. I listened to my husband's voice and became overwhelmed with a sense of dread and terrible guilt. I couldn't permit myself to think he might be dead, that he might have been one of those people dropping from the windows. I kept redialing over and over and leaving messages. "Peter, call me darling." I kept crying into the phone over and over again.

I was startled by the ringing of my phone and could hardly pick up the cover to answer it. "Peter, is that you?" I cried. "Mom, it's me Jennifer. Are you alright? Where are you?"

I became hysterical at the sound of her voice. I hadn't thought to call her. All I had thought of was what I was witnessing and what I knew had probably killed, not only my husband, but my best friend.

"Mom, please stop crying and tell me if you're alright."

I finally managed to find my voice and tried to tell her what I had seen. Every time I started to tell her more, I broke down and couldn't talk. How could I ever explain what I was witnessing? I didn't understand it, how could I explain it? I finally managed to tell her how I was supposed to meet Peter and Pat and Reid for breakfast; and how I had been detained and had seen everything from the street. "I don't know what I'm supposed to do."

"Mom can you find your way home? There's no trains, no transportation anywhere. The city is closed down. Don't stay down there. I've got the television on and it's very unsafe. Both of the towers may collapse at any moment, and they are trying to get everyone away. Please just start walking if you can. I'll go to the house. I'll be there when you get home.

Please just start walking. I'll keep trying Peter's phone and I'll call you if I get through."

I don't remember walking home, but I did, alongside of hundreds of other people. I just kept going. People along the way were gathering in the streets, needing to be with other human beings and not alone in their homes. I could hear televisions blasting from some homes, and knew when the first tower collapsed because of the silence and then cries of anguish from the people who also heard the horrific news. It took me more than four hours to reach my house. By that time, the other tower had fallen as well.

Jennifer was standing outside looking for me, and when she saw me walking to her she ran to me and hugged me, crying "oh Mommy, oh Mommy, thank God you're safe." I don't remember the last time she had called me Mommy, and the sound of her voice calling me that with so much endearment was more than I could deal with. I crumbled to the floor and sobbed uncontrollably. She sat down besides me and held me as though I were her child.

We spent the next hours glued to the television, and I knew without anyone telling me that I had lost my husband as well as my best friend. If I shut my eyes, all I could do was to visualize them in the burning building, and I imagined them trying to escape and the horror of being trapped. What had they been thinking? Oh God how I wanted to know. I wanted to have been with them. Why had I been spared I kept asking myself? What did I ever do to deserve this pass on death? I had received love from an outstanding man. Had I really ever reciprocated that love? Had I given him what he needed? I had loved him. I prayed he knew that. Was I that selfish, that although I did love Peter, I had thought about my love for you, another man, when he had given me a life I had dreamed about but never believed could exist. I was so filled with guilt and despair. Why had my dear friend Pat, who had finally achieved a worthwhile career, and seemed to have found a good man as well, died? All those dreams for her were now lost. Why?

I alternated between crying and pacing. I'd run to the front windows and look out, knowing full well that Peter wasn't going to appear. I couldn't cry anymore. All I wanted to do was to be left alone. I needed to grieve by myself. I looked at my daughter. She, too, looked exhausted. Her husband Cole had found his way to my house as well. I was so very grateful that they were together and safe. Knowing the Liz was in California was another relief. I couldn't have dealt with the thought of either of my children being lost in this horror

My son-in-law Cole left my house and, on my behalf, somehow managed to make his way down to what had been the World Trade Center, but there were barricades all around maintained by police. There was nothing anyone could do. Anyone that could have gotten out would have. It was as simple as that. The next day and the weeks that followed would tell us how many hadn't. Cole had spent the remainder of the day going from hospital to hospital in hopes of finding Peter or Pat, but nothing.

When Cole returned to my house late that night his face said everything. I begged them both to please go home. I would be alright, I insisted, and I needed to be alone.

They argued with me, but then they seemed to understand and finally started to leave, but only when I promised I'd call them if I needed them. Fortunately our cell phones seemed to be working, although sporadically.

"Tomorrow we're going downtown together. We'll bring photographs and we're going to look for them." I told them. Of course they agreed, what else could they say to me?

When they finally left, I went back into the library and lay down on the couch. I pulled the throw that always rested on the arm over me and I shut the television set. I couldn't watch any more of this tragedy unfold. I was so tired, so totally exhausted. I closed my eyes and fell asleep.

❧ 57 ❧

I awoke totally disoriented to the ringing of my doorbell. It kept ringing and ringing. I stumbled from the couch when I remembered I had sent the housekeeper home. She had a family she was concerned about, and there wasn't anything she could do for me. She had left food if I got hungry, which I hadn't. She hadn't wanted to leave me alone but I had insisted. She had promised to come back in the morning.

I didn't even think. I simply opened the door, and there you were, Matthew. The look on your face was of sheer disbelief. Tears ran from your eyes as you pulled me into your arms. You held me with such force that I felt I would break in half. I could hardly breathe, and yet I didn't want you to let me go. You finally pulled away to look at me. "Oh God Annie, you're alive. I was so afraid I'd lost you."

I just kept looking at you. Where had you come from? I wondered. Had how you gotten here?

You pulled me into the house and somehow I remembered to close the door.

You followed me back into the library and sat beside me on the couch.

I was in total shock. "Weren't you in Los Angeles, how did you get here?"

"I got stuck here longer than I expected ironing out the details for the play. I was halfway to the airport this morning, having just gotten into Queens, when we heard the news on the car radio. I made the driver turn around so I could come back into Manhattan, but by the time we got to the bridge it had shut down and no cars could come in or go out. We tried going back to where we could hit the mid-town tunnel, but that was closed too. I had the driver drop me off as close to the bridge as possible and I walked the rest of the way with hundreds of other people. I didn't have your cell phone number, so I couldn't call you and I was going crazy. I didn't know where you were, and when I finally got through to your house the housekeeper was hysterical. She said you and Peter and your guest had gone to breakfast at the World Trade Center. I thought you were dead."

I started crying and you took me in your arms and just held me. I needed you so badly at that moment, Matthew. I knew that day that, had you been the one in the Twin Towers, I couldn't have survived. I wondered what kind of awful person I was. I had been married to a man who had adored me, had spoiled me terribly and had given me everything any woman could have ever wanted, and, if I were honest, it had never been enough. In my heart I knew I had never treasured him as I should have. I sat with your arms around me and felt tremendous guilt for not loving Peter enough, and prayed that during his lifetime he'd never known how I felt.

I remembered that at times during my marriage I had wondered if Peter ever thought of you and me and our past relationship. Now as I let you hold me, I realized I had never talked to him about my feelings for you, and he must have assumed that whatever had happened between us had been so long ago it couldn't have any importance any more. That thought somehow helped alleviate some of my guilt.

A sense of exhaustion hit me and you lifted me in your arms and carried me up the steps to my room and laid me down in to my bed. You covered me with my blanket and started to leave the room.

"Don't go Matthew. Please don't leave me."

You took off your shoes and climbed in next to me and held me in your arms. I must have fallen asleep because when I opened my eyes I saw that it was morning. I almost forgot what had happened the day before, but in a moment it all came back. You weren't in the bed, but I vaguely remembered your arms around me and wondered if I dreamed the whole day and that none of it was true. I heard footsteps and thought, "maybe that's Peter," but of course it wasn't. You had a tray in your hands. You had made us some breakfast. You brought it to the bed and looked at me anxiously.

"Are you okay?"

"I don't know, did yesterday really happen? What a silly question. You wouldn't be here if it hadn't. Turn on the television please. I need to hear what's happening. How do I find out about Peter and Pat? What do I do?"

"Annie, I don't think anyone in that restaurant survived. I'm so sorry to tell you this. I've been watching the news all morning. Please don't turn on the television. It's only going to hurt you more."

I knew that in my heart, but hearing it said made it real and I wasn't ready to accept it. I didn't turn the television on. I drank the coffee but couldn't eat the toast you had made.

"You have to leave now Matthew. This is not the time for us. This is about Peter."

"Will it ever be?" you asked me.

"It doesn't matter. Don't you see? I know and you know how much we love each other. It's never going to end. It will always exist, no matter how or where our lives take us. Will it ever take us to the same place? I don't know. In the end, it doesn't matter. Right now I have to focus on the life I had and what I have to do. I owe so much to Peter. He was so wonderful to me, and Matthew I did love him. You too have to focus on your life and what you have to do."

You sat beside me, and for the next hour we told each other things we had left unspoken for many years. Somehow it was very important to us to make sure we left nothing unsaid. In the end, what we did promise each other was that we would, more than anything else, always be each other's friend. We couldn't, or I certainly couldn't, promise any more. You were entwined within my soul, and you would always stay there my dear. So as you listen to this now my dearest, know that in my heart I don't think we left any lose ends.

The weeks that followed are still a haze. I remember hugging you goodbye. I remember my children returning to the house after you left. I insisted on getting dressed and trying to make our way down to the disaster area. We were turned back, as was everyone else who was looking for answers. Eventually the answers would come to all of us.

About a month after the bombing, Louise arrived at the house. She had left her child and her husband in Paris feeling it unsafe to travel with them. She was a joy to have. She had the ability to look at life realistically and with hope for the future. She understood her father was gone, but she explained to me that knowing her father had been so happy with me during his last years made her feel so much better about his death. When she said this to me I felt such guilt.

"Are you sure he was happy?" I asked her.

"Are you crazy? He was happier and more content than I'd ever known him. Don't pull the "why didn't I do shtick Ann. None of us are perfect, including my father, and you should know that better than most."

"How'd you get so smart?" I asked her.

"Growing up in my crazy family helped." She laughed.

"What are your plans?"

I had done a lot of thinking the past month and had pretty much decided to keep the company going. I had a good staff and could certainly hire top people to join us. I told her this, and also explained that Peter had left her fifty percent of the business and a great deal of money as well.

"I'm not interested in the business. Whatever you decide to do is fine with me. Are you sure you want to work so hard? Why don't you sell it, or close it up? You deserve to have some fun. You've worked most of your life. Isn't there something else you'd like to do?"

"Like what?'

"Oh I don't know, find your self a young guy and have an affair, or go off to a foreign country, learn the language and let yourself go. Do something to make your self happy Ann. I've watched you and you always seem to be making other people happy, but I wonder about you."

I had never known how kind and perceptive Louise was. I had always thought of her as a spoiled young woman, who I envied for her sense of freedom. She was so much more than I had ever given her credit for. That day she became more than my step-daughter; she became my friend.

She had given me something to think about. I wasn't going off with some young guy that was for sure. The only young guy I had ever been interested in wasn't young anymore and once was enough for me.

The idea of going off and living in a foreign country had its appeal, but I knew myself well enough to know I'd never do it. I didn't want to be on the other side of the world away from those I loved. What I finally decided to do was sell off Louise's part of the company plus twenty five percent of my share, leaving me with a twenty five percent interest. That would guarantee me a lovely income for many lifetimes. Louise had approved, and my agreement with the new owners provided that I would still develop new projects, but only work on one film a year. This would give me ample time to travel and maybe even take the time to learn French, something I'd always wanted to do. When I visited Louise and her family in Paris I could speak to the little ones (there would soon be two) in their native tongue and that would be fun.

I hadn't seen you in months. You called me every week, late at night, and we'd talk for hours. You were my major support. When I told you what I was planning, you thought it was a great idea. You were pleasantly shocked at the Louise you had never really known.

The play had never come to fruition and in a way I was glad. I needed to build my life and, had you been in New York, I would have used you as a crutch and that would have not been what I would have ever wanted for us.

It was hard to believe that you had been married to Jeramie for over twenty years and had a bond of your own that had nothing to do with me. It seemed impossible that so many years had passed. You told me that you had tried to talk to her about your feelings towards me, but she would have none of it. Honestly, Matthew, how could I blame her? In her own way, she must love you very much and it must have been very hurtful to think she had to share your love with me.

You phoned me one Saturday afternoon, as I was coincidentally thinking of you. I had heard an airplane overhead as I was in my kitchen and looked up and thought to myself for whatever reason, "Matthew is on that plane." An hour later you were telling me you were on your way to your apartment.

"Can we have dinner?" you asked.

"I'd love to," I told you.

"I'll pick you in a couple of hours. We're going out to the Island for dinner. I want to show you something."

I was ready when you arrived at my door. As always, the moment I saw you I became a young woman that was hopelessly in love. I could feel myself change in front of your eyes. I know it had the same effect on you, because you looked at me as you had over twenty odd years earlier. You never looked at me as if to say "oh my God, who is this old woman?" It was, in itself, amazing.

You had rented a convertible, and we rode with the top down on a beautiful June evening.

I asked you where we were going, but you just grinned and kept humming and driving. You put your hand that wasn't holding the wheel on my leg, and it remained there throughout the trip, occasionally softly rubbing it. Matthew if you never did more than touch my leg it would have been enough for me. The feelings that raced through me were filled with a need that only the young think they have. They hopefully will someday realize lust is not just for youngsters.

You turned off the road somewhere in the town of East Hampton. I wasn't very familiar with the area, as I didn't spend much time out there, and so I had no idea where we were going. Peter had never wanted to spend weekends with the crowds, which was why he had sold his house.

You then turned into a driveway and I covered my eyes and began to cry. Twenty-five years came rushing back to me. It was as though it were yesterday that we had all pulled up into this very driveway. I would have known it anywhere.

You pulled me to you and held me. "Don't cry Annie, please don't cry. Let's get out."

You opened your door and got out. I unbuckled my seat belt, still crying, and got out too. You walked to the house and waited for me to follow. When I got to your side, you took out your keys and put one into the lock and the door opened. Before I could do anything you moved towards me and lifted me up.

"I may never carry you over the threshold as my bride, but I feel as though you are," you said as you kicked the door open with your foot and carried me in.

Even though it was June, someone had lit a fire in the fireplace. You put me down and put your arm around me as I looked around the room in shock. I could see the dining room from where I was standing, and could see an elegant table had been set with a lace cloth, burning candles and exquisite china.

"Matthew, what does this all mean?"

Your smile was radiant as you bent to kiss me. "It's all yours my dearest. I have tried to track this house down for years and I finally did. When I heard it was on the market, I didn't wait a moment. I wanted you to have it. I couldn't stand the thought of someone else once again owning it. It belonged to us. It brought us the most wonderful weekend I ever had in my life, and I think you felt that as much as I did."

I couldn't talk. I was filled with a love that was beyond description. If I never again have a moment like this, I have still been the most blessed person in the world. The thought of you cherishing that weekend as I have throughout the years was more meaningful than all the luxuries in the world.

You pulled my hand and took me through the house. You had somehow remembered so much of how it had looked that weekend long ago, and you had passed all this information on to the decorator you had hired. I could not believe what you had done.

"Matthew, I don't know what to say."

You pulled my hand. "Come with me. Remember Pat and her brother stayed upstairs. I have always wondered what was up there. Come see."

Up we went and there I found the master bedroom suite. A huge bed was set facing the wall of windows overlooking the ocean. "Look Annie, lie down next to me and look out the windows. You can see the waves breaking; you can hear the crashing of them as they hit the beach." I didn't get to look at the rest of the room as you took me in your arms and I rested my head on your shoulder and looked out at the ocean. It was the most soothing perfect moment, and I have never felt so safe and protected. The past months seemed to fade away, at least for that moment in time.

Eventually we made our way downstairs and discovered we were very hungry. Once we had eaten the lovely meal some unknown person had left us, I slowly walked around my new home. When I came to the room we had shared on that memorable night, you opened the door and stood back. I looked in and began to laugh. You had created it to look exactly as it had that weekend, including my flannel pajamas, which were thrown on one side of the bed, and those ridiculous red jockey shorts that you constantly wore in those days.

"Shall we?" you asked.

"Are you sure? I don't want you to do anything you'll regret."

"This is ours, Annie. This has nothing to do with anything or anyone else. No one else could possibly understand this or share this."

I understood. Others may not, but I couldn't think about that. This had been one of our most important moments, and if we had been lucky enough to be able to hold on to it for so many years and recreate it, than so be it. I couldn't let this night go by without us reliving something so important to us. I would regret it for the rest of my life if I let it go by.

I walked into your arms and we created our magic once again.

"Matthew, have I ever really thanked you enough for giving me the house and all it brought to me? Every moment I have spent here these last months of my illness have made it so much easier for me to accept. When it's all over, the memory of this will ride along with me wherever it is that one goes at the end. Thank you my love."

Sweetheart, I'm getting a little tired now. Before I end this trip down our memory lane, I need to tell you that I have no regrets about anything. We had something so few people ever have, and I have had the most wonderful life because of you and Peter. I am so lucky and so blessed.

I would want you to, if you can, tell Jeramie something for me. When you told me so many years ago, that you felt as though you had "both sides of the coin." I was so hurt. I have come to understand that one of us would never have been enough. Together we have made you complete.

If she could understand that as I do, I think she too could be complete.

I'm going to end this now. I love you my dear heart.

I believe with all my heart that we were meant to have this life. We were meant to find each other, and if indeed there is another lifetime for each of us, then I know my love we will find one another again. Just know that I will carry our love through eternity.

Her image faded from the screen but not from his heart. He would be forever grateful for the past hours and the knowledge that whenever he needed her, he had only to look and listen as their beautiful story unfolded, and he would be whole again.

The End